Estella

a novel

ALSO PUBLISHED BY DBI PUBLISHING

The Relentless Rebel Duology by Dawn Bates:
Friday Bridge – Becoming a Muslim; becoming everyone's business (1st Edition, 2013; 2nd Edition, 2017; 3rd Edition, 2023)
Walaahi – A Firsthand Account of Living Through the Egyptian Uprising and Why I Walked Away from Islaam (1st Edition, 2017; 2nd Edition 2023)

The Sacral Series by Dawn Bates:
Moana – One Woman's Journey Back to Self (2020)
Leila – A Life Renewed One Canvas at a Time (2020)
Pandora – Melting the Ice One Dive at a Time (2021)
Alpha – Saving Humanity One Vagina at a Time (2021)
Faith – Leaving Religion to Save Your Soul (2024)

Anthologies:
Break Down to Wake Up – Journey Beyond the Now by Jocelyn Bellows (2020)
Standing in Strength – Inspirational Stories of Power Unleashed by Laarni Mulvey (2021)
The Potent Power of Menopause – A Culturally Diverse Perspective of Feminine Transformation by Dawn Bates and Clarissa Kristjansson (2022)
Alive to Thrive – Life After Attempting Suicide: Our Stories by Dawn Bates and Debbie Debonaire (2022)
#ManUp Tough to Talk Curated by Steve Whittle (2024)

Memoirs/Biographies:
Crossing The Line – A Journey of Purpose and Self-Belief by Dawn Bates (2017)
Becoming Annie – The Biography of a Curious Woman by Dawn Bates (2020)
Becoming the Champion – V1 Awareness by Korey Carpenter (2020)
Unlocked – Discovering Your Hidden Keys by Carmelle Crinnion (2020)
The Recipe – A US Marine's Mindset to Success by Jake Cosme (2021)

Personal Development
51 Powerful Ps of Public Speaking by Krystylle L Richardson (2022)
Raising Grit by Beth Canalichio (2025 - No longer on sale)

Fiction Books

Sin Eater – Memories Disappear When She Arrives by Amanda Denham (2024)

Seven Feathers – There is More Life After Death by Amanda Denham (2025)

The Democ-Chu Series by Nath Brye:

Slave Boy (2020)

Blood Child (2021)

Slave Alone (2025)

To discover more about DBI Publishing, please visit https://dawnbates.com

Estella

a novel

Lara Latcham

DBI Publishing

Imprint details

"Estella: a novel" by Lara Latcham © 2025.

ISBNS:

E-book: 978-1-0682007-8-6

Paperback: 978-1-0682007-7-9

Hardback: 978-1-0682007-9-3

Illustrator: Lara Latcham

Book cover design: Jerry Lampson

Developmental Editor: Dawn Bates

1st Edition 2025

Dedication

To young people, every glorious one of them.
You are the future.
You will make the world a better place.
Thank-you.

Prologue

Within each of us coexist a number of versions of ourselves from pivotal moments in our lives. They accompany our current self as we move forward in our allotted time. In some people, perhaps because they are well-adjusted or boring (*same difference?*), the versions are nested neatly like Russian Matryoshka dolls with the youngest version at the core and chronological strata of older versions, like perfect onion layers, embracing the previous incarnation, so that all that you can see on the surface is the perfect varnished face of today's version. In other people, the versions do not sit so rigidly in order and do not layer so obediently into tightly packed onion skins, but rather, like an artichoke's leaves, they seem to be all present at once and vying for position as the current self attempts to navigate life. Certain experiences will trigger the ascendancy of a particular version, who feels that they are able to best deal with this particular circumstance. Estella is one of those people in whom her past selves are present all at once. She's happy that this is the case. Without these others, she feels, coping would not be possible.

In Estella there are seven magnificent versions; each as complex as each other and each able to cope with different situations that arise on a moment-by-moment basis because each is arrested in their own particular moment in time without the subsequent baggage picked up by their older selves.

Little Estella is seven years old, just aware that her parents don't love her unconditionally and that she doesn't seem to be like other people. She already has the nickname '*Drama Queen*' because she has a tendency to cry a lot. She feels lost and hurt.

Stel is fourteen years old, has just started to travel around the UK alone on trains and spends a lot of time in London, where she plans to move as soon as she finishes school. Anything to get away from home and her parents' constant disappointment in her. She has fallen in love for the first time and believes that they are meant to be together.

Ella at twenty-one years old, has just finished drama school and is facing the reality that her dreams will not come true and the drudgery of working full-time. She's navigating the loss of her first love and the seemingly haphazard nature of relationships with anyone other than herself. She's bored. She's romantic. She dreams in a way that she confuses her dreams with reality. She is desperate to try anything and anyone.

Esta is frozen at thirty years old, living in Spain and working for a language school. She's in love and believes that she will soon be married. Away from England she has grown in confidence and has moments of real happiness. She's optimistic and resilient.

Sella has turned forty and is back in the UK after being disabused of the idea that she would be loved and having been miserable on three continents. Her nieces and nephews can't say Stella, so she has become Sella. She is just beginning to face the understanding that she will always be alone, and she's also taking on the responsibility of primary carer for her parents who are experiencing their first major illnesses.

Stella has made it to fifty years old, has just lost her father and is caring full-time for her mother. She has lost all sense of herself and functions only in response to the needs of others.

Miss is the present-day version, fifty-seven years old and a teacher again. Teaching Spanish to sixth formers and living alone in a house that she bought with her inheritance after her mother's death. Now that she's an orphan, she isn't sure who she is, so she identifies best with her job, where the students refer to her as '*Miss*'.

Each of the Magnificent Seven might appear at any time in Estella's world. When she walks home from work, often listening to music through headphones, she is aware of the different versions responding to the different tracks that she listens to. It takes an average of eight tracks on Spotify to make the journey home. When the 80s tracks come onto the shuffle, she feels the feisty, fierce optimism of Stel and her pace quickens. When Elias starts singing *Holy*, the bitter melancholy of Ella surges through her and her inability to accept that there will be no happy ending for her; she is filled with the absurd, unfounded optimism that Ella both had and didn't have. When Luis Miguel sings, Esta is back in Spain in a relationship that she loved, and she is momentarily filled with gratitude and fulfilment. This constant hijacking by the different versions of herself is exhausting. Apart from anything else, her younger selves all walk faster than her fifty-seven-year-old body is accustomed to. She is short of breath and her legs ache. Sometimes she falls over in Stel's eagerness or Esta's confidence and she is abruptly brought back to herself, or worse, Little Estella appears to howl her outrage.

Miss has a recurring image of that figurative bag of frogs that are so mad and thinks that she is the bag and these versions of herself are the frogs that make that bag so mad. At times, the thought is absurdly funny and comforts her. At other times, she suspects that insanity is either not far away or has already taken hold. In these moments, it is Stel who takes control with a power that no other incarnation can muster, and she will shout the immortal magic words: "*For fuck's sake, women, grow some ovaries and hold it together!"* There is love in it, but there is also the self-assured arrogance of the only one amongst them who believed she was loved and, more importantly, felt that she was deserving of that love. And the beauty of Stel, is that she is arrested at a point in time where she will never realise that she was in fact wrong, catastrophically wrong.

PART ONE:
Estella and the Magnificent Seven

Friday Afternoon

"¡Bueno, ya veo que tenemos muy buena concentración esta tarde!" Miss says wryly to her Friday afternoon class of wildly distracted year twelves. Today she's in a black corduroy dress with a neon green scarf so bright that it could have an eye out. This period is always hard to teach because they are sixteen and seventeen and it's almost the weekend. Some of them are already at work in their heads, and others are counting the minutes to getting skin on skin with their loved one. All of them are exhausted from getting up and coming to college for five days in a row. There are twenty minutes left to the 4 pm bell that signals freedom for all of them, including her. She turns to a tried and tested back-up plan.

"Vale, chicos, dime, ¿qué tengo que ver en Netflix?"

There is a cacophony, mostly in English, about what she should be watching on Netflix. She hears one voice in Spanish and turns to one of the girls in the back row, "Millie? ¿Qué dices?"

"*Los Amores de Oscar*, they call it *Oscar Loves*, though. Eso no es correcto, is it Miss? It should be The Loves of Oscar, shouldn't it?"

"Literally, yes, but maybe they thought that *Oscar Loves* was snappier?"

"Hmm."

"What's it about? ¿Puedes decirme en español?"

"Erm. Es un chico guapo, like, tiene diecisiete años, like us. Miss, it's too hard. He's at college, like us... tiene un trabajo and he... vive con su padre... and step-mum."

Jacob chips in, "Canta en un erm... band, a pop group. How do you say that, Miss?"

"Un grupo pop. Muy bien, ¿qué más?"

"He's gay though..."

"Lo dices como es una cosa mala. You say that like it's a bad thing."

"Well, it... I don't know..."

"¿No sabes? ¿No sientes cómodo con gente homosexual? You don't feel comfortable with gay people?"

"I don't know any gay people, Miss." He scoffs.

"Creo que conoces a algunas, pero quizás no te han dicho que son homosexuales. I'm pretty sure that you do, but maybe they haven't mentioned that they are."

"Miss, how do you say gay in Spanish?"

"Homosexual."

"Él esta homosexual."

"Él **es** homosexual. Remember that estar is used for temporary states, ser for permanent states or facts. ¿Y qué tal los amores de Oscar? ¿Tiene un novio o está hablando con más de uno? Does he have a boyfriend?"

"Está enamorado de un chico who is, like, no es homosexual. It's kind of sad. ¿Triste?"

"¡Excelente!"

"Also, he wants to find his real mum."

"Yeah, I don't get that, his step-mum is super cool. So beautiful."

"¡En español, por favor!"

"¡Ella es guapa y super sexy!"

"¡Él es super sexy!"

"Toda la ... people ... ¿gente? Yeah. ¡Toda la gente es sexy en este programa!"

"Muy bien, pero: ¡Toda la gente SON sexy! ¡No olvides gente es una palabra plural!"

To the blessed relief of everyone the bell for the end of class and the end of the week rings and Miss waves at the class as she says, "Adiós! ¡Buen fin de semana, chicos!"

The classroom empties in seconds. Ella stands looking at the door and tears start to roll down her face. She makes no sound. She straightens chairs, picks up some forgotten pens and a few bits of rubbish as the tears fall. She goes back to her desk and sits down at the computer. She opens an e-mail to herself and types in capitals:

I AM DYING OF BOREDOM.

She deletes the word *BOREDOM*. Her fingers hover and her face shows a battle to find the right word. Time passes. She gives up and deletes the whole line and just as she is about to get up, Miss returns to the keyboard and half standing half sitting she types:

I wish my life was more exciting; like it used to be.

She presses send.

Oscar Loves

Saturday and Miss stays under the duvet for as long as her cats allow her. The cats start to yowl and she stumbles downstairs to feed them. She's close to tears, but she keeps it together. The house is full of books, colour, antiques, pictures, and stuff that she collected when she lived in other countries. The house isn't finished. It's half painted and there are still unpacked boxes shoved in corners; there are nails that seem to have no purpose sticking out in odd places that she plans to remove one day. There's stuff everywhere. There's a pair of lovely vases in the shape of women's dresses, a lamp made out of a 50s gin bottle, a basket of 60s cutlery on the dining-room table, heart shaped things, bowls of all kinds, tiles, candles, a mirrored sconce, fairy lights and occasional tables. She has lived here for two years. She tries to forget that she has a garden at the back of the house; the thought can bring on a sense of panic at the encroaching wilderness. At least in winter it isn't too rampant.

She eats a breakfast of yoghurt and an omelette at the dining table while she looks up *Oscar Loves* on YouTube. She's close to tears, but she holds it together.

She walks into town in one of her weekend dresses, a patchwork of teal silks and an orange boiled wool coat with, what the students call, her Little Red Riding Hood basket on one arm, and a set of headphones on. She keeps her eyes averted from the people around her and when people go out of their way to make themselves known to her, Stella smiles at them and speaks to them briefly while Miss cowers inside feeling distressed. In her ears, ABC are running through the *Lexicon of Love*. She buys fruit, vegetables, meat, cheese and butter in the covered market along with a loaf of bread and makes her way home. She vacuums around the cats and puts on a wash. She starts to prepare a meal. She falters as she's peeling some potatoes and the tears start. She carries on and cries through the whole preparation.

She is still crying when she moves the washing from the machine into the dryer.

She is still crying when she checks on the stew in the kitchen.

She is still crying as she cleans the bathroom.

She is still crying as she showers, but she stops as she steps out of the shower and starts to dry herself off.

She dresses in orange silk pyjamas and a powder blue dressing-gown. She goes to the fridge and pours a glass of wine. She stirs the stew and switches off the heat. She takes a seat on the sofa and turns on Netflix, scrolls to *Oscar Loves* and selects it. She sips her wine as she starts watching.

It's a small fictional town in Spain, not too far from Madrid. Esta recognises the traits of provincial Spain and the preoccupation with appearances and status.

He's a beautiful young man. Latin-American if his and his dad's accents are anything to go by. Oscar's a good person, polite and respectful, but that makes him an easy target for people who want to profit from his generous spirit. He likes to think the best of everyone, so he's often taken advantage of. He's very much in love with Nito, but he knows that Nito is straight, so he keeps it to himself. He sings in a band and he has a beautiful, pure, tenor voice and sings with extraordinary emotion. There's a wonderful warmth and depth to his voice.

He's got a great dad and step-mum and a good friend called Carmen, who is secretly in love with him, but otherwise, he's like a lamb being delivered to the slaughterhouse. He has no idea how bad the people around him are. He's endlessly forgiving. It breaks Miss's heart.

Everyone in this show is highly attractive; ridiculously attractive and also slim and well-dressed. Not a single minger in the looks department. No fuller figures. Only two genders. That makes her pretty cross. In the twenty-first century, she thinks that this kind of bullshit should be done with. A series for young people should be inclusive like the recent British *Boy Friends* and the Dutch *Liefde Verliefd/Love Struck,* both released in the last two years on Netflix. How come Spain didn't get the memo? She thinks about Esta's time living in Spain and realises that nothing has changed.

After a few episodes she starts to find them rather predictable and not particularly thrilling. Oscar's weekly song is rather the highlight, although they're always covers of older songs. He doesn't seem to have his own material. She begins to see that the dad and step-mum might not be the great people that Oscar thinks they are. She senses that they're holding secrets from Oscar, and she suspects that they might be about his mother. The best friend, Carmen, is starting to get annoyed that Oscar doesn't like her and Miss can feel that there's going to be trouble there.

She cries again, as she's thinking about what happened to Esta in Spain. She gets another glass of wine and a bowl of stew and sits at the dining table, quietly crying and eating. She puts the dishes and glass in the sink and goes up to her bedroom. She gets into bed with the cats on either side of her. She closes her damp eyes and there's a bright flash. The flash settles into a warm glow.

Esta Loves (Spain)

Esta opens her eyes. She's twenty-eight. The sky's a strong, clear blue and the sun's hot and she puts on her sunglasses as she walks down a wide pavement by the side of a white sandy beach onto which waves are gently rolling. People are sunbathing, playing volleyball and throwing frisbees. She takes some steps down onto the sand, kicks off her shoes and catches them up. She strides strongly and confidently in her form-fitting bodycon dress towards a small bar on the beach where a tall man waits for her. He's a little stout with luxuriantly curly black hair, a neat beard and moustache. His linen suit is of excellent quality and he wears it confidently. His smile widens slightly as he sees her, but she can't see his eyes behind the sunglasses that he's wearing.

"Good morning, teacher!"

"Good morning, Armando. Now, explain! Why are we meeting here?"

"It's almost summer. There is to enjoy the beach before the tourists arrive."

"Okay, but that doesn't mean we aren't going to study!"

"Of course. We study, but we study in the sun. We drink wine and we learn better."

"It's eleven in the morning, Armando, I can't drink wine now. I have hours of teaching ahead of me."

"My mistake, Esta, next time we meet on time to drink wine."

They did. There was wine. Not a lot of English was spoken. They had sex on the beach and then again at Esta's apartment. Months of happiness punctuated only by his weekly business trips. He was a sales manager for a chain of supermarkets and he spent much of the week on the road. After nine months there was an engagement ring. After eighteen months there was his wife on her doorstep screaming and shouting at her. He wasn't a sales manager; he was an accountant. He'd covered his tracks well, but she'd finally tracked Esta down. Esta stared in horror at his wife's pregnant belly. Their third, the wife informed her. At some point the wife realised that Esta knew nothing about her. She looked around the apartment and saw the photographs and things that belonged to her husband. She turned to Esta and, hands on her bump, she said, "No lo sabías, ¿verdad?" Esta, tears streaming down her face, shaking her head, held out the shaking hand with the engagement ring on it. The look of pity on Armando's wife's face almost killed her on the spot.

Not for the first time, Esta was left reeling. It was as if her legs had been taken away from her and she had been given someone else's instead. Stel had to take over so that she could work the six weeks of notice that her job required. Stel also decided that they should get as far away as possible, so when the company asked if she'd consider a job that they had in Mexico City, Stel accepted. Esta sort of came to, a little stunned, a couple of days before departure and realised that they were off to one of the most dangerous cities in the world. Ella thought it was a good thing. Stel wasn't sure but stood by her decision. Esta became Sella and went to buy a small knife and one of those money belts that you put inside your clothing.

Spain was spoilt forever for Esta.

Win Win

By Sunday evening, Miss has completed season one of *Oscar Loves* and although there remain regular hints that his dad and his step-mum aren't quite what they seem, no actual plot development has taken place in this area. Carmen has shown her true colours and outed Oscar at school. Poor Oscar has also been catfished and the local priest has informed him that he's going to burn eternally in the fires of hell.

Around 6 pm, Esta makes Miss take a shower and change out of her pyjamas into a nice stripey dress to walk two streets around the corner to have dinner with her best friend, the hilariously named Winifred Daphne Barley. What were her parents thinking? Win, is Miss's polar opposite: Win has dogs, has never worn a dress in living memory and gives not one shit about her grey hair or what anyone thinks about her. She owns an off-licence with an excellent selection of wines. What she and Miss share is: a love of good wine and excellent food, an appetite for engrossing fiction and an enjoyment of staycations featuring hot tubs with good views. They like to eat outdoors as much as possible and often barbecue.

As tonight is too cold to sit outside, they're in Win's garden room with the barbecue pulled up to the door. They start the evening with a delicious Chablis and a baked camembert with chilli flakes and caramelised red onion chutney, which they scoop up with garlic flatbread. Win tells Miss about some of the funnier customers she's had that week, and they discuss their next long weekend, which will be in April, debating the merits of a place in the woods near Bromyard and an eco-house in the Golden Valley. They decide on the latter.

The dogs beg constantly, and they both throw occasional bits of flatbread for them to fight over. After a rest, during which they open and start to drink a bottle of Picpoul de Pinet, they barbecue skewers of marinated chicken, whole sweet peppers and corn cobs. There's also a sausage for each of the dogs to buy some silence during the main course. Miss is light and enjoys the food and discussing a book that they've both just read, as well as the different books that they're both currently reading. They laugh about previous holidays they've been on.

It's a pleasant Sunday evening and Miss feels herself relax with the wine, the food and the easy conversation. Around 9 pm she becomes aware of anxiety building in her gut. She starts to fuss about the need to wake up early in the morning and make her way to work. Her lessons are planned and she has no concerns about teaching, but she worries about meeting other teachers in the staff room or the toilets. She loves being with the young people and feels their energy and potential, but her positivity for the students isn't shared by all of her colleagues. She's aware that she doesn't really fit into the team.

By 9:30 pm she's no longer good company and is straining to keep up her end of the conversation, so she pleads tiredness and takes her leave of the dogs and of Win. They do this Sunday evening meal every couple of weeks and Win's familiar with this rhythm.

Miss steps out into the cold and quickly walks the two streets to her own house, where she offends the cats with the smell of Win's dogs and gratefully gets back into pyjamas and settles down to the opening of season two of *Los Amores de Oscar*.

Can't help it

Miss tries to walk past. She puts her hands into the pockets of her grey and black plaid bubble dress and tries not to stop. She tells herself that he's not even her student, so it's really none of her business. If you asked her, she wouldn't be sure if she does it because she's nosy or compassionate, but she knows that it's inevitable.

"Are you okay?"

The boy looks like a man, but there's something vulnerable around the eyes and uncertain in his stance. He is startled. A wild animal caught in headlights. "What?"

"Are you okay? You look like something might be troubling you."

"I'm fine." He says, too fast and without any sense of conviction.

"Okay," she tells him. "That's good, but if you need anything, just let me know or talk to your personal tutor."

She takes three steps before he mumbles, "Miss..."

"Yes."

"Do you know the art department?" Her heart sinks. She knows the art department.

"I don't work in the art department," she says, by way of reassurance, "but I do know some of the teachers." She adds, "By sight." Further reassurance as she battles not to add *and by reputation*. She supposes that the art world is rather cut-throat, and they justify the way they speak to their students as training for the *real world*.

"I think that they just chucked me off the course."

"What did they say?"

"They told me to go and talk to my personal tutor about finding an alternative course."

"Are you behind with submissions of work?"

The boy winces and for a moment Miss thinks that he might cry, but he manages to say, quite steadily, "A bit, yeah."

"Do you love making art?"

"Yeah." No hesitation. That's good.

"Then why are you behind with submissions?" The boy goes to speak but stops and she can see him thinking. He rubs his forehead with two paint dirty fingers, almost tenderly, leaving a mauve mark.

"I don't know," he says, completely mystified and then a tear does fall down his cheek.

"I know that they're kind of direct and they say things a bit brutally, but if you submit work, they'll get off your back. It's as if a lack of submissions is a personal affront to them. They seem to take it personally that you haven't completed their tasks." She smiles at him, "They really care."

The boy is properly thinking now, and she can see the matter hanging in the air waiting for resolution and she watches as dispassionately as she can as he decides. "So, I could, like, do a load of work over half-term and then they might be okay?"

"That sounds like an excellent plan, to me. Do you think you could do it?"

"Totally."

"Go for it!" She continues on her way. She feels weak with gratitude and ducks into the toilets to have a small weep before she returns to her classroom.

Half Term

On the last Friday going into February half-term, she is half mad with longing for the break. She spends the day getting her classes to play games in Spanish and rewarding the students that actually use Spanish with chocolates. Millie asks her if she has watched *Oscar Loves* and she thanks her for the recommendation and says that she's enjoying it, but that it's all a bit too beautiful. "Yeah," says Millie, "makes you feel quite, like, inadequate. Imagine how much later we'd all be for college if we had to get ourselves looking like that every day." They laugh. Miss feels old and wonders when she stopped worrying about putting on mascara and eyeliner.

After the final bell and the tidying of the classroom, Miss puts on her headphones and starts down the hill. She's put together a playlist of songs from *Liefde Verliefd/Love Struck* and added in Santi Faber's latest tracks. She's deeply impressed that he can act so well in the series and also be an established pop star. The last few songs he's released have been amazing, and they transport her to a place where nothing is real, or if it is, she doesn't actually care about it. There are lines that fill her with hope and reignite a long dead feeling that there is something better waiting out there for her. She knows that it is dangerous to allow herself these moments of hope, but she is addicted to the evidence of love that the songs contain, and she plays them on a loop as Ella all but runs them down the hill home.

'When I saw the depth of love in your eyes/My heart swelled with hope and surprise'

'I did not expect to win your respect/I never dreamt we'd reach this assent/Every kiss is a pleasure that takes me deeper than ever'

'Don't try to define me/You won't outshine me/I'm just divine, me/So you can't malign me'

At her front door she is breathless with joy and excitement for her week away from work. These songs will be the soundtrack to her half-term break.

She finishes the second and latest season of *Oscar Loves* by the end of the weekend. She likes Oscar, who is also an Oscar in real life. She knows that he is never going to win an Oscar, but he's very watchable and although the storyline is formulaic, he pulls her into his fictional world and she cares about what happens to him. She wonders if there will be a season three.

She feels slightly bereft when she realises that Oscar is not a part of her evenings anymore. She decides to get out and about and takes drives to lovely locations like Ludlow and Ledbury.

Miss has a friend in London that Stel made many years before and on the Wednesday of half-term she's travelling down to the metropolis to say hello. She is wearing her favourite dress of all time. It is purple, silver and black and is made up of four contrasting quadrants and a boat neck. She feels like somebody when she wears it. She has her black velvet coat with her too. Once upon a time, in Venice, a woman stopped Sella to say that she looked 'magnifica' in this coat. She's in the quiet carriage with headphones and her book when the train pulls into Swindon and she checks the time on her mobile phone. There is a message waiting for her.

The friend, who isn't well, is experiencing a crisis and has to go to hospital and with regret has to cancel. Miss feels the quiver of concern in her stomach for her friend, and a bright burst of fear that she won't see her again. As she looks up from her phone, the train is gliding out of Swindon and closer to London. Panic suddenly catches her breath. What will she do with this day in London? She used to live in London and Ella would stride around it with purpose and swagger, but these days she feels panic rise from her stomach and into her lungs at the idea of being on its dirty streets or navigating her way around on its buses and underground trains. The very thought of the Underground sears her bowels. Buses are less disturbing, but walking is really the only option or, if she wanted to bankrupt herself, taxis.

She breathes herself calm focusing on the crashing waves on her headphones.

The fingers of her left hand run over the textured upper left quadrant of her dress, a landscape of ripples and rivulets in mauve, purple, black and silver and the thought that it ignites makes her smile. *Dress shopping*.

Just before the train pulls into Paddington, she changes the soothing waves on her headphones to the playlist from *Love Struck* and Santi Faber and once she steps down onto the platform, Ella has taken charge and guides them in strides, across the concourse and out onto Praed Street. It's only a twenty-minute walk, but Miss has to slow down and dawdle a bit as she finds herself close to the shop. Ella will wear her out and leave her a sweaty mess, if she isn't careful. She lets Esta walk them into the shop. Esta is the most beautiful of them. Esta is slim and walks with the confidence of a slim person, a confidence that Miss can only reminisce about.

Miss works her way systematically around the shop and the shop assistant, who recognises the quality of the black velvet coat and the purple dress as soon as Esta walks through the door, ferries candidates to the dressing room and checks the stockroom for the right sizes. There are ten candidates by the time Miss steps out of the miraculous purple dress and she and Esta work their way through them with acuity and consideration. The final cut is three, which is two too many, but they look good on Miss and the colours work with the shoes and scarves that she has at home.

As she makes her final decision the shop assistant asks, "I hope you don't mind me asking, but is that dress a Kozan?"

"Well spotted!"

"They're one of my favourites. Obviously after Sahara," she quickly adds.

"Do you know Ozai N Ku?" Miss asks her.

"Oh yes, they're very different."

"I'm very lucky, I live in a small town near the border with South Wales and we have the most amazing boutique. She has all the good names."

They chat while Miss transfers some money from her dwindling savings account to her current account and pays for the three dresses. Sella is complaining that one of the dresses is an evening gown and where the hell does she think she's going to wear that? Miss can't hear her. She's chatting and spending £670. Miss feels good.

Ella pushes through, out on the street, taking over and swinging the colourful paper bags that her gorgeous dresses are nestled inside, wrapped in crisp tissue and promising adventure. She is guiding them towards Marylebone High Street where she intends for them to brunch at Fischer's on chicken schnitzel, pickled cucumber salad and fries. There will be a Riesling. Miss will have to transfer some more cash from her savings account. They will spend the afternoon in Daunt Books, another bank transfer, and will need to take a taxi back to the station. Yes, there will be the need of yet another transfer of funds, but they will have lived for the day and they will return home with treasure.

It is Esta who pushes open the reassuringly heavy glass and metal door and smiles at the familiar interior and the immaculate white tablecloths. They are all reassured by the suited maître d' that takes them to a small table towards the back of the restaurant. Esta elegantly slips them onto the banquette and orders them some sparkling water whilst they decide on wine and food. It's almost mid-day on a Wednesday and the restaurant is still quiet. There are only three other tables occupied. They settle down to enjoy this moment of pleasure.

As Miss sips the water and waits to give her order, she has decided on a Grüner Veltliner in place of the Riesling, she scans the room. She blinks and takes a deep breath. She looks again. She feels a flush of heat in her stomach. It can't be.

The maître d' returns for her order and she gives it with a smile that is returned.

She glances again and sees that he is ordering coffee. He looks terrible, as if he hasn't slept or he had too much to drink last night, but it is him. It is him. It is definitely Oscar Pérez from *Oscar Loves*. His body language is telling a terrible story of pain and humiliation. She is trying very hard not to. She tries to look away, but she just can't. Inevitably she is going to get up and go to him. She tries not to.

She gets up and walks over to his table.

"Excuse me. Please forgive my interruption. Are you okay?" The startled animal in headlights.

"¿Que?"

"¿Disculpa la molestia, pero, estas bien?"

"Sí. Todo bien." Far too quickly.

"Vale, muy bien, disculpa." She turns and walks back to her table as her wine arrives. She is glad of it. He's not okay. She can feel his not-okay-ness right across the room. Something horrible has happened to Oscar Pérez. She tastes the wine and tells the waiter that it's excellent but, in truth, she can't taste it. She breathes through it and picks up a bread roll.

"¿Disculpa, puedo sentarme con usted?" He's much taller than she expected and she has to tilt her neck to look him in the face, but she manages to smile and extend a hand to ask him to be seated. She puts the bread roll back on her side plate. He's wearing a purple shirt under a teal velvet suit which looks rather crumpled and an orange woollen scarf. His dark hair is slightly unkempt and his olive skin is a tad pale and waxy. She is slightly disappointed that he has used the formal 'usted' with her. He has noticed the difference in their ages. She doesn't want that barrier to exist between them. He might never unburden himself if he sees her as 'usted.'

"Por favor, trátame de tu. Quieres tomar un vino?"

"No, gracias, tengo un café." She nods and smiles, then waits. He looks at her with something close to despair on his face. She smiles and sends unconditional positive regard across the table to him. He isn't sure if he can trust her or if he wants to. She consciously relaxes every muscle and breathes evenly. She regards his beauty and his anguish with compassion. Eventually he looks down at his coffee.

"No estoy bien."

"Lamento escuchar eso."

"Me vendría bien un amigo."

"Estoy aquí." A tear rolls down his face and he gulps down some coffee. Strangely, when he starts to speak again he has switched to excellent English with a slight American accent.

"I guess you know who I am, or you wouldn't have known to speak Spanish to me." She nods. She sends warmth and empathy across the table to him. "I have a job with Netflix tomorrow and the following day," he continues, "but I decided to come a couple of days earlier to visit a ..." he hesitates a moment, swallows then sighs. "I came to meet up with a guy that I met in Ibiza at New Years." He looks at her and she can see that he is deciding what he can tell her; he's looking for disapproval. "It didn't go the way that I had imagined. It was really... it was not okay." She furrows her brow to show her concern. He looks to his left where she suspects that he can see himself in the mirrored wall. He briefly tries to flatten his hair and rubs his face and then plunges on. "I left this guy's place in a hurry and I've left my stuff there. I need to get my stuff. I need my stuff for tomorrow." He puts his elbows on the table and puts his head in his hands. The waiter places her schnitzel in front of her and she can smell how delicious it is. "I'm sorry," he says, getting up from the table, "you're eating."

"Please sit down, Oscar. I'm sure you don't mind if I eat." He havers but sits down again. "You're frightened to go back?" She asks as she starts to cut into the schnitzel.

"Yes, I am." He says immediately and she sees that whatever happened was truly terrible.

"Then I'll go and get your stuff for you. Have you eaten, Oscar? You could share this with me. It's huge and you look as if you could do with something to eat."

The waiter brings a second plate and they share the excellent schnitzel, the delicious fries and the pickled cucumber salad and they drink the wine. They talk about the weather being so cold and how good the food tastes and Oscar begins to look more human by the minute. When the food and wine are finished, Miss asks for the address where his things are.

"I can't ask you to do this."

"You aren't asking me to do it, I am telling you that I will do it." She smiles lightly at him. "Consider it a small Thank you for the pleasure of watching you on television." He smiles at her bemusedly. "The address?" He takes his phone out of his inner jacket pocket, dismisses messages and brings up an email. He enlarges the text of the address and shows it to her. She finds her phone and takes a picture of the address.

"It's not far from here, but you'll need a car for the luggage. I'll call one. Could you bring it back here? Give me a call when you're outside?"

"Sure, can you keep my shopping here, whilst I'm away?"

"Of course."

"I'll go to the lavatory and then I'll get going."

"Lava? What?"

"Lavatory. The rest room."

"Oh, I see."

She smiles and stands suddenly aware of every one of her fifty-seven years and every pound of cellulite. She is grateful for the gentle buffer that the Grüner Veltliner has provided her with, and she lets Esta take over to avoid embarrassment. She loves the toilets at Fischer's and she enjoys the exquisite details, they all do.

When she returns to the restaurant and tries to pay, the cashier tells her that it has been taken care of. At the table, Oscar has another glass of wine and asks her for her phone to put in his number. He tells her that the car is outside and gives her the license plate and the name of the driver, Igor. He has placed her bags on the banquette and he is telling her how grateful he is. She's three paces away before she turns and says, "What's his name?"

She sees a ripple of fear shudder through his face as he says, "Parker Grove."

She smiles at him and goes out to the car, but her heart is beating so hard that she feels breathless and lightheaded. Parker Grove.

Parker Grove is every bit as handsome as Oscar, but possibly a better actor. Oscar out sings him, however, as Parker's one musical film pays testament. He's a bit older than Oscar, she thinks, maybe thirty to Oscar's twenty-six. Although Oscar convincingly plays a seventeen-year-old boy, he is almost a decade older. In real life he looks maybe twenty-one, but she knows from Google that he recently turned twenty-six. He was born in Mexico, she's not sure where, but he moved to Spain with his mum when he was six years old. When Miss is interested in something, she researches the shit out of it and will spout on about it for hours, given half the chance.

Igor is very quiet but drives well and looks trustworthy. He pulls up outside the mews house address that Oscar gave her and Esta emerges from the car wrapped in their black velvet coat and exuding confidence. She raps authoritatively on the door and stops Miss from shaking. A woman in a tabard opens the door, Philippina by the looks of it. A cleaner?

"Can I help you?"

"Hi, my name is Esta, I'm from Netflix. I've come to collect Mr. Pérez's things." The woman looks back into the house and it's clear that she's uncomfortable. She looks back at Esta, as if to say, you should probably leave, but before she can speak the distinctive tones of Parker Grove exude coldly from within.

"Who is it, Lily?"

"Lady from Netflix, sir."

Within seconds he's at the door towering over Lily and Esta. "Netflix?" He demands. "I didn't know that Netflix employed people your age." Esta has to battle Stel back.

"Good afternoon, Mr. Grove, I'm here to collect Mr. Pérez's luggage." Grove surveys Igor and the car and seems irritated. Perhaps he was hoping to see Oscar in the car.

"Why isn't Mr. Pérez here to collect his things?"

"Sorry, sir, no idea. I just got the message, the address and here I am. I've been told to collect two suitcases and a coat."

"In the bedroom."

"May I?"

"If you must." She squeezes past Parker Grove who glares at her. Poor Lily is trapped outside in the cold waiting for her chance to get back inside.

"Upstairs, is it, sir?"

"Yes."

The stairs are steep and made of polished wood. There is just one big room upstairs and the suitcases are under the window. They have wheels, but she knows that she is going to have to carry them down the stairs. They are both unbelievably heavy. She heaves them, one by one, down the steep, slippery staircase whilst Parker Grove sits on the sofa watching her with malevolent distain. She gets hotter and hotter as she struggles, but Stel is not going to let her give up or ask for help. Finally, she has both cases on the ground floor.

"Where's the coat, sir?" Esta asks, rather breathlessly.

"On the hooks by the front door." She rolls the cases to the front door and sees a beautiful, black cashmere coat hanging over the plethora of down and waxed jackets.

"The cashmere, sir?" A grunt of assent.

She opens the front door, and Igor comes to help with the cases. "Thank you, Mr. Grove, much appreciated." She has the coat over her arm and is almost out of the door when Parker Grove appears again, standing too close.

"Give Mr. Pérez a message, would you?"

"I can give it to someone at the office, sir, but I won't be seeing him."

"Aren't you taking these things to him?"

"No, sir, they're to be taken to the offices and he's collecting them from there, as I understand it."

"Little shit!"

Esta walks them to the car keeping their collective shit together. Stel is tamping and Ella is close to tears. Estella is clutching at Stel and Miss has braced Stella and Sella from the waves of ire crashing at them from Parker Grove. Calm, quiet Igor has placed the cases in the boot and is again behind the wheel. Esta gets them all elegantly into the car, holding Stel back from taking a run at Parker Grove, who watches them until they are out of sight.

"Arsehole!" says Igor and Miss can't help but snort with laughter.

"You said it, Igor."

On the short ride back to Marylebone High Street, Miss feels exhaustion washing over her and wishes she hadn't drunk the wine at lunchtime. As they get close, she calls Oscar, who picks up immediately and steps out onto the pavement as Igor pulls up. Oscar gets into the back with her shopping bags and looks at her with concern.

"Everything go okay?"

"Absolutely fine, the cases are in the back." She swaps the coat for her bags. Igor sets off. He seems to know where they're going.

"You don't look so good; are you sure you're okay?"

"Oscar, your suitcases are really heavy!"

"I'm so sorry!"

"It's okay, don't worry, it's done."

"¡Joder, no se tu nombre! ¡He estado tan egoísta!" Esta laughs at the idea of him being selfish. They all laugh. They hadn't noticed that they hadn't told him their names.

"Soy Estella. ¡Mucho gusto!"

"¡Encantado, Estella!"

The Ned

The car makes its way south while Miss relates how she dealt with Parker Grove to an awe-struck and grateful Oscar Pérez. When the car reaches Holborn, Miss starts to be concerned. "Where are we going, Oscar?"

"My hotel. We can drop off my stuff and then we can go and do something fun." Miss takes out her phone to look at the time and finds that it is somehow almost three in the afternoon. We're not going to make it to Daunt's she says to the others, and she experiences a moment of irritation. Her plans have gone awry.

"Is everything okay, Estella?"

"I have a train to catch at 5:41 pm, back at Paddington."

"You don't live in London?"

"No, I live in Hereford."

"Where?"

"About 130 miles northwest of London."

"130 miles?"

"Erm, around 200 kilometres."

"¡Joder, eso es lejos!"

"Yes, it's quite a way."

"Isn't there a later train?"

Miss feels something very odd happening inside her. She feels all of them scrum down in an intense conflab. Her heart rate is rising and she feels almost breathless as she hears herself say, "I'm sure there must be."

"Vale, entonces todo en puesto. ¡Vamos a gozar el día!"

Igor glides the car by Saint Paul's cathedral and Oscar looks at her as she draws a deep breath at the sight of it. "¿Te gusta, Estella?"

"I love Saint Paul's. This part of the city is ancient and you can feel the vibrations of all the people who have lived and died here." Oscar looks at her. He really looks at her.

"¿Verdad?" he asks, almost in a whisper. She smiles, she feels all of them smiling simultaneously, because he was really listening to her. She can't remember the last time someone actually listened to her.

"Pillar upon pillar, arch upon arch, Magnolia marbled magnificence resides amongst concrete, But where history and metropolis meet, Saint Paul's stands tall." He's still listening and his eyes show interest.

"That's beautiful."

"Not mine, a poet called Freya Townsend."

The car pulls up outside a massive creamy white mansion and Igor jumps out to get the bags as a bowler-hatted doorman strides to meet them. "Mr Pérez, welcome back."

"Thank you, good afternoon."

"Your suite is ready. If you would like to follow me." Oscar turns back to Igor.

"Thanks, Igor. See you later." She thinks how attractive courtesy and kindness are.

Their feet hardly seem to touch the marble floor as the doors are opened and it feels as if they are gently sucked through into the lobby. The doorman hands them over to Peter, who perambulates them to the lift and seemingly seamlessly they find themselves in a suite with a terrace and a four-poster bed. She sees Oscar's hand extend to Peter before he leaves and a banknote passes between them.

"Oh, my goodness! I. Am. At. The. Ned!" She opens the French windows and rushes out onto the terrace. She has read about this place. It's more lovely than she had expected.

"¿Primera vez aquí?" He stands beside her looking not at the view but at her.

"¡Claro!" She laughs. "I once stayed one night at Babington House, their place in Somerset, but this is rather grander."

"The swimming-pools here are cool."

"I've seen the pictures. So beautiful."

"Shall we go and get a drink at the bar?"

"Amazing!"

On the way back to the lift and going down she remarks on the all the beautiful things that she sees. Exiting the lift, she looks up and takes in the elegant vastness of the lobby. She delights in the patterns in the marble floor and comments on the elegant outfit of a young woman who passes them as they make for the bar. Oscar Pérez smiles. The aura of pain and woundedness has lifted and she can see why he is such a popular actor. His smile is warm and genuine and his face as handsome as you could wish, with eyes that are clear, bright and intelligent. He's wasted in the role of sheepish Oscar Martínez of *Oscar Loves*. This guy is a romantic lead or the hero of one of those action movies that she probably wouldn't watch unless it starred Ryan Gosling. She'd watch if Oscar Pérez was in it, but she guesses that *Oscar Loves* has made him a lot of money.

The armchairs in the bar are so comfortable that, to Esta's disgust, they subside into one like a landslide as Oscar seats himself with the control that his gym-trained body affords him. He is still smiling. A beautiful blonde appears and asks what she can get for Mr. Pérez. "Estella," he says to Miss, "What do you think we should drink?" She looks up at the pilasters, the burnished woodwork and the elegant lighting.

"Champagne." She declares with authority.

"Excellent," he says, "we should celebrate. What kind of champagne for the Señora?" She tries not to let the smile falter.

She turns to the blonde, "Do you have Bollinger or Cristal?"

"We have Cristal, madam."

"Do you mind if we have Cristal? I've only had it once before." She asks Oscar.

"Perfect. Cristal for the Señorita." He tells the blonde and she knows that he saw.

"I'm sorry," she says, "I'm touchy about the assumption that I belong to somebody."

"It's a reflex. It's about respect. I wasn't making any assumptions about your marital status."

"I know, I'm sorry." She looks at him. "I have noticed these days when I'm in Spain that I have become *usted* and *señora*. It's hard to accept because inside I am still the *señorita* that lived there twenty something years ago." She pauses but can't stop herself from going on. "These days I look in the mirror and I don't recognise the person looking back at me." He doesn't look away. He briefly licks his lips.

"I don't recognise the person in my mirror either," he tells her and looks down at his hands which are clasped tightly. "Do you ever feel like the outside is just the way the world makes you? I don't know if that makes sense. Like other people construct the outside of you. The inside is real, but you can't let people see that because they'll...I don't know...destroy it or try to change it?..." He searches her face. She looks back with all the tiredness and empathy that she feels and takes a deep breath.

"Yes." She feels the tears welling up and she tries to speak before they come. "Oscar, you must never let anyone get to that part of you. Even if you think that you can trust them. They will try to take it away from you. Mostly they do it by accident, but some of them do it on purpose. There will be friends that you can share some of it with, but never lovers." Her voice breaks on the word *lovers* and some tears fall, but she regulates her breath and pulls back from crying. They sit for a moment really looking at each other until the champagne arrives. They continue to regard each other as the blonde completes the ceremony of unwrapping, uncorking and pouring the sample. Oscar passes the sample to Miss, who tastes it and beams approval at the young woman.

After the blonde leaves, they sit with their glasses in hand and Oscar says, "I give you gratitude for friendship!" They raise their glasses and clink them gently before sipping. Their eyes meeting as the first sip slips into their mouths. "Can I tell you about last night?" He asks, breaking eye contact to give her time to think. She doesn't need it.

She says, immediately, "Of course you may."

"The champagne is excellent. Good choice." He says. She raises her glass to him but doesn't speak. He sits back in his chair and crosses one leg over the other and takes off his scarf. "I went to Ibiza for New Years. There was a huge house party at the villa of one of the producers of *Los Amores de Oscar*. I wasn't staying at the house, but at a villa a short walk away with a few others from the show. The party was three days. There were a lot of drugs. There was a lot of alcohol. I don't do drugs. I don't like the idea of losing control. Alcohol has a way of making me sick before I get to a point of not knowing what I'm doing. Do you know what I mean? How do you say 'mojigato' in English."

She smiles in surprise at him, "Prude."

"I am basically a prude when it comes to drugs. Actually, I am a bit of prude, period. A bit of a shock that I turned out to be bi-sexual." He runs his hands through his hair. "It's taken a while to get comfortable with that. Anyway, this party, there were guests at the big villa and guests in all the villas around the big one. There were parties in most of the villas. It was basically insane, like something out of that movie *Babylon* with Margot Robbie. My inner prude was really uncomfortable. But the thing is that *Los Amores de Oscar* isn't going to last forever and these parties are one of the ways to get yourself into a new job. Anyway, I was also asked to sing at the New Years party coming up to midnight and they were paying me for that." He smiles at her, almost apologetic, but she isn't at The Ned any longer, she is in Ibiza at the Babylonian party feeling all the fear and unease that he felt. They both drain their glasses and he refills them. He settles his gaze into the middle distance and takes up the story again. "New Year's Eve was the last day of the party. I did my set and amongst the people that came to congratulate me afterwards was Parker Grove." He pauses and drinks. Looks at the glass for a while and then glances at her briefly before resuming. "He's very charming when he wants to be. He was clearly into me. We chatted, he was very flattering about *Los Amores de Oscar*, and I told him that I had seen his Hamlet and how impressed I was. Lots of mutual admiration." He looks pained, rubs his eyes and pinches the bridge of his nose with his thumb and middle finger. He tilts forward and his voice drops. "I really wanted to have sex with him."

He looks straight at her and she sees right into him and the desire inside him. She sees that he is looking for someone to be with. He is searching for *his* person. He still believes that there is someone for everyone and every time he meets and gets intimate with a person he is hoping that this is *his* person. In that moment they are all there looking back at him with sympathy, empathy and pity dependent on their experience. He sees them all in that moment and is momentarily startled at the feeling of acceptance that comes over to him from them. He sees the tears in her eyes and takes warmth and strength from them.

"We went back to his villa for the party he was having after midnight. He suggested that we take this tablet that he said would *enhance* our time together." He pinches the bridge of his nose again. "I told him that I didn't need any enhancement. He seemed annoyed, but he let it go and got me a drink instead."

He pours them both another glass. She is aware of the pleasant buzz of alcohol in her head and her body seeming to flow better, but she is also tensed for the next words. She is pretty sure she knows what he's about to say. She sees him reliving it and trying to decide how to tell her.

"I don't remember anything else."

She feels the burn of outrage as it surges through all of them at once and she cannot stop Stel from angrily pronouncing, "Bastard." He looks up at her and they regard each other with hopelessness. Nothing will ever make this go away.

"The next day I was woken up by a cleaner at the villa. Parker was gone. It was almost evening. I had missed my flight back to Madrid. I was disorientated and my head was in a mess. I just focused on getting back to the villa where I was staying and getting my stuff. It had all been packed up and the villa was empty. There were about a million missed calls on my phone from my cast mates. I got the next flight back to Madrid and was so pleased to get back to my apartment. I got a DM from Parker saying he was sorry that we hadn't got to hang out. He said that I must have been very tired because I fell asleep in his room and missed the party. He hadn't been able to wake me in the morning and he had an early flight. He said we should hook up another time. I felt uneasy, but I couldn't remember anything!" He folds his arms across his chest and he looks even younger. He looks like poor little lost Oscar Martínez, the boy in love with his oblivious straight best friend. He looks determinedly at his foot that he is bobbing up and down.

"When I got into the shower at home...there was blood. I had little nicks and cuts and over the next few days bruises started to appear pretty much all over. I'm a prude. I was disgusted with myself. I was so angry that I had allowed this to happen to me. I have never been my own greatest fan, Estella, but this pushed me into complete self-hate." She hears him. Her heart is full of his loathing of himself and his regret for allowing himself to be tricked and cheated.

"That's why you went to see him? You wanted to rewrite history?"

He looks up sharply, "Yes. You understand?"

"If you could meet him again and have things go well, then that would make it all okay. That would erase the aberration. You'd be justified in the decisions you made." His face contorts and he starts to cry making no sound, just tears flowing down his beautiful face; his fine, intelligent eyes bloodshot and creased. She continues the story for him. "But it didn't go the way you had hoped, and you didn't get the redemption you need." Ella is weeping in Esta's arms. Ella could share a story, the story that arrested her where she remains perpetually looking for redemption and a happy ever after.

"There were other people there, last night. Vaguely familiar people. They were snorting cocaine. He made a big thing about me not touching drugs and instead handed me a drink. I pretended to be drinking it but kept going out into the courtyard and tipping it away. After about half an hour I noticed that they were all looking at me more and more often and one of them kept asking me if I felt tired. They seemed to be waiting for me to pass out. Finally, Parker suggested that we go to a club for a bit. At the club, we kissed and danced together and he kept bringing me drinks, but I managed to avoid drinking them. He was getting more and more angry and when he kissed me it was getting more and more aggressive." He looks up at her again and almost seems surprised when she is actually there listening to him. They look at each other for a while and then Miss realises that the blonde is speaking to them. She orders some sparkling mineral water and some snacks.

When they're alone again.

"There was a room at the back of this club and we all went through to it so that they could take more cocaine. I sat on one of the sofas and watched. I'm not sure how it happened. I was tired by that time. Two of them took my arms and held me down and someone, I couldn't see who, sat on my legs and started to undo my trousers. I went mad. I was an animal in need of freedom. There were four of them including him, but somehow, I got out of that room. Adrenaline perhaps? I got out of the club and ran. I ran for a while and then I walked. I walked for hours. I walked until it got light. I started to go into cafes and sit for a while and then walk again. I started to work my way back towards his house, but I lost my nerve. That's when we met." Slowly he comes back to himself, rubs his face and hunkers over, elbows on knees. The snacks and water arrive, and he gulps down water and hungrily devours the chicken tenders, mozzarella sticks, Padron peppers and fries. She too drinks the water and eats snacks.

"It's like you know me. How did you know that I needed this?" He asks with a full mouth and beginning to emerge from his hunker. She waves a hand dismissively.

"It was just a hunch." They eat a little more and then both lean back in their chairs and regard each other to see if they are both still listening.

"Oscar," she says.

"No," he says very gently.

"But, there will be others," she tells him softly. At that, he looks up with pain.

"They won't be as stupid as I was."

"You know that you don't believe that, Oscar."

"I have to believe that."

"You are not a person that can believe a lie, Oscar. Not in the long-term." She leans forward. "I understand if you can't deal with this right now, but you will have to deal with it. You have a conscience and it won't let you pretend that this never happened. You know that this is true." There is a long pause during which he seems almost catatonic.

Finally.

"Yes, I know. Pero, ahora no puedo, Estella, not now. Lo haré, pero hoy no."

"Vale. Okay."

They sit and bask in the warmth of the food. When the waitress returns, he asks for the bill and signs it to his room. Miss offers to pay her share and he looks at her with irritation.

"I have been making money since I won that goddam talent show when I was eight years old, Estella, money is not a thing for me. It's the least I can do when I have hijacked your day and told you my sadness. Please, money is not a thing."

"Thank you, Oscar, but I don't want you to imagine that I am not grateful for the excellent champagne and the delicious food."

"It's my pleasure."

She takes out her phone and a quake of anxiety shakes her calm. It's 5:30 pm. She definitely won't make the train she's booked onto. She opens the app to look for the later train that she was so sure of earlier. She doesn't want to have to change more than once and she knows that she probably won't make the 6:18 pm either. Paddington is quite a way away. She decides on the 7:48 pm.

"Estella, what are you doing?"

"Checking for my train."

"Estella, don't."

"Don't what?"

"Don't."

She looks up at him. He's leaning forward and watching her intently.

"Don't go."

She looks back at him. Her social battery is running very low. She's exhausted from the story he has shared with her, but she has also been having fun. This is the best day that they have had for a very long time. What did she type on the college computer? What has she been wishing for. Inside, Estella, Stel, Ella and Esta are all screaming at her not to go home and even Stella and Sella are finding it hard to argue against it.

"Please," he says, still looking right at her, "I could really do with your friendship right now." He suddenly sits up straight. He looks shocked. "I'm sorry, you must have people waiting for you at home. I'm being completely selfish. Please, let me get a car for you to the station." She doesn't respond and he looks at her through exhausted eyes. He puts his scarf back on as if he has suddenly realised that he's cold. She realises how much it would hurt to walk away at this moment. She really likes this young person. She would like to know him better. The idea of her house and her cats does not have its usual appeal.

"Actually," she says, "apart from two elderly cats, there is nobody waiting for me to come home. I am not working tomorrow. If you would really like me to stay, I can do that, but you must have other friends in London."

"Not like you, Estella." He looks at her with a puzzled expression. "I've never met anyone like you." He pauses and then for emphasis, she supposes, "Never." She smiles at him and he starts to grow back into himself. "I'll get another room," he says and is up and across the lobby before she can thank him. *We're staying at The Ned*, she tells them, *we are fucking staying at The fucking Ned!* They are all agog with excitement.

Dinner and Drinks with Friends

He insists that she stays in the Terrace Suite. He says he's stayed there before, and he's only down the hall. It seems to make him happy to give her the spectacular room. He wheels his cases to the door. "Dinner is at 8 pm," he tells her. "We're meeting some friends. I think you'll like them." He seems almost excited. "There will probably be drinks and a club afterwards. Is that okay with you?"

"Cool!" She thinks about the evening dress in one of her paper bags and Esta is already desperate to get her to the nearest M&S for fresh underwear and the right tights, but most importantly, for a pair of sandals. She can't go to dinner and a club in her Skechers Unos, even if they are sparkling lavender. She makes for the door to follow him out, grabbing the key.

He's startled, "Where are you going?"

"Oscar, I don't have anything with me. I'm just popping to the shops. I promise to be ready by 7:45." He still looks unsure.

"You won't leave, will you?" She puts her hand on his arm.

"I'm not going anywhere. I just need some underwear!"

"Of course," he blushes and slightly rolls his eyes, "I wasn't thinking."

Ella is in her element and gets them to the nearest M&S in ten breathless minutes. She makes a bank transfer and buys strappy sandals, pants, tights, a night gown, razors and at the last minute thinks to buy a swimming costume. There might be time to use one of the pools. She buys water and paracetamol. Ella strides them back to The Ned and they all take a collective breath as they re-enter the magnificence.

She drinks water, takes paracetamol and showers. The dress is cerise at the shoulders and graduates through pink to peach and finally a light orange. She bought silver sandals and has a silver scarf that she wore with the purple dress and she thanks the Goddess of Forward Planning for the black velvet coat that cost her half a month's wages almost a decade ago. She wonders if she should have bought some mascara or lipstick. She hasn't owned any for years. The amethyst earrings and necklace work, at least and her Pandora charm bracelet works with anything. Her hair is shiny and lively.

When he knocks on her door, he takes her breath away. He's wearing a Hugo Boss grey suit with a white shirt and a cerise tie. He wears old-school brown, lace up leather Oxfords. It feels like a miracle. He hardly sees her reaction. He sees the dress and his hand goes to his tie as the smile creases his eyes. "Was that in one of the bags?"

"Yes, rather fortuitous."

"My tie matches."

She smiles and swings on her coat. She has butterflies in her stomach for the first time in years. Earlier she WhatsApp-ed Win, telling her that she had missed her train and was staying overnight and asked if she could feed the cats for her. She feels naughty and deliciously free. Free to do whatever she likes as long as she can bank transfer the required funds into her current account. As they walk through the lobby, she is aware that people are looking at Oscar and she feels enormously proud to be walking beside him. Perhaps, she muses, they will think that she is his mother. A son like Oscar would be a thing to be happy about.

Igor awaits outside and the doorman opens the car door for Estella, tipping his hat, and wishing her a lovely evening. The car slides through the London streets and she leans her head back to watch the buildings flow past overhead with the punctuation of the streetlamps like a heartbeat on a monitor and suddenly Sella is in the back seat of a car rushing down the Avenida de los Insurgentes in Mexico DF. Queen's *Bohemian Rhapsody* is enthralling the car stereo and the man in the passenger seat in front of her has stretched his arm back to caress her ankle. She remembers the pleasure of the touch and the physical and mental pain that came so very soon afterwards. She pushes herself upright and thinks about Oscar still looking for *his* person. She needs a drink. Oscar gently touches her hand, "¿Todo bien?" She catches Igor's eye in the rearview mirror; he too seems concerned.

"Sí," she says as brightly as she can manage, "Una memoria que prefería no recordar! Nada más. In English we say, someone just walked over my grave." He shudders.

"Cocktails! What we need, is cocktails."

"Amen!"

Dinner is at The Ivy Soho Brasserie, and they are the first to arrive. The table seats six. They order mojitos and Miss lets Esta take charge because she feels overwhelmed by the sights and sounds of the busy bistro. She has suddenly begun to feel tired and all the water that she chugged back at The Ned needs to be processed. She excuses herself and he says, "The lavatory?" She smiles.

"Well remembered!"

"I Googled it. I was convinced that you were having a joke at my expense. I never heard it before."

In the lavatory, Esta gives them all a good talking to. *We're tired, sure, but when do we get a chance like this? When did we last do anything half as interesting as this? Come on! Ovary up and party like it's 1999!* Miss splashes their face, combs their hair with her wet fingers and makes an entrance back into the restaurant. The four friends have arrived. Esta pushes a trembling Miss into the back seat because she knows that she can't deal with this.

Oscar might have said something, or she might have considered that as Oscar is famous the *friends* might also be famous. She feels starstruck, sweaty and dry-mouthed. The leading actors of *Boy Friends* and *Love Struck* are seated at the table with Oscar. Including the exquisite Santi Faber.

Nothing could have prepared her for this quartet. Esta smiles. Esta is beautiful. The slimmest and most beautiful that any of them has ever been and that gives her a confidence that none other of them has, and at this moment confidence is what she needs. Esta pauses with her hands on the back of her chair, they are all looking at her, and she knows what they see. She knows what they will be thinking: *Why did Oscar invite his grandma to dinner?*

"Good evening, gentlemen, what a pleasure to see you all." Oscar leaps up and pulls the chair out for her and Esta seats them smoothly. Men often did this for Esta in her day and she nods her smiling thanks. She reaches for her mojito, "Here's to an excellent evening!" They raise their glasses and smile.

"Estella, Oscar says that you don't live in London," says Arlo Canning from *Boy Friends*. "Where have you come from today?"

"Hereford."

"Wow, that's like, almost in Wales, right?" asks, Seamus Martindale, his co-star.

"I thought it was just outside London," says Arlo.

"That's Hertfordshire, Arlo," Seamus berates. "Hertfordshire has a whole consonant that Herefordshire doesn't!" She giggles at that.

"Very clever. It's an easy mistake to make though, Arlo."

"What brings you two to London?" she asks the other two friends. "Haven't you just finished a tour, Santi?"

"Yeah, how did you know that?"

"I'm a fan. I wanted to go to either the Bristol or Birmingham concert, but work got in the way. I caught up on YouTube. They looked amazing. You gate-crashed the London concert, right, Bram?" She smiles at Santi's love interest in *Love Struck* to show that she's ragging him.

"Yeah, that's right. I just had to get a bit of attention, you know?" They all laugh.

"Happy to be back from New York, Arlo?" His smile is tired, but he nods happily.

They order food. Santi and Seamus are picky about their orders, but Oscar, Bram and Arlo are straight forward. They talk about ordering wine, but Esta tells them that she's sticking to cocktails. Santi smiles at her and says, "Me too." She feels like she knows him from Miss's research around *Love Struck* and from listening to his songs. His smile is like a light that lifts your soul.

They talk about Arlo's recent run on Broadway and Seamus's experiences making American TV in Hollywood. Bram's recent projects and his frustrations around his current opportunities. Oscar is very quiet.

"Oscar, is there going to be a season three?" she asks. He meets her gaze and smiles.

"Yeah, they're announcing it tomorrow."

"Great. Does he find his mother?"

"I don't know. I don't think they've written it yet. Filming starts in August."

"Estella," Bram says, "what do you do? Are you in television?"

"No," she laughs lightly, "I'm a teacher. I teach A Level Spanish."

"¿Hablas español?" Santi asks excitedly. Although he's Dutch now, he lived in Colombia until he was seven years old.

"¡Claro!" she smiles at him, "¡Eso es porque me contratan!"

"Have you lived in Spain?"

"Yes. Sevilla, Andújar, Oviedo, Almería y Menorca. I also lived in Mexico for a few years." She finds Oscar looking at her.

"¿Conoces DF?"

"Yes, I lived in Mexico City in San Cosme, and I worked close to the World Trade Centre."

"I was born in Coyoacan."

"No! I had friends who lived near La Casa Azul." They beam at each other.

"¿Has estado en Colombia?" Santi asks and before Miss can stop her Esta divulges more information than Sella would like.

"No, I haven't been to Colombia, but I did have a Colombian boyfriend once." Arlo saves the day.

"More cocktails, anyone?"

The drunker they get the more disjointed the conversation becomes, but they all seem to be having a good time. They're all very tactile and laugh easily. It's a joy to be around them. Miss comes out and lets herself just relax and talk to them about their lives. Oscar is never far from her. She feels like a talisman for him. From the restaurant they have to go to a club, where Santi is going to perform three songs. They have to take two cabs and Miss ends up in a cab sitting next to Oscar with Santi facing them on a pull-down seat; he's finding it hard to sit still. It's as if there's a soundtrack that only he can hear and he's dancing to it.

Santi tells her that the club had been helpful during the recent tour and he feels he should do this for them, but that he feels pretty tired. He can't decide what to sing.

"Open with *Surprise*," Miss suggests, "go into *Deeper* and finish with *I'm Just Divine*." He looks at her appraisingly.

"You really are a fan!"

"I don't lie."

"She doesn't," says Oscar and she feels his hand slip into hers under the flap of her coat. He squeezes her hand and she squeezes back. She feels like his mother, reassuring him that everything is alright.

"Well, Miss Estella, I think I will take your advice." Santi tells her and his smile is beatific.

The club is horrific. So many people. So much noise. Ella has very vague memories of coming here maybe forty years ago when she first moved to London from Hereford. It's cleaner and more organised, but Esta has to take over and even she feels the need of Oscar and when the opportunity arises, she takes his hand. He looks back momentarily at their hands clasped and then at her eyes and smiles. He keeps hold of her until they arrive at the stage area and they have a little space around them. As he lets go, he leans in and shouts across the noise around them, "¿Todo bien?" She nods gratefully.

There's a lot of faffing about with mics and Santi changes his shirt. She tries not to, but she does look. They're brought drinks. Finally, the DJ stops and Santi is announced. She looks out at the excited crowd and wonders at how many people go clubbing on a Wednesday night in February. Santi is about to sing when Arlo asks if she wants to get onto the dance floor. They make their way to the area in front of the stage with Bram and look up as Santi starts singing *Surprise*. Then they start to dance. There's Arlo, Bram and Miss, but here come Ella and Esta. '*When I saw the depth of love in your eyes/My heart swelled with hope and surprise'*. The music inhabits her as it always has and she is moving with it and letting it take her as far away from herself as it can. She feels every beat and nuance and her arms and legs are not her own but belong to the music. Happiness pours through her and washes away the years, the tears and the wounds. The words transport her, and she feels as if she is momentarily a part of Santi up there on the stage. During *Deeper*, which is a slower number she, Bram and Arlo look up at Santi and sway as his sincerity washes over them and makes them wish that he was singing to them. Their smiles are huge. But here it comes. The three of them glance at one another and then they're singing *I'm Just Divine* with Santi. They are Santi. Santi sees them. He sings to them. He sings with them and she is somewhere that doesn't even exist. If she died now, this would be heaven, it would be bliss to feel this way forever. She feels the emotion of Santi's words and the emotion of the music and she has passed through to a place of warmth, love and acceptance. As Santi finishes, she, Bram and Arlo erupt into applause. Arlo pulls her back towards Oscar and Seamus. She sees Oscar looking at her. As she comes up the steps to them, he takes her hand.

"Wow," he says, she sees his mouth shape the word, then he leans close to her ear, "you dance like no one is watching." She feels the bliss dissipate. What does that mean? None of them knows what that really means and for a horrible moment she thinks that she is going to cry, but suddenly Santi is there.

"Hey, Miss Estella, you rock!" He's hugging her. "We need more cocktails and we need to take Estella dancing!"

Arlo and Seamus are deciding where they should go. As they set off to leave the club, Oscar takes her right hand, and Santi takes her other arm. Bram follows close behind. She knows that the crowd are staring at the young people, but she also knows that some of them will be looking at her and wishing they were in her place. The bliss is back and all of them are taking this moment to live in the present and feel the comfort of these lovely people taking care of her. She breathes deeply and smiles.

It's wonderfully cold outside and she turns her face to it as some would turn their face up to the sun. She realises with a twist in her stomach that there is some discord.

"It's Wednesday night," says Seamus, "that's the problem. There aren't a lot of places open."

"Hey," she says, "let's not worry about dancing. I've always wanted to go to Soho House, you guys are members, right?"

That unites them and off they go in two taxis to Dean Street. This time she finds herself sitting between Santi and Oscar, who are singing a Luis Miguel song, *Amarte Es Un Placer*. She is struggling to stay in the present now. These two young people have no idea what this song means to Esta. Fortunately, the trip is short, and they are soon disembarking at Dean Street.

She marvels at the pleasures that money can afford you. She enjoys the beauty of the place and the people, but most of all the exquisite delight of the care that these young people are taking of her. She is installed on a comfortable sofa, Santi on one side and Oscar on the other. There are endless cocktails, and they endure her questions with equanimity; she feels comfortable and complete.

"Estella, there's a party tomorrow night." Oscar tells her.

"Yeah, you should come," Santi chips in.

"It's a Netflix party," Oscar explains. "They're announcing shows that have new seasons and some new projects that are coming up. There'll be lots of people there and there'll be dancing. Santi and I will both be singing. Would you like to come?"

She looks at him. She wants to just yell, *Hell yes,* but she feels like she might be outstaying her welcome. This evening has been a dream come true. Perhaps she shouldn't push her luck. She realises that they are all looking at her now.

"You don't want to come?" asks Bram.

"No," she says, "it's not that I don't want to come. It's just that, well, you have all been very kind this evening and I don't want to impose."

"Impose?" Santi puzzles.

"Outstay my welcome."

"Ya basta de tonterías," says Oscar, rather heatedly. "You're coming!"

"That told you," giggles Seamus. And that is the end of the discussion.

Oscar gets up and tells her ostentatiously that he is going to the *lavatory*. She explains the joke to the others. The group ebbs and flows, but one of them is always there. Oscar, however, does not come back from the *lavatory*. She decides to pay a visit herself and on route sees Oscar surrounded by a group of handsome men. He looks different. There is something hard in his face and she realises that one of the men surrounding him is Parker Grove.

She pays her visit and, on the way back, puts herself in Oscar's line of vision. She sees that the hardness is just a front to cover the panic beneath the surface. His eyes lock on hers and she feels his self-disgust and knows that it's undermining him in every way. She tries not to. She tries to persuade herself that it's a bad idea, but it's inevitable. Esta elbows her way into the group.

"Excuse me, gentlemen, but I'm afraid I must insist that Mr. Pérez comes with me." She pushes past Parker Grove, but he catches her arm.

"Excuse me, grandma, but you don't get to insist on anything, this is a members' club and I'm fucking certain that you aren't a member." It is Stel that turns on Parker Grove with a low growl that only he can hear, venom dripping from every word.

"You will unhand me now, or you will regret it, Mr Grove. If you cross me, I will finish you." Parker looks like he's going to laugh her off, but Stel continues soto-voce, "Don't fuck with me, or I'll convince him to go to the police." At that, he drops her arm.

"My goodness, Oscar, what a frightful dog you keep!" smirks Parker Grove and then, out of nowhere, Oscar's fist connects with Parker's jaw and, caught off guard, he crashes to the floor.

"How dare you insult my friend!" He turns to Miss, "Are you okay, Estella?"

"I'm fine, you really didn't need to..." but she trails off because she knows that actually he really did need to. Security is there in moments, but Oscar's already shepherding her towards the cloakroom and their friends are following.

"Did you just punch Parker Grove?" Asks Arlo. Oscar doesn't speak, she doesn't suppose he can just now, but he nods tightly. "Well done, mate, that guy is a total arse."

"Yeah, he touched up a friend of mine at an event round at Greek Street. He's a real jerk."

"He's a shit singer too!"

They are all out on the pavement now. Miss turns Oscar's wrist and sees that it's almost 1 am. "Oscar, should we head back to The Ned?"

"We're staying there too," Bram tells them.

"I think Netflix has the whole place booked out," says Arlo. "We're all there."

Two more taxis. Oscar doesn't let go of her hand. He doesn't speak. Santi leans his head on her shoulder. His mood has dropped. At The Ned they all agree to meet for breakfast later that day at 9 am. Oscar's still holding her hand. He still hasn't spoken. She gets him into the lift and takes him to the Terrace Suite. They stand for a while just hand in hand. She leads him to the ottoman and pushes him to sit down. She strokes his hair with her free hand. He tilts his head against her stomach and the tears start. He releases her hand and wraps his arms around her. She feels the heaves of his sobs and the warm dampness of his tears. She stands there for what seems like hours, but is probably only twenty minutes, until she feels his arms loosen and the heaving sobs reduce. She takes a step back holding his shoulders so that he won't fall forwards. She takes his hands, pulls him up, and puts him into bed. He's under the covers, but as she moves away, his hand shoots out from under them and grabs her arm, "Please, don't leave me!" He is a husk, and his voice is barely there.

"I won't leave, Oscar. I'll be back from the bathroom in a minute." She sees him mouth the word *lavatory*. "That's right," she says, "back in a minute."

She lies beside him on top of the covers and keeps her hand against his shoulder. She's sure that he can feel it through the fabric. Miraculously, they both sleep. She dreams that she is back at the club dancing in front of Santi and that she is bathed in the light of his smile. She sleeps soundly, which is not normal. When she starts to wake, she feels her mouth pulled into a smile, which is not normal.

Morning

She opens her eyes and sees that light is coming through the curtains. She turns and sees that his eyes are open. He's smiling at her. "You stayed."

"I stayed." She is smiling back. "How are you?"

He takes a moment, "I'm okay, I think. My hand hurts a bit."

She laughs, "I'm not surprised, that was one hell of a punch."

"I've wanted to do that for a long time." She realises that the punch wasn't about Parker Grove's betrayal of him.

"Tell me."

"My dad used to hit my mum," he says. "When he grabbed you, I saw red." He was punching his dad. He was settling old scores. "Are you hungry?"

"Starving."

He flips back the covers and jumps out of bed, "I'll knock for you in half an hour."

Ella races them to the shower. Esta grabs a dress from the other bag. They are breathless but ready in a very short time. She suddenly thinks to look at her phone, which she can't remember looking at since she texted Win. She didn't even take it with her when they went out last night. There are some missed calls. First from Anna, the friend that she was going to visit the day before and the second from Win.

"Hey Stel, if you are still in London, I'm in hospital. St Thomas's. Come and see me?"

"The fuck you missed your train. What the hell is going on? How did you meet Oscar Pérez?"

Confusion. How could Win possibly know that she had met Oscar Pérez? There's a knock at the door. She opens it to experience another breathtaking moment. They both laugh. Today's Ted Baker suit is mauve and so is her dress. "Come on, we're late!" She looks down at her phone. It's 9:15 am. She chucks the phone on the bed and they go hand in hand to breakfast. A symphony in mauve.

"Don't you two look cute in your coordinated outfits," Seamus says. He looks well rested, but the group is not as animated as they were last night. There are hangovers, but they are all still impeccably polite and well dressed, just a bit subdued. There's a lot of silence while they eat and scroll their phones. Estella orders eggs Benedict and Oscar an egg white omelette. She supposes that he does trade on his looks and they drank a lot of calories last night, but she can't imagine being that committed to her look. She'd rather be round than give up the delights of butter and sugar.

"Hey, Estella!" Bram breaks the silence. "We can't find you on social media to tag you. What do you call yourself?" She smiles.

"I'm not on social media." There's silence.

"Not even Facebook?" Asks Seamus.

"Not even Facebook. I don't really like it. I understand that it's good for business and for people like you, but I see what it does to my students and I don't think it's healthy." It's a tumbleweed moment. If she needed to remind them of the age divide, this was the way to do it. As soon as they have finished eating, each dedicates all their digits to their phones and are engrossed.

"What's on the agenda for today," asks Arlo, suddenly putting his phone down as if it's a bit too hot, "I think we don't have to be at the party until seven tonight?"

"I have some work to do on my socials." There's a general consensus that they all have this to do.

Oscar addresses her, "Estella, I have a rehearsal this morning."

"Okay, I actually have something that I need to do this morning."

"Great. See you for lunch?"

"Sure. What time?"

"12:30? I'll book something and let you know where to meet."

"Great."

Oscar gets up, buttoning his jacket and looking at his phone. He bends and kisses her on the forehead, "See you at lunch. Guys, see you later." Murmurs from the others. Estella doesn't look at them, but she is aware all the same that they are looking at her and exchanging looks amongst themselves. Bram gets up next. Shortly after, Seamus and Arlo leave too, but Santi remains.

"So," he elongates the word, "Oscar Pérez doesn't kiss people in public. What's your secret, Miss Estella?" She looks at his beautiful, mischievous face, and smiles.

"I think he thinks of me as a surrogate mother. He had a bad day yesterday and I happened to meet him just as he needed a friend."

"Estella," he leans towards her, "if he looked at my mother the way he looks at you, I would be having a serious talk with him."

She laughs, "Don't be ridiculous, he doesn't look at me like that." Santi shakes his head.

"Oblivious. You're one of those people that has no idea who they are."

"I know who I am," she says a little snappily.

"Oh yeah? Who are you?" She leans across the table and beckons him forward. He leans in.

"*I'm just divine*." It's a line from one of his songs. He cracks into laughter.

"Okay, it's none of my business, but seriously, if you really aren't aware of how he looks at you, you need to pay attention."

"Santi, I'm probably older than his mother!"

"So?"

"It's not appropriate."

"Appropriate? You might be older than his mother, but you ain't his mother. You aren't anything to him that would make you an *inappropriate* person to be with."

"I'm a teacher."

Santi laughs at her, "Honey, you ain't his teacher. Sounds to me like you're looking for excuses not to enjoy being with him." She holds his gaze and feels anxiety seeping into her joints. She looks down at her almost finished eggs Benedict and realises that she's lost her appetite.

"Hey, Estella, are you really not aware of how he looks at you?" She looks back at him and gently shakes her head.

"He doesn't," she says quietly. Santi looks back.

"I'm not trying to piss you off, but you need to be aware, or a bomb is going to go off in your face and you'll have no idea what's going on."

None of them knows what to do. Miss is left to try and decide what she should say. As it turns out, she doesn't need to say anything.

"What are you doing this morning? Can I come?"

"I'm sorry, I'd love to spend some time with you, but this is something that I need to do by myself. I'm going to visit a friend who's in hospital."

"Okay, but I'm going to see you later and you're going to dance with me tonight, right?"

"Wouldn't miss it for the world."

"Hey, if I can't DM you, can I get your number? You're kind of fun."

Win

When she takes her phone off the bed she sees another missed call from Win. She calls her back.

"Hey."

"What the actual fuck is going on?"

"I saw him yesterday, in a cafe. He looked really upset."

"So, you did the Stella thing and asked him if he was okay?"

"Yeah."

"So, how did that become going out on the town with the guys from *Boy Friends* and *Love Struck*?"

"How do you know about that?"

"Seriously? You're all over Instagram!"

"What?"

"You're on all their feeds. Oscar posted a video of you dancing in a club last night and they all shared it and after that you started to pop up on feeds from people in the club and somewhere called Soho House." Estella feels cold.

"They don't mention my name, do they?"

"Erm, I don't think Oscar did. He said, if his teachers had been this much fun, he might have done better at school, but I don't think he mentioned your name." Estella, smiles, she was right, he doesn't see her as anything other than a caring adult.

"Hang on! Santi hash tagged you as...Miss Estella. He called you a superfan."

"Am I recognisable in the pictures?" She hears Win snort with laughter.

"Of course you are! They're videos and photos of you, although I must say that you look quite glamorous."

"It's the company."

"Maybe, but you look good, mate. Are you having fun?"

"Yes. I'm staying at The Ned."

"No way!"

"You don't know what that is, do you?"

"Obviously not."

"It's amazing. I'm in the Terrace Suite. Google it."

"With Oscar?"

"No!"

"Why not?"

"It's not like that."

"Why not?"

"Win! He's twenty-six and I am fifty-seven, do you seriously think he would think about me in that way?"

"He seems to like holding your hand."

"What?"

"In a lot of the pictures, he's holding your hand."

"But that doesn't mean anything."

"Doesn't it? I can't remember the last time I held someone's hand. It's a very...intimate thing."

"I'm a surrogate mother."

"Oh, he's said that, has he?"

"No, but he treats me with great respect."

"Listen, love, you have not exactly picked princes for your partners. Just because he isn't treating you as shittily as your previous boyfriends have, it doesn't mean that he isn't into you. You're kind, intelligent about anything that doesn't concern you and you're fun. I have seen you dance on tables."

"Last night he said that I dance like no one is watching. Do you think that's a good thing or a bad thing?"

"Love," she laughs, "you've seen those plaques people put up in their houses! It's practically one of the fucking ten commandments."

"Fuck! I don't know what I'm doing."

"I repeat: are you having fun?"

"Yes."

"Are you...well? You're not..."

"No, I'm well. Nothing like that, at the moment."

"Well, good. Just have some fun!"

"Can you feed the cats again?"

"What're you doing today?"

"There's a Netflix party tonight. Oscar asked me to be his plus one."

"Wow! Red carpet type thing?"

"Shit, what do I wear?"

"Asking the wrong person, Stella, you are asking the wrong person. Are you planning on coming home any time soon?"

"Tomorrow. I'll come home tomorrow."

"Call me and I'll collect you from the station. We'll have a drink."

"Thanks, Win."

"Enjoy yourself tonight."

Anna

She's putting on her coat when a text arrives. "Igor free for the morning. Text him to take you where you need to go. X" She clicks on the contact that Oscar has sent and asks Igor if he can take her to St Thomas's. She messages Oscar: "Thanks so much." She hesitates before sending it and adds an X then sends. Igor tells her that he's outside. Walking through reception on her way to the car she almost trips up. Matthew Daddario is checking in. She feels herself flush and hurries towards the door.

In the car, Igor asks her if she is well. She says yes and asks if he's okay. He says he's good, but why are they going to the hospital. "Last night, when you go out, something happened. I saw in the mirror."

"Oh," she remembers catching his eye when Sella took them back to Mexico City. "Igor, don't worry. I just thought about something that I hadn't thought about for a while and I wanted to forget it quickly. You know, sometimes memories aren't good."

"I understand." He starts the car.

"I'm visiting a friend in the hospital," she tells him. "I was meant to go yesterday, but she wasn't well enough for visitors."

"Okay."

Anna has always been beautiful and even in illness she has a glamour about her. Estella has stopped to buy flowers and cigarettes for her friend, who is pleased with the cigarettes, which Estella quickly puts away in the locker by her bed. The flowers are superfluous, and Estella asks a nurse if she could donate them to someone else. Anna doesn't currently look as if she can manage to get out to smoke a cigarette, but she's a fighter. It has been a long illness and there have been crises before, but today Anna looks poised despite the weariness that she wears with dignity. In fact, she looks arch.

"What's going on?"

"I think it's me that should be asking you that question, Estella Lisle Marks!"

"Wow, full name, you're either angry with me or you're about to interrogate me."

"I hope that interrogation won't be necessary. Perhaps the right question will get the right answer. Why, my dear, are you still in London?"

"I missed my train yesterday."

"Stel, I've been on Instagram! Why're you being so coy?"

"Coy! I'm not being coy. I don't have anything to be coy about."

"So, you're telling me that you're not having a fling with Oscar Pérez?"

"What? No! We had dinner."

"Where did you stay?"

"At The Ned."

"Fancy! Did you share a room?"

"Yes, but not like that."

"He was too drunk?"

"No!"

"You were too drunk?"

"No!"

"Then, why on earth, was it not *like that*?" She asks, putting her hands up in air quotes at the appropriate moment.

"Because he's twenty-six!"

"Oh, Stel, as my twenty-one-year-old says, why do you have to put a label on it?"

"Not you too!"

"Me too? Who else is telling you that you should be having fun?"

"Santi Faber."

"Oh, he says you're a superfan. You never mentioned him to me before."

"Well, it's weird for a fifty-seven-year-old to be obsessing over a twenty-five-year-old. I refer my honourable friend to my previous comments." They sit looking at each other for a long time.

"Stel, you haven't exactly had an easy time of it. I know that relationships haven't been a source of joy to you. I know that your mental health isn't the most reliable. But...can't you just have some fun?" She feels the tears coming and puts her head in her hands hoping that she can refrain from an outburst. Tears for her own situation seem totally inappropriate when her friend is so ill.

"I don't think I am capable of just having some fun, Anna. It always starts out as fun and laughs, but I always end up...in a mess. Mentally or physically or both. I have a job and a house. I haven't been in hospital for years now. I'm having fun, but tomorrow I have to go home and be Miss and teach Spanish and be respectable and careful."

"Yes, but tonight is yours!"

"But will tomorrow still be mine," her voice breaks, and the tears start, "if I do something that triggers my mental health tonight? I almost flipped last night. I almost took something the wrong way and nose-dived."

"Okay, I get it."

They talk a little longer and when Estella sees that Anna is starting to get tired, she takes her leave. Anna tells her to take care of herself and she feels momentarily angry, but only for a few seconds. She does take care of herself, but that doesn't always make a lot of difference to outcomes. She has never been able to predict when she will become unwell. She has often been in manic episodes for days before she understands what is happening. She is better at recognising depressive episodes, but not good at asking for the help she needs. Who, after all, would she ask? She can't burden friends with her mental fragility; it simply isn't fair to them.

Igor is waiting for her outside. "You are crying," he says as she gets into the back, "your friend is very sick?"

"Yes, she's very sick."

"I am sorry."

"Yes, me too."

"Oscar tells me to take you to meet him for lunch. We go now?"

"Yes, please, Igor. Thank you."

She watches as the beautiful buildings slip by and she allows herself to cry a little more. It's cathartic. She demands of all of them that they live in the moment. She asks Esta to take over for a bit while she rallies. By the time they pull up outside a shiny chrome building, she is back in the moment and determined to enjoy the rest of the day.

"Thirty-sixth floor," says Igor. "The Darwin Brasserie. He's waiting for you."

Lunch

The thirty-sixth floor. As she rides up in the elevator Sella is plunging them all back into memory. She is telling the younger ones about the Grand Hyatt in Shanghai where the atrium alone was thirty-three storeys, and the bar and restaurant were on the eighty-seventh floor. The brasserie is rather noisy, but Oscar has secured them a table with a view of Saint Paul's, and she is grateful for his thoughtfulness. She says all of the right things and makes all the right sounds of awe and shows that she is impressed. Miss has to keep Esta from remarking on the very ordinary furniture and the paper serviettes. He is trying to please her, and he is the first person to do this for a long time.

They order steaks and a bottle of Pinot Noir. Oscar asks for a salad with his and no sauce, but she goes for the fries and the sauce.

"I hope your rehearsal went well."

"Yes, I think it'll be okay. I don't perform live very often these days and I get a little nervous. How was your morning?"

"I've been to visit a friend in hospital. That's what I was supposed to do yesterday, but she wasn't well enough for visitors. That's how I met you. If everything had gone according to plan, I would have been at the hospital when we met."

"Then I'm a very lucky man. I don't want to think what my day would've been like if you hadn't come to ask me if I was alright."

"Someone else would have asked you."

"Do you believe that?"

"I believe that we get what we need, but not always what we want."

"Then I lucked out. I got both."

"That's a kind thing to say." The wine is uncorked, and he asks her to try it. It's delicious. She raises her glass. "To good fortune!"

"And guardian angels." The glasses meet and he looks her in the eyes and smiles at her. They sip. "Is your friend very ill?"

"Yes. She's been ill for a long time and there are fewer good times now."

"How do you know her?"

"We met in 1977 at school in Hereford. We both lived in London in the 1980s, but even after I left we kept in touch. We lost touch for a while when her son was small, but we got back in contact a couple of years ago. During the time we were out of contact she had several cancers. I feel bad that I wasn't there for her." He looks stunned. She imagines that he is considering that she was alive so many years before he was born, but she's wrong.

"My mother has cancer. Well, she's in remission, but I worry all the time that it will come back." He swirls the wine in his glass.

"That's something that must be there all the time for you. Does she worry too?"

"I don't know." He exhales. "My mom doesn't speak to me. She hasn't always had the best life, but she made some decisions that weren't great for me. I know that she was frightened that she couldn't survive. I don't think she'll ever trust men again in her life. She's close with my sister." She feels his pain and senses his conflict.

"What happened to your mum?"

"She was married young to a violent man. Her life wasn't very happy." He looks out to the view of the city, but she knows that he doesn't see it. "To get away from her husband, my dad, she became the mistress of a rich Spaniard who visited Mexico City regularly for business. She managed to persuade him to take her and me and my sister to Madrid and set us up in an apartment. Once we were in Spain, he lost interest in her. He would forget to pay the rent. Mom got a job in an office, but she hated it. My dad was rich, she hadn't had to work before." He looks resentful and irritated.

"So, how did she make money?"

"When she realised that I could sing she kept putting me into competitions. I was eight when I won a competition on TV." He glances at her. "It was one of those shows where you get coached by a successful artist or producer. Each week you perform, there's a vote, and one act doesn't make it to the next week. You live from week to week on your nerves. It was exhausting and she put a lot of pressure on me. Luckily, I won. There was a record deal and tours. Endless fucking tours. Mom stayed home with my sister and there was a succession of older female chaperones. Some of them were nice. Some of them were just not caring. Nothing terrible, but I missed my sister. By the time I was fourteen I was, well, good looking, I suppose. There were some films, a couple of TV shows, loads of adverts, endorsements and modelling. I never saw any of the money. When I was at home, it was by that time a big apartment in the centre of the city." The steaks arrive and they eat a little. "Well, that's not exactly the best steak I have ever had," he says.

"No, but it's edible. Please continue with what you were telling me. You were fourteen?" He shrugs as if to say, *what does it matter?* But he continues.

"I worked pretty much all the time. TV series. Guest appearances. Opening supermarkets. Tours. Modelling. I've pretty much done it all. I was miserable. I didn't get much education. I didn't get to make friends. I didn't get any say in what I did. I had a bank account and an allowance was paid to me each month. But, honestly, I had nothing to spend it on. I was always being sent clothes and shoes and video games. I just had to put the stuff on my social media. I asked my mom about the money from time to time, but she told me that I didn't need to worry about it. We had a recurring argument where I would say, *I earned it, so I want to know where it is*. Then she would say that I was ungrateful. Didn't I know how hard she worked to keep me in work? I would say that I wanted a break. She would say that I could have a break when I stopped being in demand. It wasn't her that did the work anyway, it was her lawyer that handled my appearances." He pushes his half-eaten steak away and takes a mouthful of wine. "When I turned eighteen, I spoke to a lawyer. When I explained my situation, she was outraged. She spoke to my mom's lawyer. My mom had probably been expecting that this would happen. She didn't contest the demand. There were millions of Euros. They got transferred to me, but my mom didn't have to move. She still has a really good income, so I guess she made investments or there was an account that we didn't find?" He waves his hands around and when he speaks again, he's angry. "I wouldn't have made her move. I would have paid her a generous allowance and paid for the apartment. I just wanted to be in control of my own money. I did the work. But, she was angry. She turned my sister against me. She told me to move out." He tops up their wine glasses.

"I was eighteen. I moved into my own apartment. There were huge amounts of money. I was so lonely that I used to call my lawyer and take her to lunch just to have contact with a person. There was a lot of press coverage. Mostly the articles were in my favour because there were other stories about exploitation of young performers at that time, but there were some horrible articles about what a bad son I was. She got cancer a year after she kicked me out. Her lawyer told my lawyer that my mom believed it was the result of my betrayal." He swallows the rest of his wine.

"I was really lonely and I felt guilty. Suddenly, there were a lot of people who wanted to be friends, but I had learned really young that being famous and rich doesn't attract the kind of people you can trust. It's very hard for me to trust people." He reaches out and puts his hand over hers. "That's why you are such a miracle for me, Estella. I knew I could trust you the moment I looked you in the eyes." She smiles at him, but her heart is beating a little too fast from the anger that is still emanating from him. So much to be angry about.

"The first couple of years were hard. I slowed down with work a bit. I read a lot of books. I hired some tutors. Improved my English. I kept trying to get a relationship with mom, or at least my sister, but they wouldn't see me. I heard about the cancer from the lawyer and I transferred money for her treatment, but she sent it back." He pours more wine.

"I did a couple of pilot movies in the States. The pilots didn't turn into anything, but I met people who had money. People who I could be sure were interested in me instead of my bank account or my connections in the industry. I fell in love. I had sex. I got heartbroken. I got an STI. I realised that I'm bisexual. I battled with my self-loathing. Then four years ago I got a part in a soap opera which lasted two seasons. Then *Los Amores de Oscar* started." He looks at her.

"Whenever I'm in Madrid, I visit my mother and sister, but they never let me into the apartment. I ring the bell, but they never let me in. Sometimes I hear them on the other side of the door. Footsteps approaching the spy hole and then retreating. Every birthday I send a card and flowers. Every Christmas I send a card and a hamper. The cards always say the same thing: *I love you and I hope to see you soon*." He takes a deep breath and exhales, turns to her, swivelling in his chair. "But I don't want to see them. They're shitty people who took advantage of me. If, one of these days, they opened the door, I don't think I would go in. If I did, it would be to shout at them. Sometimes, when I'm recording a song, I ask for twenty minutes alone in the sound studio, and I scream and shout and say all the things that I'd like to say to them. It makes me feel better."

She takes his hand and very gently kisses it and then cradles it in both of hers. "That's too much for anyone to bear, Oscar. You must be weighed down by so much anger. That your mother won't engage with you is intolerable. You have no outlet. No chance to redress the balance."

"Apart from my lawyer, I've never told anybody about this. I've always been worried that this happened to me because there's something wrong with me. That I'm fundamentally unlovable. But you see me. You hear me. You don't find me abhorrent, do you?"

"No. You are a lovely, thoughtful, kind person." He takes his hand from hers and touches her cheek, a brief caress with the back of his fingers.

"Gracias, Estella. That means the world to me. Now, let's get out of here. We have stuff to do."

On the way down in the lift he makes a brief phone call. All she hears is, "Hi, it's Oscar...is it okay if we come in the next thirty minutes?...Great. Thank you." Igor is waiting for them outside.

"Estella, I hope you don't mind," he says rather sheepishly, "but this evening is a black-tie event." She thinks for a moment that he's about to say that he's thought better of her coming, but she doesn't have long to realise that, as usual, she is wrong. "The dress from the other night is great..."

"I'm so glad that you said something! I have been worried about what I can wear."

"There are places where you can hire evening wear. I get sent a lot of suits. I have another Ted Baker for tonight, but I was hoping that you would let me rent something for you to wear. Is that presumptuous of me?"

"No, Oscar, it's very kind and thoughtful." She hesitates. She wants to say that she will pay for it, but she isn't sure how much it's going to cost.

"Please don't think about the money, Estella. You know now how little that means to me, right?"

"Thank you, Oscar."

"¡No hay de que! It's my pleasure."

Igor pulls up outside a Victorian townhouse somewhere near the British Museum with a discreet plaque that says *Dressed to the Nines*. The door is opened by a middle-aged man in a beautiful suit with a tape measure slung around his neck.

"Good afternoon, Oscar."

"Good afternoon, John. It's good to see you. May I present Estella."

"Nice to meet you, Estella. My goodness, you do look sweet in your coordinated colours." He smiles warmly. "Oscar, take a seat in the waiting room, it's just through there." John indicates a beautifully polished wide wooden door. "Estella, you must come this way." He ushers her down a corridor and then into the basement where there are comfortable looking sofas, mannequins displaying stunning dresses and a modesty screen.

"Sit down, my dear." She carefully seats herself and then looks at John with all the anxiety that is knotting her stomach.

"John, do you even have dresses for people my size?" He looks pained for a moment, and she expects that he's about to tell her that he will try to help, but that he can't promise anything, but, as usual, she is wrong.

"Estella, what size are you? Twenty-two? Of course I have dresses in your size. Not all my clients are like Oscar. Not that he has ever needed to hire clothes from me. He came to me for advice about what to wear. He gets sent a lot of clothes and when he was younger, he wasn't sure what was good and what wasn't. He wanted some rules to follow. That's how we know each other. Tonight is a black-tie event, right? Do you know what he's wearing?"

"Ted Baker dinner suit."

"Okay, so he's traditional black tie. What do you think about wearing black?"

"It's classic. It's slimming. Makes sense." She suddenly realises something. "John, I don't want to let him down!" He rolls his eyes and purses his lips.

"You won't. Trust me! I need to see what you've got. Are you shy?"

"Not as shy as I ought to be," Esta says and takes off her dress. "Slip off too?"

"How reassuring that some people still wear the correct undergarments. Slip off please. Thank goodness that you have a proper bra." He regards her with equanimity. "I bet you were a cracker in your thirties, Estella."

"Actually, John, I was pretty good right up to about forty-two, but things have slipped a bit since fifty-five."

"How old are you?"

"Fifty-seven."

"Great skin!"

"Thanks."

"I thought you were about forty-five."

"Yeah, right."

"Actually, I'm telling the truth. I suppose your hair is dyed?"

"To within an inch of its life."

"You must go to a good salon; it's a very natural colour."

"Thanks."

"I'll be back in a minute."

The dress is a whisper of almost weightless black silk velvet, cut on the bias with shaping around the bust and a V neck that doesn't plunge too far. There are jewels and beads around the bodice and the thing that really makes it is a cape of delicate soft black feathers that fall like capped sleeves over the arms and on the back of the dress are subtle appliqued angel wings. It fits beautifully without constricting her. He pairs it with simple black strappy sandals and a gold necklace that looks like angel wings and matching bangles, one for each wrist. She looks at herself in the mirror and then looks at John looking at her.

"You're a genius, John."

"Pleased to be of service. Do you want him to see it?"

"No, let's make it a surprise, shall we?" He nods approvingly.

"Where are you staying?"

"The Ned, the Terrace Suite."

"Shall I have it sent over there? He said something about having to go to Selfridges this afternoon."

"Okay, if that's not too much trouble."

"All part of the service. I'll send someone to collect it tomorrow. Leave it with reception. Okay?"

"Perfect!"

Socials at Selfridges

Oscar explains that he has contracts with certain brands to feature their products on his social media and that in return he gets all the clothes, shoes, watches and gadgets he could ever want. They're on their way to Selfridges so that he can get some of these posts recorded. "Estella, it's going to be a bit crazy in there," he says. "People are going to want selfies and they're going to want to talk. When they're casting shows they often look at our follower numbers when they decide on casting, so I have to keep my followers up. It might seem shallow, but it makes a huge difference to my career."

"I'm not judging you, Oscar!"

"I know, but I'm kind of judging myself. I don't feel entirely comfortable with this bit of my life." *Nor many others,* Stella wants to say, but the others keep her quiet.

"Actually, I have stuff that I need to do," she tells him. "When I'm done, I'll go and get a drink at the bar in the accessories hall. Let me know when to meet you." He looks dubious. "Oscar, I've been doing this sort of thing all on my own for the best part of forty years. Don't look so worried." His brow furrows, but he makes no further objections.

When Igor leaves them at the kerb and drives away, Oscar gives her one more sceptical look before assuring her that he won't be too long. "Take your time," she assures him. She follows him into the store and within ten paces he has been stopped by admirers. She smiles and makes her way to the beauty hall. John has made an appointment for her. Whilst she waits her turn, she has been shoehorned into a full schedule, she receives a text message.

Santi
R U in Selfridges? Santi. X

Yes, how did you know?

Santi
Oscar on Insta. Where R U?

Beauty Concierge. I have an appointment.

Santi
C U there in 5.

She does a double take when she sees him. He's wearing jeans, a bomber jacket, trainers and a baseball cap. He laughs at her look.

"I'm incognito!"

"You certainly are!"

"I just wanted to do some shopping."

"Totally understandable." A beautiful young person calls her name, and she is seated in a swivel chair.

"How can I help you, today, Estella?" Esta takes charge.

"I'm going to a party tonight. I haven't worn make-up for years, but I don't want to let the friend who invited me think that I don't appreciate the invitation. I was thinking about something to open out my eyes a bit and a good lipstick."

"I understand. John said that you have a dress from him for tonight. What colour are you wearing?"

"Black."

"How do you feel about eye liner?"

"I always used to wear it. A liquid flick on the top lid and mascara. The jewellery is gold and I wondered if there could be gold eye shadow or a shadow line in gold?"

"That sounds like a good plan. What about foundation?"

"I'm in menopause, so that wouldn't last five minutes. The mascara and eyeliner need to be waterproof."

"I understand. What colour lipstick?"

"Deep red," says Santi. "Something dark. She can take it." The young person looks at him for the first time and Estella sees the blush bloom at the recognition and a moment of confusion before professionalism returns.

"Very good. Let's get started."

They do an excellent job. Her eyes look much bigger and the touches of gold will work brilliantly with the jewellery. Santi is admiring. "Classy!" She eschews putting the lipstick on until later, but Santi chooses the colour from half a dozen samples slashed across her inner arm.

"I just want to pick up some perfume, I haven't had any all day and I feel improperly dressed."

"What do you wear?"

"Usually Shay and Blue, Atropa Belladonna or Black Tulip, sometimes Saltworks, Neroliander or Ocean Drive."

They have fun trying the different perfumes and they both end up buying more than they had intended.

They seat themselves in The Fount Bar and order champagne. Santi keeps his baseball cap on, and the barman asks for ID. Estella has to laugh, and Santi takes it in good part, but it's the barman who ends up feeling embarrassed when he finally realises who he's just ID-ed.

"Happens all the time, man." Santi tells him, "No problem."

"Does it really?"

"Yes, Estella, it does." She sees how this might have undermined his self-possession slightly. She asks him about how his day has been and he tells her he's been bored. She tells him that he ought to read, but he makes a pained expression.

"Santi, I saw Matthew Daddario checking in when I left The Ned this morning. Do you think he's going to be there tonight?"

"I don't know, probably, he did the *Shadowhunters* thing, right? Was that Netflix?"

"It was streamed on Netflix, but it was made by Freeform."

"Why are you so interested?"

"He used to be the most beautiful man in the world."

"And now?"

"He's the second most beautiful man in the world."

"I see. Oscar has taken over now, is that it?" He smiles cheekily.

"Did I mention Oscar?" They pause for a moment, then Esta takes charge. "Shall we have another?"

They're halfway down their second glasses of champagne when Oscar appears quite suddenly at their table. "Can I get one of those?" Estella signals the barman. Oscar looks frazzled.

"Are you okay?" He looks at her with a tense smile, but his jaw drops.

"Wow! Your eyes look amazing. Is that what you had to do?"

"The dress deserved it. Are you okay?"

"I'll be fine, when I have a drink. I didn't think it'd be so busy in here on a Thursday." The champagne arrives and he gulps down half the glass instantly.

"It's half-term, Oscar. That's why I'm not at work. The schools are off all week. Lots of families visiting the metropolis."

"Makes sense." He drinks the rest of his glass and signals for another. "Buen disfraz, Santi. ¿Ha sido efectivo?"

"Muy eficaz. Fan free all day!"

"I love my suits," Oscar says, "but I think I need to take a leaf out of your book."

"Sometimes it's good to just be an extra." They drink in contented silence, but Stel has been waiting for the right moment to get what she wants out of today.

"Hey, is there any chance that we could get back to the hotel? I really want to go for a swim."

"Estella, Igor can take you back now and you'll have plenty of time for a swim, but Santi and I have to go and do a sound check for tonight."

"Okay, well, you two take Igor, and I'll catch a bus." Oscar, looking affronted, is about to speak when Santi cuts in.

"I have a Suzie; she can take us to the sound check and Igor can take you." Estella thinks of all those nice black cars that you see illegally stopped all over London and begins to see the whole industry that must exist around getting the rich and famous from one pleasurable experience to the next. She realises that she has been a part of that pleasurable world for over 24 hours.

When they part, Oscar again kisses her forehead just before she ducks into the car. Igor checks that she's belted and comfortable before launching back into the traffic. She looks through the back window and sees that Oscar is still watching the car, a teenage boy in a baseball cap standing next to him. Appearances are so deceptive. Nothing is ever what it seems. She goes to rub her eye but remembers the make-up just in time. She almost laughs. Case in point, she thinks.

At a red light, Igor turns back to look at her. He gestures towards his eyes, "This is for tonight?"

"Yes. The dress is..." she hesitates. How should she describe it? "It's like a costume from a play. I felt like I should be somebody else." She wonders what she is trying to say. Igor doesn't interrupt her thoughts. Finally, she understands, "I wouldn't feel comfortable going to this party tonight as me. I don't think I belong at this party. I'm going because Oscar wants me to go. For some reason, he thinks he needs me. So, if I have to go somewhere that I don't belong, surely, I need protection?"

"He needs you. You need protection." Igor says. "He needs a friend. So do you. Who is your friend?" She sees Igor's emphatic eyes in the rearview mirror. She thinks of Win, her drinking buddy, her partner in partying and the person who visits her in hospital when she is in an episode, but who never asks her directly about her condition. She thinks of Anna, who will ask and listen, but who she sees only occasionally. There were other friends, but the episodes took their toll and there are not so many close friends these days. There are the women from Book Club, with whom she is sociable. They are mostly people she has known practically her whole life. There is love and friendship, but in truth, she uses her mental fragility to stop herself from becoming close with others. Win is the closest to her precisely because she knows that she won't ask about her mental health and because Win rarely shares any of her own feelings or concerns.

Estella is bone weary from the ups and downs of her emotional waves, the constant second-guessing and the never-ending stream of emotions that rampage through her from everybody she meets. It is as if, at the very core of her physical body, there is a magnet to which the feelings and particularly the distress of others is attracted. There have been episodes of hospitalisation for mania or depression that she is pretty sure did not even originate with her. The magnet drew in these extreme emotions from the people around her, leaving them relieved and cleansed, but taking her to the verge of insanity. She does not know how to rid herself of the magnet or even how to reduce its pull. The only way to protect herself is to go home and lock the door and stay away from people, but Estella also needs people. She likes to think that she doesn't, but deep inside she is still, against all sense and reason, looking for someone who will see her, hear her, respect her and love her. She thinks of how much she knows about Oscar. How much he has shared with her. She wonders what he thinks he knows about her. He says that he needs her, but she feels that actually any kind person would have done, but for some reason, it was her. Did she make that happen, or was it pure chance?

"Estella?" She looks up and realises that Igor has pulled up outside The Ned. "You need a friend," he repeats. "You have my number." They look at each other and she sees his kindness.

"Thank you, Igor."

"Don't cry," he says. He gets out of the car and comes round to open her door. When she is standing beside him on the pavement, he says very quietly, "Don't let him take all your energy. He will take it all if you let him." She looks him in the eye and feels the truth of what he is saying. She nods and walks back into The Ned.

Swim

A few paces into the lobby Bram places himself in front of her. "Hey, Estella, come and have a drink with us." She's so taken up with her inner thoughts that she just follows him over to a huge group of cast members from *Love Struck*.

"Hey, everyone, this is Estella. Santi and I went out with her and Oscar Pérez last night." Four girls jump up and hustle her into a seat, their cosy friendliness makes her smile. She looks at them one by one.

"Let's see if I can get this right," says Miss, "Mila... Eline... Beatrix and... Fenna?" They smile and nod at her seeming to be pleased that she knows who they are.

"What's Oscar like?"

"Very handsome, very kind and very quiet. Easily frightened. So go easy on him, girls."

"Isn't he with you, Estella?"

"No! We're friends. I'm a lot older than he is."

"So?" Miss looks at them with her best, *come off it* face.

"But Santi said..."

"Yeah, and Bram said you shared a room with him last night." Miss sighs.

"It was a big room and a very large bed, and it was completely innocent, ladies. We're friends." They look unconvinced. She can understand, they trust Santi and Bram. "Listen, I don't mean to be rude, but I am desperate to have a swim," Stel says. "Do you mind if I go and have a swim and catch up with you later?"

"Sure, we'll see you later."

"Thank you for understanding." She feels the nervous energy coming from the four young women. They are all looking for their opportunities. Oscar is a catch. She needs to get into water and try to wash away the emotions of the day.

She showers, taking care not to get her face wet, and shaves her legs and puts on the swimming costume that she bought the day before, pulls her dress over the top and heads down to the indoor pool. When she gets there, she cannot believe her luck. The pool is empty. She steps into the water and submerges all but her face. If it weren't for the make-up, she'd be all the way under the water.

Water.

She has very few memories before the age of six, but there is one of standing on a beach. She must have been quite little because she is not very steady on her legs and she is holding onto her mother's leg to support herself. She is looking out at the calm, turquoise sea and feeling the power coming from the little waves running to and from the beach. She suddenly makes a dash towards it. Within a few paces her mother has caught her up and takes her back. She has always wanted to get into water.

There was a waterfall on a coffee plantation near Cuetzalan. Sella had stripped down to her bra and knickers to the horror of her friends and waded into to the icy water. There was a woman selling bottles of cold drinks to the men working on the plantation. She had the bottles on strings in the water; that's how cold it was. She swam up to the waterfall and behind it and back to shore. It was so cold that she started to lose the feeling in her legs. When she walked out of the water she could hardly walk for cold, and her friends had to point out that at some point her knickers had left her body. She remembers the hysterical laughter and the sense of having been cleansed. She has a photograph of Sella sitting with the woman who sold drinks. They both have their heads thrown back, mid-laugh, and as she pushes through the water and feels it streaming around her, she can feel the intense happiness of that moment so long ago.

She completes five lengths before anyone else arrives. She completes five more before she floats on her back for a few minutes and then makes her way out of the pool, takes a hot shower and wraps herself in the fluffy towels provided. She is renewed. She wonders what it would be like to be able to swim in a pool like this, alone, every day.

Rafaela

Coming down the corridor to the suite running her hands through her damp hair and feeling renewed she encounters Oscar. "I was looking for you," he smiles and brushes a hand lightly over the damp shoulder of her dress. "Was it fun?"

"Delicious!"

She opens the suite door and they go inside.

"Come and sit down. I have something for you." He sits on one side of the sofa and indicates the other. She sits feeling well and light. He has a small Pandora bag, "I noticed that you have a charm bracelet, and I wanted you to have a charm to remind you of our meeting and what you did for me yesterday." He holds out the bag. "I hope you like it."

The charm is heart-shaped, and each bulge of the heart is studded with small stones in the form of angel wings and a white stone dangles from the bottom. She thinks of the dress. Another coincidence? She smiles up at him, "Thank you! I love it."

"Do you know about the angel Rafaele?"

"A little. He's the healer, isn't he? Also, the patron saint of mental health?"

"Amongst other things," he says rather sadly. "Yesterday, you were my angel Rafaela. You even kept watch over me through the night. I'm not sure how yesterday would have turned out without your kindness. This charm is to mark the start of our relationship, Estella. Well, sabes que, te voy a llamar Rafaela. No, Rafa. Rafa, mi ángel personal." She leans to kiss his cheek in thanks and finds herself in his arms. Her face nestled into his neck. He smells good and his neck is reassuringly warm. She feels the strength and solidity of him and how good it is to be held. She cannot remember the last time that somebody held her like this. She lets herself relax into him and they stay like that. She hears the tiny ticking of his watch. She feels him kiss her forehead.

"Well, Rafa, we have a party to get ready for!" They slowly move away from each other. He hesitates a second, but then he's standing and heading for the door. "Pick you up in forty-five minutes."

"Fuck!" She says. He laughs, but not unkindly.

"Chop chop! As you Brits like to say." And he is gone. She puts the charm onto her bracelet.

She tops up her mascara and eyeliner and reapplies the gold highlights. She steps into the dress. She puts on the jewellery. She brushes back her still slightly damp hair. She slips on the sandals. She applies her lipstick.

There's a knock on the door as she is blotting her lips. Santi stands there. Oh, bloody hell! Black leather trousers, black boots with heels, dinner jacket with bejewelled lapels and no shirt. Just smooth, delicious skin and a silver chain. She tries to keep her eyes on his lovely face, but she can feel the blush subsuming her own. Esta takes over, "Great styling, Santi. You look magnificent."

"Hmm, well, thanks, but you aren't doing too badly yourself. I think I picked up your perfume by mistake." She suddenly realises that in Stel's haste to get to the swimming pool she must have left her Selfridges bag on the bar table and Santi has miraculously picked it up.

"Oh, my goodness, you're a life saver! I hadn't even realised that I didn't have it."

"What have you put on your hair? It's cool like that."

"It's just damp."

"Well, that's not gonna work! It'll dry out and you'll look like you've been electrocuted. Two minutes. Don't let him take you before I get back."

She leaves the door ajar, gets the perfume out and applies liberally. The orange note in the fragrance cuts through and she has a sense of wellbeing. A brief knock and he's back with a pot of gloop. He has his hands in her hair. Oh, bloody hell. He grabs her hairbrush and gently pulls it through her hair. He gives her an appraising look and nods approval. He washes his hands in the bathroom. He's gone. "See ya later!"

In the mirror is somebody that she doesn't know, but who, she has to admit she would take a second look at if she saw them in the street. The door again. It's still slightly ajar after Santi's departure. There he is. Slim-cut classic dinner suit, patent lace-up shoes, crisp white shirt, slim matt bow tie; he could be James Bond. They look at each other for some time. She turns so that he can see the wings. She feels him run a hand along one. "Rafa!" He says. She turns back. They smile. "You smell good." He says. "You're beautiful."

"So are you."

"We'd better get going."

"Could you put my lipstick in a pocket without spoiling the line of your suit?"

"Sure, I can put it in the inner pocket."

"No, it's going to make a bulge."

"It'll be fine. Look!" She can see it, but she realises that she can also see the outline of his phone. Maybe he just doesn't care that much about spoiling the line of the suit. "Do you want me to take your phone too?"

"No, I'll leave it here."

"But you won't be able to take photographs."

"What would I want to photograph?"

"Well, Matthew Daddario is going to be there...don't you want a selfie?" Santi must have said something to him. Surely, he wouldn't have told him what she said about who she now thinks is the most handsome man in the world. She doesn't want Oscar to feel that she is disloyal. She laughs, but doesn't quite carry it off.

"No!"

"Why not?"

"I hate photos of myself. I'm not sure why people are so obsessed with photographing everything. We have memories for a reason."

"I would like to have a photograph of you and me together."

"Well, I'm not going to say no to having a photo taken with you, Oscar. That's different. We're friends."

"Good," he says, but he doesn't sound happy. It feels like they have just had an argument. She's not sure how that happened.

"Shall we go?" He holds out his hand to her and they make their way downstairs. His hand is warm and careful, and she feels excited, but he is walking very fast. In the foyer, the bars are packed and there are gaggles of people. The noise is tremendous. Almost everyone is taking pictures or videoing with their phones. She's aware that some of them are filming Oscar and her as they make their way to the door. It crosses her mind that in this dress and with the hair and make-up her students probably wouldn't even recognise her. She catches sight of Matthew Daddario and the other Shadowhunters and blushes yet again. It has been a day of it.

"Oscar!" It's the guy that plays Nito, the straight best friend. "¿Come va, hermano?" He's very handsome and clearly happy to see Oscar.

"¡Víctor, me alegra verte!" Oscar clasps the other man's hand, palm to palm, with his spare hand in a brief dip towards each other. "Te presento, Estella."

"Mucho gusto, Víctor."

"Hola, Estella." looking only briefly at her and then back at Oscar with concern. "¿Hermano, no vas a venir con nosotros?" He sounds disappointed that they will be travelling separately.

"Disculpa, pero tengo que estar allí antes para prepararme para la canción con Santi." He doesn't sound like he's sorry. Something has changed in Oscar since they have stopped to talk to Víctor.

"Aquí estoy!" and Santi is with them. "Wow, you smell good, Estella!" With a wink.

"I didn't know that you two are singing together." Estella says.

"Last minute thing. He sings. We sing. I sing..." Santi says casually.

"*I'm Just Divine?*" She asks. He smiles.

"Yeah."

"Víctor, disculpa, nos vemos allí, ¿vale?"

Víctor doesn't look like it's okay, but he doesn't stop Oscar from leaving. Oscar's hand, now more clamped to rather than clasped with hers feels tense and she tries to make eye contact with him, but they are really rushing now for the door. Santi is getting left behind. "Oscar! Please. Slow down." She tries to keep her voice neutral, but the tension is seeping into her from his hand. When he turns to face her, she thinks for a split second that he might shout at her. He looks miserable. "¿Que pasa, Oscar?"

"Nada," he says crossly and unconvincingly. Then, after a brief pause, "Estoy nervioso. Disculpa."

"¡Oscar," says Santi, "no hay de que! The rehearsal went really well."

"I don't have your confidence, Santi."

"Let's get there and we can just relax."

"I'll relax when it's over." He says angrily.

"Oscar, what do you want to do?" She turns him to face her. "Would you prefer not to do this?" He looks at her and smiles tightly.

"I'll be fine when I'm on stage, I just hate the run up to it. I'll be fine. ¡Vamos!" He almost jerks her arm out of its socket as he makes off again.

"¡Oscar, vas a romperle el brazo!" Santi asserts. "¡Ten más cuidado!" Oscar turns to glare at Santi, but then softens and speaks quietly to her.

"I'm sorry, Estella. Is your arm okay?"

"Maybe it would be better if I didn't come tonight," she says, feeling quite on edge with the discord. A good night's sleep feels very attractive at this moment. But his response is instant.

"No, Estella, no puedo hacerlo sin ti. Por favor, quiero que estes conmigo esta noche. Por favor, perdóname. No puedo hacer esto sin ti." The desperation in his voice is palpable. "I'm sorry, I didn't mean to hurt you. I can't do this without you. Is your arm okay?" She looks up at his anxious face and suddenly wishes that she was at home with her cats watching something on Netflix. His anxiety is being drawn into the magnet at her core and all the benefits of her swim are dissipating. Truth to tell, she's tired. So much has happened in the last two days. Santi keeps quiet and watches them. She glances at him and he gives her a small smile. "Estella?" asks Oscar.

"I'll come, but please can we just walk at a normal pace?"

"Yes, of course. Thank you. Is your arm okay?"

"Nothing that a cocktail wouldn't sort out." He suddenly steps forward and scoops her into his arms. She feels his mouth near her ear speaking very quietly

"Rafa, I'm sorry, I'm being selfish, but I need you here with me. I promise there will be cocktails and dancing." His body against her. The warmth of his breath in her ear. One hand at her waist. The other at her neck. Desire stirs and turns her liquid. Shame floods through her. She feels like she has betrayed him and made herself ridiculous. But she does not push him away. Her hands, she finds, have grasped his shoulders. She cannot decide if she is fire or ice. He moves away and she has to brace herself so as not to fall. He kisses her forehead. "Gracias, Rafa," he says quietly and starts walking towards the door again. He doesn't take her hand this time, but he is walking more sedately a couple of paces ahead of her and Santi.

"Surrogate mother?" Whispers Santi. Then he makes a gesture with his hands like a bomb exploding.

"What did you say to him about Matthew Daddario?" Esta hisses.

"I told him that you think that he's handsome."

"And did you tell him that I think that you are more handsome?" Santi gasps slightly.

"You never said that, Estella, so I didn't know it until right now. Not for sure." He takes her arm, "I appreciate the compliment." Her face is on fire, yet again. She feels stupid and vulgar and completely out of her depth.

"Breathe," Santi says, "for fuck's sake, breathe."

Red Carpet

In the car she is seated between them. The car isn't as wide as a taxi and their proximity is making her feel deeply uncomfortable. The thigh of the man she has literally just confessed to adoring is up close and personal with her own right thigh. The right thigh of the gorgeous, complex and thoughtful Oscar Pérez is up close and personal with her left thigh. She suspects that she is having an out of body experience, either that or she might be about to have a stroke. She is becoming light-headed, and she can hear her heartbeat thudding rapidly in her ears.

"Oscar," she hears Santi say, "I think she's going to pass out!"

"What?"

"Estella, you need to take a breath."

"Estella, what's wrong? You're so hot. Santi, she's burning up."

...

The next thing that she knows is that she is waking up alone in the back seat of the car. The doors on both sides are open and cold air rushes through to her blessed relief. At first, she thinks that they have run away and left her. Then she hears them outside. She hears Igor's steady voice, "Give her minute. She needs to cool off. She have a difficult day."

"A difficult day?"

"Oscar, she's awake."

"Estella?"

"Calm. Be calm."

"I am calm."

"You're not calm, Oscar. That scene back at the hotel was not calm."

Esta is really pissed off now. This was supposed to be a really fun night. This is not how tonight is supposed to go. She is determined to salvage this. They have wanted a life more interesting for a long time and now it's here, they're not coping. Igor bends his head into the back of the car.

"You okay?"

"Yes, thank you, Igor. Do you have any water?" He ducks out and she hears him speak to Oscar.

"Wait. She need water. Wait." He hands her a bottle of cool water and she takes a drink. Another.

"Oscar, give Santi my lipstick." Santi appears.

"Want me to do it?"

"Yeah. Is my hair okay?"

"Look at me." He fixes her lipstick and runs his fingers through the righthand side of her hair. "It's good."

"Right. Let's go." Santi gets back into the car and closes his door and cracks open the window. Oscar gets into his side, "Estella..." Esta holds up a hand.

"Enough! Let's get this over and done with." She nods imperceptibly at Igor in the rearview mirror, and they resume their journey. Oscar is rigid beside her. When Igor pulls up, Esta turns to Santi. "Would you mind making your entrance alone?"

"Of course not. Are you okay?"

"Grab a cocktail for me. We'll be in shortly."

Santi gets out of the car and she hears the fans go wild. "Igor, take us round the block, would you?" The car moves off and Esta pushes herself across the seat to put a space between her and Oscar.

"Oscar, do you want to be at this party?" He moves his neck around and she hears it snapping with tension.

"Not really."

"Then why is it so important to be here?"

"They're announcing season three and I'm contracted to be here. I'm being paid to be here."

"Do you want me to be here with you?" He looks at her sharply.

"Yes. I told you; I can't do this without you."

"Okay. Oscar, this is showtime. Are you ready for this? Can you walk that carpet at a sedate pace and be charming to people? Are you ready to be the handsome, polite and caring Oscar Pérez that your fans adore?" He seems to straighten and grow a couple of inches.

"Yes. I am. Sorry."

"Good. Let's do this. Igor, if you would be so kind."

A few minutes later they are pulling up again. Oscar bounds out of the car and opens her door with a flourish. He offers and Esta takes his hand. She swings their legs elegantly from the car and she takes a moment to make sure that everything is as it should be before she nods the go ahead to Oscar. He holds her hand as they walk the red carpet, and they stop to be photographed; she tells him quietly to go and sign some autographs. Seamus and Arlo are there and come and talk to her. The *Love Struck* cast arrives with Bram at their head. Then Oscar takes her hand again and they are walking into the building. She has no idea where they are, but a few moments after they enter the enormous space, Santi places a glass in her hand and Esta drains it in one smooth chug.

"Gracias, Santi, muy amable." She says. "Your compadres have just arrived, if you want to go and join them on the red carpet..." He smiles and returns to the crowd.

Oscar introduces her to his cast mates, and they chat in Spanish. He seems to be okay, but she sees some tension in his jaw and he keeps running an index finger over his left eyebrow. It's a tell that she has noticed in herself when she feels overwhelmed. He says he has to go and get ready to sing and he kisses her forehead again. His cast mates look askance. She's going to have to ask him to stop doing that. The tables allotted to *Oscar Loves* are crowded, but she finds a spare seat next to the actors that play Oscar's dad and stepmother, and she asks them about series three, but like Oscar they have no idea what it holds. She is on her third cocktail by now and Miss is feeling pretty relaxed.

"Well, I think it's going to be explosive," she says in Spanish. "I mean, all those breadcrumbs that they've been putting into the previous two series."

"Breadcrumbs?" asks Oscar's dad, looking at his on-screen wife, who Esta would bet is his off-screen mistress.

"You know, all those bits at the end of scenes when Oscar leaves the room and you two look at each other like you think he's on to you." They both look non-plussed and Miss starts to think that maybe she's remembering it wrong, but then a woman a few seats away from her, catches her eye.

"We thought we were being subtle," she says. "Was it really that obvious?" Miss wonders if she should really say what she thinks. *Oscar Loves* is basically formulaic. In fact, it's pure soap opera. She can imagine its storyline on a telenovela, but she decides to play nice. She doesn't want to put Oscar in a difficult situation.

"I studied drama," she says, "I was trained to look for these things." She wonders if this makes any sense. The woman seems to accept it, so she can avoid being rude about the predictable storyline and the quality of the scripts for the show.

"And you think that series three will be explosive?"

"Absolutely! He's going to find his mum and he's going to find out that his dad...hmm...maybe his stepmum too...have been lying to him about his mother." She smiles at the woman, who is watching her intently. Miss's glass is empty and she's about to get up and hunt for another cocktail, but the woman reaches out her hand to shake Estella's.

"Hi, I'm Nuria Almendras García, I'm one of the producers on *Los Amores de Oscar*." They shake hands. "It sounds like you have some interesting ideas about how series three could be made more exciting." Miss smiles and laughs.

"In my head," she says, "I have the whole thing mapped out. Plot twist of the decade!" Nuria makes Oscar's dad move, which seems rude, but he does it meekly so this woman must be important.

"Tell me."

"Well," says Miss, feeling that this is an important moment that she doesn't want to waste, "let's just say that my idea involves adultery, gaslighting and a whole host of mental health stuff that would be very on point with current media preoccupations." She decides that she has to give her something for free. "Oscar's dad and stepmother were involved before Oscar was born. His real mum suffered post-natal depression, and they used it to get rid of her..." Nuria's eyes light up.

"Perhaps we could discuss this further?" The producer suggests. "I suppose that Oscar can put me in touch with you?"

"He has my number," says Esta and to ensure that Nuria knows that she's not an idiot, she gets up to search for a drink and fails to find her way back to the table. She bumps into Seamus at the bar and spends the next half an hour meeting the *Boy Friends* crowd.

She's still sitting with them when the lighting changes and music starts to play and the room starts to applaud as a couple of older men take to the stage. It's a Netflix celebration and various programmes get mentioned and iconic moments viewed including *Los Amores de Oscar*. Then the suits leave and after the stage goes briefly dark the lights come up and there is Oscar looking relaxed and suave. The band strikes up the overture and Esta pushes Ella in front of her. He is about to sing *O Tu O Ninguna*, which is significant for Esta in ways that she does not want to think about.

Ella waits for the song to finish and when it does and through the applause, she sees Santi coming onto the stage to join Oscar. She hears the overture starting and there are dancers appearing behind the two young people. Oscar and Santi sing Take That's *Greatest Day* and the entire audience is up and dancing and loving every second. Miss is there, dancing with the *Boy Friends* cast. More applause, and Oscar leaves the stage to Santi and *I'm Just Divine*. Miss and the Boy Friends sing at the top of their voices and dance around their tables as if they have no troubles in their lives at all.

After Santi leaves the stage, there are some more announcements and congratulations and finally food is being served. Miss has no idea how much she has drunk at this stage, but she goes to the bar for another drink anyway. She can feel tiredness from her toes to her eyeballs. She wants to eat something, but she isn't sure where to sit and she wants to find Santi and congratulate him...and Oscar too, of course.

She's at the bar waiting for a mojito, when Víctor joins her. He looks miserable. "Hey," he says, "having a good time?" His English is very good.

"I think so," Esta says. "I've had so many mojitos that I'm not actually sure anymore." They both laugh. "Víctor, are you okay?" He looks at her.

"You're with Oscar, now, right?" She shakes her head and is distressed to find that her vision momentarily blurs.

"No, Víctor. I just met him yesterday. We're friends. I'm very much older than him."

"He really likes you. I can see it."

"Yes, but as a friend." It's Víctor's turn to shake his head, she bets that his vision isn't blurred.

"He used to look at me like that." So that's how it is. She waits. "We used to be in a kids' show together when we were in our teens. We were inseparable. He didn't know he was bi until we kissed." He puts his hands in his pockets. "He wasn't very happy about it." She stretches out a hand and places it gently on his shoulder.

"I'm sorry. It sounds like it was painful." He nods.

"When I got this job, I thought it might be a second chance."

"No go?" He shakes his head.

"He barely speaks to me. He's very polite, of course..."

"Of course."

"We're not even friends anymore." He asks the barman for a drink. "Now we're going to be doing a whole new season together. I should be excited to have the work, but I've been thinking of asking them to write me out."

"Don't turn down work because of this, Víctor!" she berates him. "Nobody can afford to do that."

"Oscar could."

"Yes, but Oscar is the exception that proves the rule." She spots Oscar a few meters off scanning the room. "Oscar is coming this way."

"Fuck."

"Run, if you want to."

"Gracias, Estella." He goes.

It's a few more minutes before Oscar spots her. He keeps being stopped by adoring fans. She doesn't wave at him or call out. She knows that it's inevitable that he will find her. She feels weary, also hungry and nervous. She's aware that tomorrow is coming faster than she might have liked and she will be going home. She feels a certain amount of dread at the idea and it's creating an uneasy sensation in her belly. As Esta pointed out earlier, they have been wanting more excitement in their lives, and this is excitement of the very best quality.

When their eyes meet, he smiles and she finds herself smiling back. As soon as he's within earshot she says, "You were fabulous. Your voice is lovely."

"Gracias, Rafa." He looks embarrassed. "You'll think that my nerves were hysterical." Sella wants to say that his mood had probably been more to do with Víctor, but the others tell her to back off.

"Not at all. There are a lot of people here tonight and a duet must make you feel as if you have less control over your performance." Miss offers.

"Santi was very easy to work with. He's very professional."

"Do you feel more relaxed now?"

"Yes. ¡Tengo hambre! ¿Tu?"

"Starving."

"Shall we get out of here?"

"Absolutely." Although something dies inside as she thinks that she will never see the *Boy Friends* and *Love Struck* cast members again. Their progress to the exit is hampered by people stopping to congratulate Oscar and as a result she does get to say goodbye to Arlo and Seamus and the others. She meets Bram and the girls. Part of her insides revive. She keeps scanning the room for Santi, but he's nowhere in sight. Just as they are leaving, Nuria catches Oscar's arm.

"¿Oscar, te vas?"

"Sí, Nuria, Estella tiene hambre y tengo que levantarme temprano mañana para nuestra reunión."

"Vale. Estella, fue un gran placer conocerte. Estoy deseando hablar contigo sobre tus ideas para la tercera temporada. Oscar me dará tu correo electrónico."

"Perfecto. Hasta la próxima," Estella replies.

Igor is waiting, but so are the fans. She persuades Oscar to go and sign things for people. It's a freezing cold night and these fans must have been standing here for hours. She climbs into the car.

"Are you okay, Estella?"

"Yes, Igor. Thank you for asking. A little hungry. Have you had a chance to eat?"

"Yes. I eat at friend's house. His wife make fantastic food from home. I am very fat." She laughs and he laughs too.

"Sounds great."

"Food is the thing I miss about home."

The door opens and Oscar slides in next to her. Igor drives and the streets slip by and she has no idea where they are, but doesn't have the energy to be inquisitive. She lets her head loll back and she almost falls asleep. She feels his warm hand cover hers, but she doesn't open her eyes. When the car stops, she finds that they are back at The Ned. The lobby seems absurdly quiet now after the earlier pandemonium. She wonders if he has decided that they won't eat.

"We're eating in your suite," he says as they get into the lift.

There are patio heaters on the terrace and the cafe style table has a cloth on it and is set for two people.

"Do you think it foolish to eat outside?"

"Not at all, I love eating outside."

She grabs her coat and they step out onto the terrace. There is a young man and a heated trolley. He serves them with prime rib, mashed potato, creamed spinach and there is a jug of delicious red wine jus. There is a beautiful bottle of Tignanello. She tells him about her time in Italy when she was Sella and she lived at the top of a palazzo in Firenze and all the restaurants she used to go to with her rich students from the English school where she worked. Her frequent trips by train to Venice and the autumn when she went with a friend to tour the Prosecco vineyards. She doesn't tell him about who the friend was or what he did to her in the back of his limousine. She has spent years trying to forget that.

He asks her if Italy is her happy place and she thinks for a second that she might be sick, but she breathes and plays for time by looking as if she's considering the question. "No," she finally manages. "My happy place is Menorca."

"I have to admit, I've never been to Menorca."

"It's very beautiful. I used to go as a child, and I have some friends there still. There's a wonderful house in the middle of a field that you can see from the main road on the way to Ciutadella. It's called Bonanova. It has a fabulous flight of steps up the front to the first floor. It's been abandoned for years, but I always dreamt that I would live there one day." She smiles at the thought of the derelict farmhouse with its grand entrance. She has been dreaming about it for forty years.

There is a hiatus in the conversation and the young man returns to take their plates and deliver a dessert trolley. As they dig into their desserts, Oscar asks tentatively, "What did you tell Nuria?"

"Sorry, Oscar," she suddenly realises that she might have spoken out of turn. "I was talking to the couple that play your parents in the show and I said I thought that season three would be explosive because of the breadcrumbs."

"The way they keep looking at each other as if they're hiding something?"

"Exactly. Nuria heard me talking to them and was trying to get me to tell her what I think's going to happen." She luxuriates a moment at the taste of the chocolate mousse. "I get the feeling that they haven't decided on the plot yet."

"I think you're probably right." She smiles at him.

"I have this really great idea."

They talk for half an hour about her idea. She hadn't realised how much she had been thinking about it. She finds that she has a detailed plan in mind, and she also has some strong feelings about things that the characters will say. Oscar gets quite excited. She doesn't tell him the whole idea, though. Now that she has met Víctor, she thinks it might be best to keep that part of the plan to herself for the time being.

"So, it's okay for me to give your e-mail to Nuria?"

"Yes, absolutely."

"You could make some money out of this, Rafa. This is a really good concept."

"Really? Do you really think that they'd pay me for the idea?"

"Yeah. They'll pay you for it and they'll want you to work with the writers."

It's almost 1 am when Oscar finally says goodnight and, after some argument, goodbye. She insists that she must go back to Hereford the next day to start preparing to go back to work.

He tells her that he will book a late check-out for her as she will need to sleep. He has meetings all day tomorrow and has to do some Instagram posts. At the door, he pauses, turns back and scoops her into his arms as he did in the lobby before they left for the party.

"Gracias, Rafa. Nos vemos muy pronto, ¿vale?"

"Of course," she assents, but she suspects that they will not meet soon. In fact, she wonders if they will ever meet again. This was a moment. He was in crisis and she saw his pain. She was in the right place at the right time. The crisis has passed. He will get back to Madrid and life will resume. He will try to visit his mother. Maybe he will come to his senses and spend some time with Víctor.

He lets her go and she suddenly feels bereft and cold and more tired than she has ever been. He slips out of the door and is gone.

She stands a little while looking at the door before she locks it. She pulls off the dress and lovingly replaces it in the garment carrier. She goes and stands under the hot shower and removes the gloop that Santi put in her hair. She removes what she can of the make-up without a cleanser, it's waterproof after all. She wraps her hair in a towel and puts on her night gown. She sleeps and sleeps. She dreams that she is dancing at Santi's concert. She is bathed in his music and the light of his smiling face. She wakes up to pee at about 7:30 am and brushes out her hair and gets back into bed. She sleeps some more.

Wake-Up Call

She's woken by a knock on the door. She has no idea what time it is and wonders if she has overstayed the late check-out. She scurries out of bed and opens the door. Oh, bloody hell, it's Santi. He peers at her and touches her face with his fingertips, "Not fair!" he complains. "When I got out of bed this morning, I had spots and a rash. It took twenty minutes to conceal it all." He walks into the room and looks down. "You have a note." he bends down and picks up an envelope, which he hands to her. "So, he didn't stay here last night," he states. "Great room."

She looks at the envelope.

"Cat got your tongue?" asks Santi.

"Sorry," she croaks. Her throat feels like sandpaper. "I was asleep." It's all that she can do not to add...dreaming about you, but commonsense prevails.

"Well, chiquita angelita, it's almost lunchtime, you're going to have to check-out soon. Oscar said that you're leaving today, but you can't go until you have lunch with me."

"Oscar said that?"

"No, obviamente no." He rolls his lovely eyes. "He said you were leaving. I say you have to have lunch with me."

"Okay."

"Thanks for the enthusiasm!" He laughs. "I'll be in reception. Try not to be too long."

She unpacks the third dress she bought before this extraordinary experience started. She pulls on a simple relaxed shirt dress in powder blue with a white grid pattern. As she packs up the things she has accumulated over the last couple of days she finds the envelope. She opens it and takes out a sheet of thick creamy paper.

'Rafa, querida.

I'll be back in the UK in two weeks. Please can we meet then? I know that you will be working, so maybe I can come to Hereford?

Text Igor when you are ready to leave. He says the drive is about three and half hours and he has never seen Hereford. He will take you home.

I'm sorry for last night's drama. I know that you know that it wasn't just nerves. I will explain.

I'll call you next week. I have to fly back to Madrid tomorrow and I have a TV appearance on Sunday, so Monday will be easier. Besides, you probably need a break from me!

Gracias, otra vez, Rafa.

Oscar. X'

She feels absurdly grateful. He's going to try to keep in touch. She really can't ask for anything more than that. She receives a text. "Hurry up!" As she hasn't been able to remove the make-up, she tops it up, minus the lipstick that she can't remember what happened to. She says goodbye to the Terrace Suite and says thank you for the good times. She goes down to the lobby, returns her key, and leaves the garment bag and the box with the shoes and jewellery at the desk. She's put a note inside for John with her thanks.

"You have some really good dresses," Santi tells her.

"I know. I do a great dress."

"Where for lunch? Shall we get Mexican food?"

"Hell, yes!"

Santi is incognito, but there are still a few people who recognise him. Igor drives them to a place in Shoreditch, where they have tacos. He asks her about her job, her family and what she does for fun. He asks a lot of questions about her cats and her house. She asks back. The only thing that stops them talking is eating and exclaiming over the delicious tacos, guacamole, black beans and corn cobs. They laugh a lot. Their conversation slips seamlessly between Spanish and English and she learns a couple of Dutch words. It's like a breath of fresh air. She feels relaxed, happy and refreshed. When the time comes to leave, they both feel their mood drop. They tell each other that they had great fun. She gets into Igor's car, and he gets into Suzie's.

"He is good friend," says Igor.

"Yes," she agrees. "He gives energy." Igor nods his agreement.

Estella loves watching the London streets whizzing past her. She smiles at the familiar buildings and thinks of the positive experiences that she can associate with them. At Ealing, she smiles broadly at the Hoover Building and recalls the numerous times that she passed it being driven to or from drama school by one of her parents. She and Igor chat. He is a kind, interesting man. Around Oxford, he suggests that she sleeps for a while. She is tired, she thinks, and dozes for a while.

At Gloucester, she suddenly remembers that she needs to call Win.

"Hey, are you back?"

"I'm at Gloucester. Oscar's driver, Igor, is driving me back."

"Fancy shmancy!"

"Yeah. I know."

"Shall we use the vouchers I have for Bao to the Broth tonight?"

"Great idea. The cats will probably murder me in my sleep tonight."

"Yeah, the fat one almost scratched my eyes out this morning."

"Sorry."

"I'll knock about 7 pm."

"Great. See you then."

Looking at her phone, Estella can see that she has emails, but she really can't be bothered, and besides, she will be sick if she reads them in the moving car. She leans back once more and naps for the rest of the trip. She wakes on the road from Ledbury to Hereford and Igor is eager to tell her how beautiful he thinks Herefordshire is. She tells him that he should see it in spring and summer when there are so many hues of green that it's quite overwhelming. He nods.

At her door, she invites him to come in to have a drink and use the bathroom. He drinks some coffee in her living room and says he likes her house. He pets the cats and looks at the books. They chat about owning a home. He has one in Croydon. A flat in a high-rise, but all his. He tells her that growing up in Kiev he never imagined that he would have his own place. He tells her that he almost lost it when he got married and she turned out to be manipulative. He says he's much happier being self-reliant and she understands completely.

After she has thanked him for all his kindness and he has left, she realises something significant. She is standing in the hallway having just shut the front door. She cannot decide if this something is amazingly good or if it is the most disturbing thing that has ever happened to her. Another moment of ice and fire competing. Miss has been alone all day. She has not been hijacked or supported once. All day, with Santi and Igor, she has been just herself. She has had no need of any of the others. She can't remember the last time that this happened.

There is a knock at the door. Win shouts, "Come on! Hurry up!" It's standard operating procedure. Miss laughs and opens the door.

On the stroll to the restaurant, Win grills her about the party and who she saw and met. It's not until they are seated and have ordered that she asks, quietly, "What was the stuff at the hotel before the party all about? Oscar looked angry." Miss remembers all the people with phones in the lobby and realises with a burn in the gut that it must have all been caught on video and posted. She suddenly feels exhaustion flooding through her veins.

"He was really nervous about singing at the party and he was acting kind of weird. Santi called him out on it. For a while I thought that we might not even go to the party."

"There's a lot of chat about it on Insta."

"What are they saying?" Her friend looks sheepish.

"Love triangle."

"What?"

"You, Oscar and Santi."

"You're kidding me!"

"The way he grabs you; it looks pretty intimate."

"But..."

"I know, but there's no sound, it's just what it looks like. And then Santi posted today that you were having lunch together..." Miss thinks of poor Santi being dragged into this. This will put an end to any friendship they might have had. It would be far too complicated.

"Miss!" It's one of her students from year thirteen.

"Hi Milo, how are you?"

"Good, miss. Have you just got back from London?"

"Yes, how did you know that?"

"I saw that you were at that big Netflix party last night. I didn't know that you knew those people."

"I only just met them."

"But you're going out with Oscar Pérez, right?"

"No! No, Milo, I'm not. He's a friend." Milo hesitates.

"That's not what it looks like on TikTok, Miss."

"Yes, but Milo, you know that you can't trust what you see on social media."

"Yes, Miss." he says heavily. "Bye, Miss."

The meal is something of a trial after that, but the food is good. Win tries to steer the conversation into other avenues and they successfully talk about their up-coming trip and decide to see each other a week on Sunday for a meal at Win's house. They walk slowly back to Estella's and say goodnight.

Inside, Estella goes to her phone and opens her e-mail. There is a mail from the principal of the college where she works.

'Dear Miss Marks,

It has been brought to my attention that over the last 24 hours a number of social media posts have been made which include photographs and videos of you. The posts portray behaviours that might be deemed unseemly for a teacher in charge of the education of young people aged from sixteen-eighteen. The matter will require investigation by the college board of trustees.

In the meantime, before this investigation can take place, I am writing to inform you that you are suspended with pay until the investigation has reached its conclusions.

You must not, under any circumstances, come to the college premises during this investigation, unless expressly invited. You must not communicate with any colleague or student of the college during the investigation.

I will contact you again when necessary.

Principal David Mallory.'

Estella drops the phone. She stands arrested in shock and shame. She feels them all waking up inside her and there is a cacophony as they make their feelings heard. After the silence of today, it is all too much. She roars with anger, confusion and fear. She balls her fists and beats her head. She goes to the kitchen and pulls a knife from the block, pulls up the sleeve of her beautiful blue dress and slices a horizontal cut into the flesh of her inner forearm. She cries out in pain and tears roll down her still made-up face. She holds the arm over the sink and watches the blood drip and feels the agony. She runs the tap hot to wash the blood away and clean the knife. The pain is excruciating. She feels lightheaded. When the blood stops dripping and is clotting around the wound, she takes a wad of kitchen towel and blots the cut.

She leaves the back door open for the cats and tips a pile of biscuits onto their tray. She goes up to bed with a bottle of wine and a packet of over-the-counter sleep medication. She puts a bucket by the bed. She carefully pulls off the dress and hangs it up. She opens the wine and swigs at it. She pushes out three tablets and takes them one by one with swigs of wine. She keeps swigging until she has to lie down. Then she sleeps and dreams that she is dancing to Santi's songs and bathed in the light of his smiling face.

She weeps as she sleeps for the loss of everything that she has worked so hard for. She weeps for her stupidity and lack of judgement. The only relief is that her parents are not alive to see what an utter mess she has made. She hopes not to wake up, but when she does, she simply chugs down more wine and pills. It's the only thing that will shut them up.

END OF PART ONE

PART TWO:
Miss Takes the Reins

Monday Morning

While Estella is sleeping, the Internet is at work. While Estella stumbles sleepily and trips on her way to the bathroom banging her head on the landing banister, posts are being made, shared, turned into memes and reshared. While she shuffles on her bottom down the stairs to put food out for the cats and takes out a chunk of her leg on a protruding nail, rumours are circulating and theories being put forward as facts. When the others try to berate her and break through to wake her up, she presses brutally at the cut on her arm to make them back off. While she staggers, one eye swollen closed from the banister incident, back upstairs losing her footing and falling to the bottom in a heap of bruises, Oscar is trying to reach her on the telephone that ran out of battery long ago. When she finally manages to get back up to the bed and chugs the last of the wine and the sleeping tablets, Oscar has left Madrid and is on his way to London. It's the small hours of Monday.

Win, passing Estella's house on her way back from walking the dogs at 8 am on Monday morning, sees a small group of people standing outside with cameras and wonders what the hell is going on. As soon as she is out of earshot, she calls Estella and gets a message telling her that the phone is switched off and that voicemail is unavailable. She takes the dogs home, texts Estella's neighbour and then goes back to Estella's road. She quietly turns down the side passage of the neighbour's house to the gate into the back garden, which the neighbour has unlocked for her. She walks down to the end of the garden and squeezes through a gap in the fence shared with Estella's property and walks through the wilderness of Estella's back garden to the back of her house.

She finds the back door ajar and steps into the living room. The cats are sitting on the sofa and they start mewing as soon as they see her. The house is icy. It's -3^{0}C outside and it doesn't feel much better inside.

"Stella!" Her voice sounds frighteningly loud in the cold, still house. She takes a step closer to the sofa and feels something underfoot. She picks up the dead phone. She sees the bags that Stella must've brought back from London. One of the cats is nested on the black velvet coat that Stella always meticulously hangs up but which is now in a heap on the sofa under the cat.

"Stella!" Win hears her own fear. This has happened before. Only once. Once was more than enough. She's edging through to the hall and bracing herself to go up to the bedroom when she sees a smear of blood on the floorboards at the foot of the stairs. She's about to shout out to Stella again when she's startled into dropping the phone by a bang on the front door. She hears the cats scram through the back door as the shout permeates the hallway.

"Estella! Please open the door. It's Oscar." Another bang. She takes the few steps to the door, unlocks it and opens it. "Est..." Oscar stops. He's so tall and good looking that Win just gawps. "Is this Estella's house?" Win can hear the reporters outside calling to Oscar and the flick of camera shutters.

"Yes. I'm her friend. Come in." Oscar squeezes past her and then another tall, broader man comes in.

"Igor," he says. Oscar is looking at the blood.

"What?"

Win secures the door.

"I don't know. I just came in from the back garden through the neighbour's fence. I haven't been upstairs yet." She sees Oscar pick up the phone and tap at it, seeing that it's dead. Igor has gone to the back door and is securing it. Oscar looks up the stairs and then climbs them.

"At the front. Her room's at the front." Win doesn't think that she can face going up those stairs. It wasn't in this house that it happened last time. It was a different house, but she's sure of what's upstairs. She'd never seen a person that broken up close before. She's occasionally seen homeless people who'd passed over into some kind of madness of matted hair, cuts and bruises, but she hadn't had to pull the duvet away from their scabbing wounds, dab damp cloths at their swollen eyes or attempt to pull a brush through their blood-encrusted hair. She recalls the metallic tang of the blood and the mustiness of her sweat as she unwound her from the duvet.

"Are you okay?" Igor asks her. He can see the answer. "Please, you can put heating on? Feed cats. Make coffee." She nods. She watches Igor climb the stairs. Then she hears the crying. As if someone had just turned the volume up. It's a keening. She knows instantly what to call it although she doesn't think she knew what the word really meant before now. Between agonised notes she hears him saying the word *Rafa* repeatedly. Her tears fall then and she rushes to busy herself in the kitchen.

...

Igor follows the sound of agony and comes into the room. Oscar is sitting on the bed, rocking slightly. There's the smell of blood and sweat and Igor opens the window. Oscar has a very pale, bloodstained hand in his. The rest of the body is under the duvet, but it isn't moving. Igor gently peels back the duvet from where he thinks the head should be. It's her hair, but there's dried blood. He pushes back a little more duvet and brushes back the hair and finds her face, swollen and bruised, one eye closed by swelling the other flickering as if she's dreaming. There are still remnants of make-up around her eyes. She's burning up. He uncovers the arm of the hand that Oscar is holding and finds the cut sliced across the inner forearm. Oscar lets out a wounded howl. The cut is angry red and hot to the touch. There is bruising on the tender flesh around it and scratches. He covers her up again, carefully. He doesn't think he can do any more just now. There are memories stirring that he would rather not revisit. He takes his phone out and calls 999.

Thursday

She wakes up on Thursday just after 3 pm. She has no idea of the drama that has been unfolding around her. Oscar, who has never used a hospital in his life, is shocked to discover what an NHS A&E department is like and cannot understand why they have to wait for Estella to be seen and treated. Igor has strong words with him, but as soon as she's patched up and injected with antibiotics, Oscar arranges for her to be moved to a private hospital, where she has a room of her own and there's a comfortable armchair where Oscar and Igor take turns to keep watch. When off duty, they return to Estella's house to sleep. Oscar takes first watch and Igor erases all traces of the *incident* so that when Oscar arrives at the house he sees only Estella's colours, books, things and feels the warmth and comfort of her home. Oscar sleeps in her comfortable bed from which every sign and smell of what happened has been expunged. He cuddles her furry rabbit toy, which had been splattered with blood until Igor took it in hand, and fancies that he smells her on it.

Oscar is in the hospital chair, scrolling through his social media on his phone, when he hears a sharp intake of breath followed by a dry, painful-sounding cough. Apart from some bruising, her face is almost back to normal. Three days of sleep, antibiotics and anti-inflammatories will make that happen. She hasn't opened her eyes. He puts the edge of a beaker of water against her lower lip, and when she tilts her head, he lets a little water dribble into her mouth. Still not opening her eyes, she feels for the beaker and takes it from him and continues to take little sips of water. He goes over to the window and closes the curtains. It's not exactly a sunny day, but she's had her eyes shut for a long time. When he gets back to the bed, her eyes are open. She stares straight ahead.

"I didn't want to wake up." Her voice is a faint grating rasp.

"I'm so sorry about your job, but they haven't done the investigation yet. You might still..." He trails off. He knows that it'll be very hard, maybe impossible, for her to go back to that job. The journalists were outside when the ambulance came and took her away to hospital. They got photos of her face as the stretcher was taken past them. It's all over the Internet. There're still a few journalists outside the hospital. They photograph him coming and going.

Oscar's lawyer has been in touch with the college; the investigation won't take place for a few months yet. Estella will be paid until it happens, but this isn't the same as having her job. He sees how much her work meant to her. He hopes that she'll never know that they had to pump her stomach out. He hopes that she'll never know that the police came and investigated if the injuries had been inflicted by someone else. He had proof that he was in Madrid on a live television show until almost midnight on the Sunday, and that he arrived at the house after Win. Win had proof that she contacted the neighbour before entering from the back garden. Igor showed them the bloody nail, identified the knife she must've used. Her phone, once it had been charged and unlocked showed all Oscar's messages, the email from the principal and several messages from Santi Faber.

"Nuria wants to set a meeting to talk about your ideas for season three," he tells her. When she doesn't answer, he realises that she's fallen asleep again and the water has tipped over her scarred left arm.

It takes days. He has to cancel photoshoots, guest appearances and an audition that had taken months to set up for an independent Spanish film, but he knows that this is his fault. In the end, the following Thursday, after showering and dressing herself, she is discharged and, in the car, on the way back to her house, she asks him when Nuria wants to meet.

"Next week would be good," he says. "Tuesday?" She nods.

She makes him leave without getting out of the car. She thanks him and Igor for their help, but it's mechanical and dull. When Oscar tries to embrace her, she puts out a hand to stop him and turns her body protectively as if she were fending off a blow. He can't speak. He thinks he'll cry. Igor takes her to the front door, shielding her from the journalists. He wants to remind her that she has his number, but he knows it's useless. He opens her door for her, hands her the keys and closes it as soon as she's inside. He waits until he hears the mortice click as she locks it.

In the car, Igor says, "She needs time, Oscar. She don't want to live. She have to want to live again. She needs time." Oscar nods.

He calls Nuria, sets up the meeting and explains what's happened to Estella. He knows that she's seen the coverage, so there's nothing to gain by trying to cover it up. He assures her that Estella is well and ready to work. He gives her the email address she needs to mail the tickets to and suggests a hotel that they might put her up in.

"She won't be staying with you?" asks Nuria. He hangs up without replying.

Family

Estella has a brother and sister. They both love her very much, but she keeps them at arm's length. Estella has spent her life rushing from one experience to another and ricochetting from the highs of success and achievement to the lows of failure and loss. There had been few times in her life, until she became carer to her parents, when any kind of equilibrium had been achieved for a sustained period. She's adept at masking the issues and the Magnificent Seven are one of the mechanisms that have helped her to appear reasonably balanced to people who don't know her well. Therefore, it follows that she cannot allow people to know her well and that includes her family. She spent years living at distance in London or abroad to manage the subterfuge, and when she returned to the UK she hid in her role as carer for her parents. Her siblings know that she's not quite like other people and certainly not like them, but, in truth, they've no idea what she's really like. It makes it very hard for them to have a relationship with her.

Estella's recent explosion on social media means that her nieces and nephews have been seeing her in a number of situations that they would never have imagined their aunt, and even her brother and sister have seen the posts feeding through to Facebook. It was then, she supposes, inevitable that one or both of her siblings would end up getting in touch.

Inside the house, after dismissing Oscar and Igor, she sits for a long time with the cats. There are still journalists outside, so the curtains are closed at the front of the house. Igor escorted her to the door on her return, so she didn't have to speak to anyone, and he had already closed the curtains. He's such a kind person. She hopes that she'll never hurt or inconvenience him. She dozes for a while with her fat cat sitting on her stomach and the skinny one on the carpet by the sofa, vigilant.

When she has to go to the toilet, she decides to look at her phone which Igor has left on charge in the kitchen.

She sees messages from Santi. Heat surges through her at the desire to read them. She imagines how lovely it would be to spend time with him. She deletes the messages without reading them and blocks his number. It's for the best. *Love triangle*. That idea has to be squashed.

There are missed calls from both of her siblings and her nieces. They're all broadly supportive, but there's strain in the voices of her siblings, Bella and Richard. They both say that they wanted to come to the hospital, but they didn't know which hospital she was in as it said in the press that she wasn't at the County. She thinks carefully about what they might know and what she doesn't want them to know and realises that they probably already know far more than she wants them to. She rehearses her sane voice. Tries a couple of different messages. Eventually, she sends them both a voice note; she detests talking on the telephone, it's too hard to speak to someone when you can't see their facial expressions.

"Hey. Sorry for the drama. I just came home from the hospital. I'm fine. I don't know what you know. I went to London on the Wednesday of half-term. I met Oscar Pérez completely by chance. He had a problem that I was able to help him out with. It was just a favour, nothing important, but he showed his gratitude by inviting me to stay a couple of nights in London and go to a Netflix party with him. Win tells me that there're all sorts of rumours going around on the Internet. He's a friend. There's nothing going on. The social media stuff has got me suspended from work pending an investigation. I suppose that I'll lose my job. The email telling me that I'd been suspended triggered an episode. I'm coming out of it. Please don't worry. I'll start looking for another job. Please let the kids know that I'm fine and I'll be in touch when I'm stable again. Okay? Sorry."

A few minutes after she has sent the message, her phone pings.

Richard:

Must've been a bloody big favour. Let us know if you need anything.

She tries not to cry. She knows how she appears to them. She's the youngest and has always been *a worry* to them. Just as she is battling the tears back, her phone rings.

"Hey."

"Hey, Stel, I'm glad you picked up. I thought maybe you wouldn't."

"Sorry, Bella, I didn't have my phone in the hospital."

"Have they given you medication this time?"

"Bella, you know my feelings about that; I don't want medication."

"London was a manic episode, right?"

"No!"

"You looked pretty manic dancing in that club, Stel."

"What? I was just having fun."

"Stel, your idea of fun, is never in line with other people's. You looked like you were in a trance. Tripping!"

"I was having a good time. The music was amazing. You know I don't take drugs."

"You're nearly sixty, Stel."

"So?"

"When you took on the responsibility of caring for mum and dad, I really thought that you'd turned a corner. You did us all a huge favour and I'll always be grateful for that, Stel, but are we going back to the bad old days?"

"Bella, don't do this."

"Don't do what, Stel? Don't point out that this is the fourth time that you have been hospitalised for manic depressive behaviour? Don't say that it's a huge disappointment after twelve years of calm?"

"You think that I wanted this to happen?"

"I'd like to say no, but it just seems like you need attention."

"And you think that I did this for attention?"

"I'm never quite sure, Stel. I'm never sure why you get into these peculiar states. You've always been a bit of a drama queen..."

Estella ends the call. She goes to her contacts. She blocks her sister's number. She blocks her brother's number. With regret, she blocks the numbers of her nieces and nephews because she doesn't want them to be pawns in her siblings' games. She pants. She fights the urge to go into the kitchen and slice open her arm again. She goes out into the cold wilderness garden and paces back and forth like a caged animal. She repeatedly raises her arms above her head and tries to breathe deeply. She hears her phone ringing inside the house. It's a distraction. Her breathing starts to regulate. She begins to feel cold. She puts a cold hand on the nape of her neck and feels her body begin to relax. She paces a little more and then walks slowly back into the house.

On her phone is a missed call from a number in Spain and an e-mail with her plane ticket for Tuesday and a message saying that a hotel has been booked for her. The voicemail is from Nuria, saying that she's looking forward to seeing her on Tuesday.

She needs a plan.

She considers letting the capable Esta take charge, but as she feels her moving forward, she stabs her thumb into the still tender wound on her left inner forearm until she knows that Esta has retreated. It was them that got her into this mess. They were the ones egging her on to enjoy the excitement without a thought for how she would pay the bills. She needs to be careful now. She can't depend on their judgement.

She cleans the wound and washes her thumb. She can't afford another infection. She's going to have to appear reasonably normal in five days' time. She pours a glass of water and sits down at the dining-room table with paper and a pen.

She makes a list.

- cat sitter
- hair
- long-sleeved dresses
- pack for a week
- lipstick
- perfume
- cleanser

getting to airport?

She goes upstairs and squints down to the front of her house. There are still a few journalists outside. She phones the hairdresser and makes an appointment for the following day. She texts her neighbours to ask them if she can use their side passage in the morning and apologises for the journalists hanging around. She Googles cat sitters and e-mails a woman about looking after the cats while she's in Madrid. She's going through her wardrobe picking long-sleeved dresses for her trip when her phone pings.

Igor

Check in Tuesday 04:10 am at Heathrow. Oscar book me to collect from your house midnight Monday. See you then.

She texts her thanks and crosses one of the items off her list. She selects seven dresses and assesses for cleaning and repairs. She puts on a wash, stitches on a loose button and fixes a hem. Her phone pings.

Win

Home? Need anything?

Home. Have everything I need. Dinner on Sunday?"

Win

Fab.

Win came to the hospital, but she was frightened by the state of her and overawed by Oscar and Igor. As Estella hadn't exactly been communicative, Win hadn't stayed long. Estella feels bad. She goes onto Tommy Banks' Oldstead at Home website and orders them a food box for the weekend: Onion, Duck, Douglas Fir. She arranges delivery to Win at the Off License so that she knows that she doesn't have to shop. They usually reserve this for birthdays, but Win deserves a boost. She phones up the Beehive and arranges a delivery of flowers to her poor, long-suffering neighbours. She transfers some money from her savings account to cover the spending.

She's exhausted.

Whilst she waits for the washing to go into the final spin, she wanders disinterestedly to the fridge. She finds it full to bursting. There's smoked salmon, jamón serrano, eggs, pasta, butter, apples, Manchego, olives, a flatbread. It's so kind. It turns her stomach. She has no appetite at all.

Once she's emptied the washing machine, she goes back upstairs and goes to bed. It's only three in the afternoon, but she's exhausted and she needs to leave the house by 9:45 in the morning. She hovers by the bed, remembering when she last slept here and how little she'd wanted to wake up. She puts on her pyjamas, climbs into the fresh sheets, and hugs her bunny to her chest. She's asleep in seconds, bathed in the light of his smile.

She wakes around four in the morning with a banging head and supposes that she hasn't drunk anything for rather a long time. She upsets the cats and carefully goes down to the kitchen to drink some water and take some paracetamol. There is no paracetamol. She looks in all the places she keeps them. All the packets of pills that she once had around the house have gone. No painkillers. No sleeping tablets. She feels irritated. She goes to her handbag and gets the packet of ibuprofen that she keeps there and takes those instead. She goes carefully back to bed and sets the alarm for 8 am.

When it goes off, she resets it for 8:45 am. At 8:45 she snoozes for ten minutes and finally drags herself out of bed to shower and dress at 8:55 am. She feeds the cats. She considers breakfast but rejects the idea. It's raining. She puts on a hooded raincoat, wanders down the garden, squeezes through the break in the garden fence, makes her way to the back of the neighbours' house and through the gate and onto the street. She walks straight past the journalists who are huddled miserably under their umbrellas.

The hairdresser is amazing and asks her no questions, just does his usual fantastic job on her roots and tidies up the cut. He's very careful around the wound on her head, which he only discovers when he starts to put the colour on, but doesn't ask what happened. It was the same twelve years ago. He suggests that she might want to let it air-dry, the only oblique reference to the wound that would burn under the heat of a dryer. She puts the raincoat back on and slips back out onto the rain-soaked street in anonymity.

Chave and Jackson has the same lipstick that she lost in London, and she buys a new perfume because she can't use the one she bought with Santi again. Too many memories. She buys make-up remover and paracetamol. One of the assistants looks as if she might say something, but she manages to get out without any conversation. She practically runs back to the house. She passes the journalists again, ducks down the alley, locks the gate after she's passed through and is soon back in her own house.

She makes herself drink some water and eat an apple. She dries her hair. She irons the dresses that she washed the day before. She goes into the cellar, finds her suitcase, and puts it in the utility room to air out. She goes back to bed. She sleeps.

It's four in the morning and she's suddenly awake. She paces her bedroom. Anxiety has woken her up and is tormenting her. Who is she to tell the executives of *Los Amores de Oscar* what to do with their season three? She's nobody. She carefully peers through the side of the curtain and finds that there are no journalists outside her house. It's cold and wet out there and there is definitely nobody waiting for her. She scans the cars and they all look empty. She pulls on a rare pair of trousers, t-shirt, sweatshirt and trainers. She grabs her waterproof and puts up the hood. She opens the front door and steps out into the rain and she starts to walk. She walks fast, propelled by fear and anxiety. She keeps to the streets that are lit. Her mind is racing with ideas, scenarios and fears. She can hear words that need to be said and the specifics of the plot start to become clearer as she walks. She just keeps turning and turning and finally she sees that light is breaking through and there are a few flakes of snow mixed in with the rain. Her feet feel cold and her legs are starting to ache. She heads home. She finds that there are still no journalists as she lets herself through the gate and back into the house. She sheds her wet coat and shoes, puts on the heating and makes a mug of hot chocolate. She sits down at her laptop and crafts a plan for season three of *Oscar Loves* and writes the first scene between Oscar and his mum.

By the time she looks up from the laptop, it's almost midday and when she checks the screen she has close to twenty pages of plan and scenes. She gets a glass of water and heats the flatbread, putting a wash of underwear on. She edits the pages while she picks at the bread and sips at the water. She transfers the washing into the dryer and works on scene two between Oscar and his mum. Then she writes the scenes between Oscar and Nito. After printing the scenes out, she reads them aloud and makes some adjustments. She feels pleased with what she's crafted and realises that the pleasure that writing gives her is restorative; a positive energy that seems to heal her.

Early in the evening, she folds the dried wash and takes it up to the chest of drawers in her bedroom. She looks at the photograph she has on the wall of her sitting outside Florian in Saint Mark's Square, Venice. She has a vivid recollection of the pure joy of being there with a glass of Prosecco in her hand regarding the perfection of the basilica.

She goes back to her laptop and opens a new file which she names *At Florian*. She writes. She makes herself eat a little smoked salmon around 9 pm and at midnight, when she hears the church bell toll, she makes herself go to bed. She sleeps deeply in the only way that she now knows how to sleep and feels herself healing in that wonderful light. Hope begins to work its way into her mind and into the thrum of blood in her veins. There's a sense of a possibility of a chance of reinvention and, maybe, redemption. Like the tiniest chink of light in a pitch-black room at the dead of night. Like the faintest trace of sweetness in an underripe blackberry. Not enough to raise a smile, but just enough to create a little electricity to quicken her heartbeat.

The following day, she revisits the work she has done for *Oscar Loves* and then sets to writing again. *At Florian* flows well and she's aware that she's had this story in her mind for a long time. By the time she goes to shower and prepare to go round to Win's, there are about twenty thousand words, and she knows exactly where the story is going. Thinking about this story makes her feel calm and strong.

At Win's, there's excitement over the unpacking of the meal and reading the instructions for cooking it. They access Tommy's playlist and open a bottle of Barolo while they prepare the starter of French onion soup. They don't talk about what happened. They cook the main course together and exclaim at the flavours. It's not until they're sitting with the chocolate crémeux that Win says, "How're you feeling?"

"Better, much better. Thank you." She's glad that she doesn't have to lie. "I'm sorry, Win. I'm glad that it wasn't you that had to find me this time."

"He's a lovely bloke, Oscar, isn't he?"

"Yes, very kind and..." Estella hesitates. What else does she think of Oscar? She knows that he's kind, but everything else that she knows is not necessarily positive. He's complex and moody. He's damaged and angry. He's unhappy, and like her, living out of alignment with his real desires and interests. She repeats, "He's very kind."

"And very handsome!" Win chips in. "He's obviously got the hots for you."

"It's not like that," she says wearily.

"If that's what you want to think, it's up to you." Win holds her hands up and the dogs go wild thinking that she is going to throw something for them. "Shut up, you lot!" she bellows through the barking. "I'm just saying," she continues, "he could be good for you. It'd be nice to be looked after for a bit, wouldn't it?"

She thinks of how he takes care of her. She considers the week or ten days he spent with her at the hospital and which she suddenly realises he must have paid for, but these things do not evoke pleasure in her. She's aware of a tension around her chest relating to these caring kindnesses that make her feel beholden and obliged to him. She recalls him telling her that money was not a thing for him and how small she felt with her diminishing savings account and her habit of living beyond her means. But he is kind, she has to remind herself.

"Sorry," says Win, "I know that you're fresh out of hospital and probably not in the mood, but I think you're onto a good thing there." Estella wants to shout at her friend. Wants to tell her that nothing good has come from her association with Oscar Pérez, but she can't because, actually, all sorts of good things have happened; and who knows what more might come. She manages to smile at her friend, but there's no real warmth in it. The uneasiness in her chest won't shift.

Estella explains to Win that she's found a cat sitter, who's coming round the following day to get a key and learn the ropes. Then she explains that she's going to be away for five days in Madrid. She tells Win about her conversation with Nuria.

"That's amazing," says her friend, "you've always wanted to be a writer." Estella doesn't tell her anything about *At Florian*, not yet. She'd like to tell someone, but she won't be seeing him again, so best to forget about that and keep this to herself for the time being.

A little later than usual, Estella doesn't have the idea of being up for work tomorrow looming over her tonight, they part with a tentative plan to meet the following Sunday for a debrief of the Madrid trip, as long as she isn't exhausted. Her return flight is set for Saturday afternoon. When she arrives home, it's almost 10:30 pm and she goes straight to bed.

In the morning, she packs and puts her case by the front door. The cat sitter seems nice; her fat cat takes to her at once. She transfers funds to pay for the five days from her savings account and then makes the payment to the cat sitter. She writes until 10 pm and then goes to shower and change. She's wearing the purple dress that she bought recently but it feels rather large on her. There isn't enough headspace to think about this at the moment. She puts on mascara and eyeliner and puts it, along with the lipstick, in her hand luggage with her laptop and charger. She puts in the printed sheets of the work she did on the show. She's tired, but she's calm. The writing helps her to feel calm. She makes herself eat a couple of slices of apple and a small piece of cheese and drink some water, but it curdles in her stomach and she has to battle not to be sick. Soon, Igor is at the door and she smiles at his reassuring presence. He has a hot drink and uses the bathroom, and then she says goodbye to the cats. Taking her black velvet coat and her hand luggage, she steps out into the night and her next adventure.

Madrid

From the moment that he meets her at the airport, there are photographers everywhere. When she exits arrivals, he's standing there in clean, smart dark jeans, a crisp white shirt and a soft green leather jacket that she's pretty sure is Givenchy. As always, he takes her breath away, but she's uncomfortable with the press. They kiss cheeks rather formally and he wheels her case to the waiting car.

"Flight okay?"

"Yes, very comfortable."

"You look a little pale, Rafa."

"I didn't sleep last night. Igor picked me up at midnight." He turns sharply.

"Oh, mierda, I should have told them how far you live from the airport. They could have put you up at Heathrow."

"It's fine. I can sleep later."

Oscar's demeanour changes after this exchange. He seems to be cross with himself and she can feel disappointment, but not with her, so she assumes that he feels that he has let himself down. She knows that feeling and she feels the pull to reassure him, but she hasn't the energy to do it. In truth, she feels exhausted and ill-equipped for the meeting that she's going to.

She's no idea how to handle the discussion and make sure that she can make some money to support her until she can find work again.

The car's right out front with a female driver, who nods and smiles at Estella, putting her bag in the back of the vehicle. Inside the car is a woman more or less Estella's age, who extends a hand, "Mucho gusto, Estella, my name is Elvira. I'm Oscar's lawyer. I hope that you will allow me to be yours too?" Her English is heavily accented, but good and leaning towards a British accent rather than Oscar's American. Estella shoots a grateful glance at Oscar.

"What a relief, Elvira. Encantada conocerte." Then to Oscar, "Gracias, Oscar, eres tan atento. I was very worried about the meeting."

"No hay de que, Rafa." He has never called her Rafa in front of other people. She understands his trust in Elvira at once.

Estella and Elvira discuss what she has to show the representatives from *Los Amores de Oscar* and they discuss what she wants from the deal. Estella lays herself open to Elvira's guidance as she's no idea how these things work. When Elvira suggests the minimum figure that Estella agrees to for the work that she's done so far, she's stunned and wide-eyed. Elvira enumerates the services that the production company might ask her to fulfil from consulting on the script to being on set to help with interpretation and dialogue, and how much she should charge the company. At some point during the discussion, Oscar has taken her hand and he holds it gently but firmly in his own. She's glad of its warmth; she feels cold and fragile.

When the car stops and Elvira gets out, Oscar briefly kisses her hand before they follow her. Inside the glass and chrome building, Elvira and Estella wait for visitor passes, but Oscar tells them that he has another meeting and that he'll see them later. He seems to have his own pass. Estella feels a moment of panic as she sees him disappear into a lift, but Elvira touches her arm.

"Are you well, Estella? I told Oscar that I thought this might be too soon for you." She sees the genuine concern in her eyes and feels warmth and positive regard fill her belly.

"It's better if I keep moving forward." Elvira nods.

"May I take a look at the script that you wrote?" Estella hands it over and closes her eyes for a moment. She feels quite lightheaded.

"Apologies for the delay," says the receptionist in Spanish, "one of the producers has been caught in traffic. Can I get either of you a coffee while you wait?" Elvira asks for a cortado and Estella asks for some water. She closes her eyes again. She's so tired that she can feel them trying to break through. She knows that they're only trying *to help* but she doesn't trust them anymore. She puts her hand into the fold of her dress and viciously pinches a bit of flesh on the outside of her thigh. She doesn't know why, but physical pain always banishes them.

She feels a hand on her arm and opens her eyes to find Elvira's eyes filled with tears and a look of anguish. Elvira holds up the pages she's been reading.

"These are incredible, Estella. You write beautifully. This is really powerful. We can get much more for this. I don't think that anyone on the current writing team could write this quality."

"But is it sufficiently of the style of the show?"

"Yes, I think so, but easy to change a few words to make it blend if it isn't." She takes out a beautiful, lace-trimmed handkerchief and carefully wipes her eyes and blows her nose, drinks her tiny coffee and repossesses her professional bearing. "Does Oscar know about the scenario with Nito?" Estella shoots Elvira a glance.

"No. I'd rather that he doesn't know just yet." Elvira smiles at Estella and nods.

"Good strategy. I think they'll like that outcome, it's so unexpected, but I'm not sure what Oscar will think."

The receptionist lets them know that the meeting is ready for them.

There are five from the team present and their lawyer. Thank goodness that Oscar asked Elvira to come. Estella switches on classroom mode and pitches her idea to the team broken down into what happens in each of the eight episodes for season three. She does it all in Spanish and only flounders for vocabulary a couple of times. The writing in Spanish must have really tuned up her skills. Teaching A Level means that she doesn't get to use the whole gamut of vocabulary that she once possessed, or rather that Esta possessed.

They are asked to move into a side room for a while and Elvira is complimentary about Estella's pitch. They aren't excluded for long, and when they are seated again, it's Elvira's turn to do the talking and the negotiations begin. Estella listens mesmerised by the unthinkable sums of money that are being discussed for the purchase of her concept and the script that she's written. A price is agreed. Estella feels slightly guilty about the liberality of the decided fee and feels relief that she'll soon be able to get to her hotel and crawl into bed. Any adrenaline she might have had is rapidly ebbing away and exhaustion is winning.

"Estella, we have a secondary proposal for you," says Nuria. "I see from your CV that you've done some acting in the past. In fact, you studied at drama school. You have a very unusual look about you. We'd like you to play Oscar's mother. It's a small part, as you know, but it needs someone who can carry it off. We'd like you to do it."

For a moment, Estella thinks that her Spanish comprehension has failed her. She thinks that she's just been asked to act in season three. She must have misheard. That would be ridiculous. She feels her lungs closing and her breath shortening.

"You wrote some very powerful words for the role of Oscar's mother," Nuria continues, "and I think that you could deliver them with power too. Naturally, we would pay you a handsome fee for this."

Esta is desperately trying to push through to accept the offer. She knows that Miss is close to a panic attack and this is her opportunity. There's a common dream held by Esta, Ella and Stel before their confidence was obliterated and Sella, worn down by the constant losses and betrayals, let go of the last shreds of their self-belief and took them forward as a passive being. She had to. They know that she had no choice, but they still have the confidence that knows that living in the power of other people's emotions makes them ideal actors. They can become whoever they need to be.

Elvira asks for them to retire to discuss the offer; a figure, so unbelievable to her, that she can't comprehend it has been mentioned. Elvira guides her back to the side room and looks Esta in the eye. Estella pushes up the arm of her dress and thrusts the nail of her thumb into the still tender wound on her arm. She hears Elvira's sharp intake of breath, and Esta backs off.

"Estella?" Shock and fear. Estella fights to regulate her breath. Sits and allows a few tears to fall.

"How did they find out that I used to act?"

"Your CV is on a couple of job websites. I found it myself. When I saw that you were spending time with Oscar, I Googled you. There's not much on the Web, but your CV is there and there's a video of you teaching at a language school in Mexico City."

Estella has visions of the over-populated online world. Facts, fictions, photos and information just floating around waiting for a Google search to land on it. She recalls the promotional video for the school in DF that Sella, still looking like Esta, had made. It was just a few short months before...before the incident on Insurgentes. An image of them in the back of that car, the caress of her ankle. She presses into the cut again.

"Estella?"

"Sorry, perhaps this was too soon."

"Filming won't be until August or September. There is plenty of time. They are offering a good amount of money."

"Why are they doing that?"

"Estella, you are all over the Internet. Having you appear in the series will draw thousands of viewers. We could even ask for more money." She thinks of all of those posts and reposts that Win has described to her and she feels overwhelmed. She's everywhere and strangers are judging her and making comments about her. How do people do this? How do they, no, ***why*** do they let the world see them on social media? It's outrageous. She thinks of the video of her dancing to Santi's song and everything that's happened as a result of that single post.

The door opens and Oscar rushes in. He takes in her arm and her bloodied thumb. He leaves. She thinks that he's run away and feels that this is good; he's finally got it and decided to run away, but, as usual, she's wrong. He returns minutes later with a first-aid kit, pulls up a chair close to hers and starts to clean the wound and her thumb. He speaks quietly and calmly in Spanish.

"Rafa, querida, why don't you want to do this?"

"You knew that they were going to ask?"

"Yeah."

"Why didn't you say anything?"

"I wanted you to sell your idea first and get that deal sorted before you...before you reacted to this idea."

"Why do you want me to do this?"

"Because you'll be exceptional. You'll elevate the whole thing from soap-opera to drama." He looks her in the eye. "When people think about *Los Amores de Oscar* after the third season, all they will remember is those scenes between Oscar and his mother."

"No pressure, then," Estella says.

"But you won't even need to try, Rafa. I know you can do this. You just have to be there. There's the money too. You'll be...secure...you won't need to worry about getting another job for a while."

She thinks about the numbers that have been talked about and the freedom that they would give her. She's started to think about money in terms of how long it will keep her from having to go back to her old working routines. At least a couple of years, maybe three, without having to take nine to five work. She could travel. She could finish her house, which has been arrested in its development since she ran out of energy two years ago. She could write. She remembers *At Florian*. She won't need to do the filming for at least five months, and she has the work to do collaborating on the script. There's time to prepare, rehearse, perfect.

She looks at his beautiful, earnest face and then into his eyes. His belief in her is frightening. Esta would have basked in it and grown in confidence and happiness, but she feels the pressure of it and she feels something else behind his belief that scares her even more. She can't quite understand what it is, it's nebulous but looming.

"Okay," she hears herself say. "I'll do it." She feels a change in atmosphere instantly. The tension that she felt coming from Elvira and Oscar suddenly dissolves and if she were not seated, she suspects that she would have collapsed at the loss of its density and intensity. Oscar, however, is in control of himself and although he smiles, he asks her very quietly if she's sure. She nods. He leans towards her and kisses her gently on the cheek.

"Gracias, Rafa."

Elvira and Estella return to the meeting room and the relief on the faces of the executives is almost comical when she agrees to their proposal and at the fee they've offered. Elvira had wanted to ask for more, but Estella baulked at the suggestion. She's struggled with money her whole life and she feels guilty asking for such huge sums for what, to her, are things that don't constitute hard work. Elvira isn't happy but agrees to act to her instruction on this matter. There are handshakes and congratulations. Estella vibrates with the strength of emotion in the room. She's desperate to sleep. Oscar joins them in the room and places a supportive arm around Estella's waist, which she can't object to because she's not sure how she'd stand up without it.

Elvira leaves them in reception and says that she'll be in touch when they're ready to sign the contracts, which will probably be Friday. She takes Estella's hand and tells her that she's so pleased to meet her. She hands her a business card and tells her not to hesitate to call if she needs anything.

Oscar shepherds her to the car, saying, "Let's get you something to eat." Her stomach turns.

"Oscar, I really need to sleep. Please can I go to my hotel?" She sees a flash of anger in his eyes, feels in her belly his desire to take her to lunch, but she's hollowed out and he can see it.

"Sorry, Rafa," he says a little stiffly. "I'm being selfish again. I'll take you to your hotel."

In the back of the car, she lets her head fall back and she closes her eyes. She's almost asleep when the car pulls up. He takes her into the hotel, a steadying hand at the small of her back and wheeling her case until a porter takes it from him. He deals with her check-in and hands the keycard to the porter. He takes such care of her.

"Are you free tomorrow, Oscar?" Her words almost slurring with exhaustion.

"I've kept the whole week free for you, Rafa."

"Come and get me in the morning?"

"I'll be here at 10 am, okay?"

"Perfect."

"Sleep well, Rafa." He kisses her on the cheek, and she follows the porter into the lift and to her room. As soon as the door closes behind the porter, she falls onto the bed and lets the tears course down her face and very soon she's asleep. She's bathed in the light of his smile, her arms and legs moving to the instructions of the music; transported to a place where nothing matters.

A Day in the Sun

She wakes feeling drugged and finds that it's dark. She's not sure when she came to the hotel, but she thinks it was early afternoon. She locates her phone and realises that she hasn't turned it back on from the flight. When it comes back on, she learns that it's 11 pm. She uses the luxurious bathroom and finally pays attention to her surroundings. The room is exquisite. Dark marble bathroom. Room panelled in wood. Terrace with a wonderful view of the city streets. She finds a menu for room service and discovers that she's staying at the Thompson. She orders a double cheeseburger and a piece of cake. She unpacks and changes into pyjamas. She feels lighter. Room service delivers on a trolley and she sits in an easy chair and devours the burger and half of the cake before she starts to feel sick. She can't remember when she last ate. This is a bit too much for her. It's too stodgy. She goes back to bed setting an alarm for 8:30 am and cradles her stomach. She expects to lie there in discomfort for hours, but she next wakes when her phone alarm goes off.

Today he takes her breath away in Adolfo Dominguez, navy chinos, a matching jacket with a Mandarin collar, desert boots in a natural suede and a pop of colour from his orange scarf. It's supposed to be a relaxed outfit, but she understands that relaxation is a foreign concept to Oscar. He stands perfectly straight, like a mannequin, one hand neatly in a trouser pocket, the other resting on the handle of an elegant umbrella. He smiles broadly at her. She's wearing her orange dress. The same orange as his scarf. They laugh and he kisses her cheek. He crooks his arm and they walk out into rain under his umbrella.

"Did you sleep well, Rafa?"

"¡Como un tronco!"

"I'm so pleased. Are you up for a little day trip?"

"Sounds wonderful." She feels light and rested and he seems to feel the same.

"Ávila or Toledo?"

"I've been Toledo, but I've never been to Ávila. Can we go there?"

"That's my first choice."

The driver is called Rocio and she gets them to Ávila in a little over an hour. Estella is entranced on the journey by the buildings in the city and the countryside of La Mancha. She exclaims at the windmills, the castles and the cute little towns that they pass at speed. When they arrive at the walls of Ávila, she is dumbstruck by the majesty and power they exude. As they get out of the car to walk into the city, the sun suddenly breaks through the clouds and the walls seem to be lit from within. Estella feels the power of the sunlight and turns her face up to meet it. When she opens her eyes, she sees Oscar looking at her. The expression on his face speaks volumes and she feels a little trickle of dread as it sinks in.

"I know," she says wearily, "how is it possible that I'm the same person that you found at the house a fortnight ago?" He flushes deeply.

"I'm sorry." She doesn't speak. She lets him ask. "This is the person that I met in London. How did the person I met in Hereford...happen?"

"Let's walk. I'll tell you. Let's see if you believe me."

They set a course through the narrow stone streets and the sun feels like a blessing as she tries to dredge up the words to explain to him what she is. She's tried to explain it many times in her life to many people, but however eloquent she is they just don't seem to be able to or want to get it.

"I've never met anyone who understands this, Oscar. People seem to want to not believe me when I tell them what it's like being me. At least you know that I'm not a liar. You told...you told Santi that I don't lie. I hope that you really believe that." Saying his name brings back the pain of losing his friendship and the sweet memory of the day that she came back to herself because his company was so soothing.

"I'll always believe what you tell me, Rafa." She breathes deeply and decides to try, despite the nagging doubt that he won't take her seriously.

"My experience of life seems to be different to other people's. I'm sure that there must be other people like me, but I just haven't met them yet. I feel emotions and atmospheres very intensely. I feel my own emotions, but I also feel the emotions of others around me and a lot of the time I don't even know if what I feel is mine or theirs. When I was a kid, I used to run towards water because I felt the power of it. On mountains I'd take off my shoes and socks and stand in the mud to feel the heartbeat coming up through my feet and synchronising with my own. I'd run out into the rain and dance in it for the pure joy of the release of tension that rainfall brings to the earth and sky. But I learnt very quickly that other people didn't feel this way and that when I did these things they would look at me in a way that made me feel wrong and uncomfortable. I learnt to stop doing these things; to behave. It killed a small part of me or, at the very least, locked it up in a place where I wouldn't easily find it."

They stand at the door to the cathedral and the power of all the beliefs of all the souls that have passed through this door washes over her. She stops and looks him in the eye.

"But nothing stops me from feeling everyone else's feelings. The desires, the fears, the excitement and the hatred of other people is a constant assault on my nervous system."

She sees him wince with the force of what she's saying. She walks ahead of him into the ancient building and tries to see the beauty instead of feeling the rush of sibilant, desperate prayers for assistance, forgiveness and mercy. When she feels the tension of his presence behind her, she turns and offers a small smile of apology.

"I spent much of my younger life running from one experience to the next. I was desperate to live, love and experience and because I don't seem to have the filters and alarm systems that most people seem to have, I put myself in untold danger. Again and again." She looks him in the eye again. She needs him to hear this so badly. "I've allowed people to do terrible things to me. Emotionally. Physically. Sometimes I tried to stop them, but not always. I never succeeded in stopping them when I tried so I stopped trying after a while. There was always the fact that I'd blundered myself into the situation, so I deserved what I got. And when I get hurt, I don't just bleed, I don't just cry, I disintegrate."

She looks away. Her voice has become hard and angry. She deliberately softens it. "You've seen it." She shoots him a small glance and sees that he's close to crying, but she can't let up. She needs him to understand. "After I disintegrate, I have to find a way to pull all my atoms back together and reform into a person of some kind. It's a kind of reinvention. A new me for a new attempt at life. There's a new version for each disintegration." She prepares herself. She has to tell him everything. "But the person I become is never the right person. I'm never the person that another person could love for what they are and want to be with them, just as they are. I'm always a person that others want to change. So, I learned to be alone. I learned to give up on being with someone."

She sits in a pew and looks up at the astounding vaulted ceiling and feels the terror and delight that people have felt for hundreds of years.

"I spent years learning to be alone. It was a slow process and along the way I met people that I thought would be different. I fell in love with them and thought that they'd see me, love me, care for me. I made so many mistakes and then had to reinvent myself again. Finally, I learnt to behave respectably and get up and go to work every day and do a good job. I managed my distress at the constant flow of people's emotions and only allowed tears to fall the same amount that other people do in public but otherwise kept them for home, when I couldn't be seen. I created a smiling, efficient and caring persona that I could use in my professional life so that nobody would have to deal with the real me; reckless and spontaneous like a wildfire. I do genuinely care about other people and I want to help them, but I don't have boundaries like other people and I do too much, say too much and exhaust myself in the process. I lose myself."

Snapshots of her more rash and heedless moments flash through her mind with the usual mixture of nostalgia, awe and disgust. Each emotion vying with the other for precedence like the Magnificent Seven fighting to be in charge at those same defining moments.

"I listen to people at work talking about their home improvements and how they enjoy watching TV dramas and reality shows and having a couple of weeks on a beach somewhere hot once a year and I just don't understand. When I watch a TV drama, I want to be in it and my heart weeps that my life is so fucking mundane. Every weekend when I have two days away from work I long to be in Shanghai or DF or any other fucking place that is not the place that I have been in all week long. My desire for stimulation is insatiable. My capacity to be bored is vast. I'm a monstrous, reckless, stroppy, ill-mannered teenager. Inside. Inside, that's what I am. The real me. The me that I have to hide. It's exhausting."

She sees that he cannot process everything that she's telling him. She thinks that she should stop, but she doesn't think that she can. He has to hear it all, even if he doesn't understand it or believe it. She owes it to herself to at least give him the full story. She feels his confusion, tinged with irritation but also his fear. He thought that she was something else. Something worth his time and effort. She swallows and ploughs on.

"Sometimes it's just too hard to hide how bored and lost I am, and then I have to hide myself away. It's exhausting keeping things hidden. It's so boring, too. The last few years, since my mum died, I've been ambivalent about life. I've thought about whether I have the courage to end my life and all the mess, but there's this tenacious, bullying, tortuous hope that, just around the corner, is something that will change my life into what I need. I cannot kill the sensation that there'll be an opportunity to do something that lets me be myself."

She turns on the pew so that she is facing him and she places her palms on his chest. She looks into his eyes and he holds her gaze.

"You've given me the best opportunity of my life. Writing this script and the chance to act in this show is the best thing that's ever happened to me. This isn't mundane. I'm loving the creativity and the freedom. I feel happy for the first time since we met in London. Before then, happiness had been a stranger for years. But, I'm not fixed, Oscar. I'm still the same messy, fucked-up teenager inside. The person that you met in London is only a part of me, you need to know that she could just slip away at any time and you'd be left with the mad one. The one you met in Hereford. Nobody wants the mad one, Oscar. Believe me, I know and you know too. You've seen her."

He does the most unexpected thing. He puts his arms around her and crushes her to his chest. She hears his voice in her ear through the curtain of her hair.

"I was frightened by the Estella that I met in Hereford, Rafa, but I didn't hate her. She confused me and I was hurt that she didn't trust me, but I didn't stop loving her. I didn't understand, but it makes sense now. Going back to Hereford after all the excitement in London and finding that you were suspended from work; it must have a been like someone throwing a bucket of water over you. Such a shock. Why didn't you call me? Why did you hurt yourself?"

He holds her shoulders and pushes her away from him so that he can see her eyes. "Why didn't you call me?" She sees the hurt in his eyes. She feels his disappointment.

"It never occurred to me to call you, Oscar. I make a rule of not depending on other people."

"Why?"

"Experience. In my experience, other people can't be depended on."

"You can depend on me!"

"I know that now," she says and tries very hard to believe it. She'll need to teach herself to trust again. It's been a long time.

"I'll prove to you that you can depend on me, Rafa."

She smiles at him. She really smiles at him and she sees his face light up with the pleasure of it. They hold hands and look up at the light and airy vaulted ceiling and let this moment of trust sink in. She vows to learn to trust him, to be the mother that he lost, or perhaps never had. To call him for help. To let him help her. She thinks that she can manage that, if she puts her mind to it.

He takes her for lunch at El Almacén, which is a delight to the senses. They have tempura prawns and mushroom and ham croquettes with a Martin Codax Albariño. She eats carefully after last night's belly ache and his appetite seems capable of wolfing up the remaining food. For their main course they have the most delicious rib-eye steak and fries and a beautiful Portuguese Vina da Costa red.

"Now, this really is a good steak," he says referring to their questionable London experience.

"You're right. I think it's the best steak I've ever had."

When they've finished the steak, neither of them has eaten many of the fries that came with it, he tops up their glasses with the delicious red.

"Rafa, why did you hurt yourself? Have you done that before?" He gently indicates the inside of his left forearm. He meets her eye.

"I used to do it a lot, when I was in my teens and early twenties." She lets the memories come. The boy who loved Stel and who she couldn't love because she was already in love. His disappointment, pain and sadness. Her friend, who loved the boy, so angry with her for rejecting him. So hurt that he hadn't chosen to love her instead. All these emotions running through her along with her own love that was not always returned, but which she could not get rid of however hard she tried. Her friend yelling, "*You don't even know what love is. You're just hiding in a fake relationship. Your 'boyfriend' doesn't give a shit about you.*"

She had escaped from the room where everyone was displeased with her. She didn't dispute that the friend might be right that her *boyfriend* didn't give a shit about her, but that didn't mean that *she* didn't love ***him***. She'd loved him from the first moment that she saw him, years before, and from that moment in her life he'd been her first thought every morning and last thought every night and many of the millions of thoughts in the in-between. She couldn't shift the need for him. Stel had shut herself in the bathroom, seething with all of the emotions that were caught inside her; hers, theirs and others that she couldn't identify. She wanted them to know that she was hurting, but she also wanted the hurt to go away. It had not been a conscious thought. She just picked up the razor and dragged it across the back of her hand. The instant pain blanked all thoughts from her head. All she could do was concentrate on the pain and the blood which was pouring out of the back of her hand. It had given her relief in so many ways. She'd needed to clean it and cover it and care for it, and it had been just what she needed to take her mind off all the emotions assaulting her nervous system.

"I'm sorry," she hears him say, "I shouldn't have asked."

"No, it's fine. I'm glad you asked. I was just thinking about it. It provides a huge relief to me when my nervous system is overwhelmed with my emotions, other people's emotions and when...and when my critical inner voice becomes too loud to cope with." She takes a sip of the wine. "When you cut yourself, there's pain to distract you from your thoughts and feelings and then there's the process of cleaning the wound and making sure that it isn't so deep that it needs stitches. As the pain dulls, then there comes the disappointment in yourself that you've done it and then the fear that someone will discover what you've done. But, in the moment that you do it, it feels like there's no alternative. It's the only way to stop all the crap that is going on inside your head. A moment of stillness in the eye of a storm."

He nods.

"Have you ever?"

"No," he says without managing to remove all of the disgust from his voice, but at least he tried. "I knew some kids in my teens that did it, but I never felt the need. When I feel anxious or overwhelmed, I use my punchbag or go for a run." He looks at her and drops his gaze. "I don't think I feel things like you do. I certainly don't feel other people's emotions. I find other people quite difficult to read. Sometimes I feel like my emotions aren't really a part of me...I don't know how to explain it...as if I can stand on the outside and look at them as if they're external entities that someone else can deal with. They don't seem to be important."

"So, you don't feel emotions unless you choose to?"

"Sort of, I think."

"You told me how angry you are with your mum and your sister, for how they treat you."

"Yeah, but mostly I don't even think about them or how I feel about them. It might come up when I go to the apartment, but lately it just feels like going through the motions. I remember that when I spoke to you about it in London, it felt more real than it had for a long time. I suppose anger is probably the only emotion that I regularly feel." He thinks for a moment. "Yeah, I get angry quite a lot, but that's what the punchbag is for."

"Do you think that you're suppressing the emotion because you have no outlet for it?"

"Maybe. I really have no idea, but I definitely don't pick up on other people's emotions like you do."

"When I saw you in London, I felt that something terrible had happened to you. I was really worried. The older I get, the more it happens. I try to stop myself from interfering, but the compulsion is usually overwhelming. It feels like it's my mission to help when people have reached that ghastly moment from which they can't move on. As if I might give them a word or an idea that'll help them move forward."

"You did that for me."

"Then I spoiled it all by being a nutter." She laughs sadly.

"But that was my fault, Rafa. I started that problem. I should never have posted that video. I should never have asked you to come to the Netflix event with me. I was selfish. I never thought for one moment about how it would impact on you. You made me feel so calm and capable. You were the only thing keeping me grounded."

"Oscar, I'm an adult with free will. I didn't do anything that I didn't want to do."

"But it might lose you your job."

"Yes, but I made all those decisions. I chose to go to the event with you."

"You didn't choose for me to put that video of you on TikTok and Instagram. That's what might lose you your job. My decision. That's what pushed you into hurting yourself this time." She shakes her head.

"No, Oscar, it wasn't like that."

"It was, Rafa."

"There were so many things, Oscar, and you have to remember that I have a history of this kind of breakdown."

"Rafa, the video changed everything and that was my responsibility."

"Oscar, you aren't responsible for what happened. You're not responsible for me. You didn't make me breakdown. I was ashamed of my behaviour. You'd been so kind to invite me to do all of those exciting things, but I should have refused. You're a young man; you don't need a surrogate mother following you around. When I got back to Hereford, Win and I went out for a meal and one of my students came up to me in the restaurant. He asked me if I'd just got back from London. Said he'd seen me on social media with you and... and the others. I suddenly saw myself through his eyes. I must have looked ridiculous to him. A woman old enough to be his grandmother, dancing in a club in London with a group of beautiful young men who were too polite not to include her in their night out."

"Rafa, that's not how it was. Your student wouldn't have thought that. ***We*** didn't think that. You're a person and we liked you. We liked being with you. We wanted you to be there. We should've taken better care of you and not posted you all over fucking social media without asking your permission. We...***I***... messed up your life."

She sees that he believes what he's saying.

"Oscar, I'm not your responsibility. Putting me on social media didn't break me. I've had a fault line in my mind since I was a teenager, and these incidents happen from time to time. This incident happened to coincide with our meeting."

He stands and walks away. She sees him paying the bill. Her heartbeat is thrumming in her ears. She realises that he won't be pacified. She sees his honour and his sense of responsibility and remembers how attractive his kindness to her and others is.

She thanks the maître d' and steps out into the cold. He's standing looking down the street. She stands behind him and places her right palm in the centre of his back.

"Okay, Oscar, you win. Putting that video on social media has destroyed the life I had before. In truth, I don't think I'll ever be a teacher again. I did feel as if there was no way forward. I was terrified that I'd lose my house, again. I lost my house some years ago at another difficult juncture in my life. Another breakdown. But you'd already started to give me the possibility of another life. A life better suited to my... my personality. If I hadn't gone to the Netflix event with you, I wouldn't have spoken to Nuria and I wouldn't now be about to enter a creative new job that is paying me the equivalent of years of my previous salary for literally a few months of work." She leans her head against his back and wraps her arms around his waist. "When I saw that e-mail from the college, I thought that my life was over. I wanted my life to be over. I tried to make it be over. But really, it was just a new life waiting to happen and it happened because you made it happen." He turns and they hold each other. His chin rests on the top of her head. She can hear his heart beating a little too fast. "You see, if you hadn't posted the video, none of this would have happened. I would still be dying a slow death of boredom, in Hereford." She feels his chest heave.

"Rafa, if that is what you choose to believe then I'll try to believe it too. Okay?"

She nods against his chest. She feels him kiss the top of her head. She pulls away.

"Shall we ask Rocio to take us back to the city?" He nods and takes her hand, and they walk back to the car. She can feel his relief that they've talked about it, but she thinks that he hasn't forgiven himself. There's something still troubling him, but she's exhausted. She longs for a swim. As they are driven back to Madrid, she dozes and she feels him take her hand in his. She's grateful for the warmth.

On the Town

On Thursday they spend the day visiting museums and walking around the city centre. Estella almost stops noticing the journalists and photographers, and by the evening, they seem to have become bored with the respectful distance between the two of them. That evening, Estella wants to go dancing and she hears that a band she enjoys are playing at a club just around the corner from her hotel.

"What kind of music is it?" He asks her. "Such a strange name, *El Diábolo de Shanghái*!"

"It's sort of punk, I suppose," she says. "One of the musicians is from Menorca. I knew him when he was a kid."

"Punk?"

"Yeah." She laughs. "It's the kind of music that you can jump around to; it's great fun."

They've had some dinner, and Estella has decided to have a night of gin and tonics. She likes the generous measures that they pour in Spain, and she feels super hydrated even though she gets smashed. Oscar is also drinking gin and tonics, and she's really hoping that he's going to enjoy the band. This will be her first dance since the infamous boogie to Santi's set at the club in

London, and her brief bop with the *Boy Friends* cast at the Netflix event.

He's smiling, but she feels his discomfort. When the band plays, she can hardly sit still in her seat and when people start to dance, she asks him if he wants to dance. He shakes his head diffidently.

"You don't mind if I dance, do you?" She asks. He says of course not, but she senses some discomfort. She goes to the dance floor in front of the stage and joins the mash of people gyrating and jumping around. She lets the music take her and she feels the joy of abandoning herself to rhythm and expression. At the end of the set, she returns to Oscar, smiling, sweaty and satisfied. The smile that he returns doesn't quite reach his eyes.

"How do you do that?" He asks, incredulously. "You really don't care what people think, do you?"

"What people?"

"Any people."

"Oscar," she laughs, "I'm not you. Nobody's watching me. Even if they were, they don't know who I am." She stops as it hits her. "Or, at least, they didn't until recently." She sees the shadow cross his face and she feels compelled to save the day. "Anyway, I don't care. I enjoy dancing almost as much as I enjoy swimming."

"After season three, everyone will know who you are, Rafa." That leaves her feeling gutted, but she manages to smile at him. She hopes she has faked it well; it's better than his, at least, she wagers. They finish their drinks, and he escorts her back to the hotel. Tomorrow afternoon, she's going to sign the necessary contracts at the production company's offices, and Oscar has planned a special evening out for them; she's pretty sure that it won't include a punk band and dancing.

Friday morning, she has claimed alone-time to do some shopping; she's visiting El Corte Inglés department store, which she has long considered to be her spiritual home. She elects to walk for almost an hour to get to their huge store in Castellana. She enjoys the walk and rewards herself with a drink in the cafe on arrival. Then she shops. She buys a pair of earrings and a bracelet from Vidal & Vidal, and a couple of scarves from Lola Casademunt. She looks at dresses but can't even find anything that she wants to try on. This leaves her feeling rather flat. The morning disappears in a flash. She grabs a cab to meet Elvira for a briefing before signing the contracts with the production company.

Elvira's office is in her house but has a separate entrance from the street. It's close to the centre, so Elvira must be doing well for herself. She runs efficiently through the contract with Estella and is pleased when she makes notes of the salient points. Estella gives Elvira her bank details and learns that Elvira's fee is a modest five percent.

Estella asks if their conversation is confidential, to which Elvira responds that it will always be confidential and that nothing Estella says to her will ever be discussed with anybody, including Oscar. Estella is reassured by the fact that she chooses to name him, showing that she's understood what she's asking.

"Elvira, I need some help with other matters. I'm writing a novel. Can you recommend a lawyer in England to support me with that? I think that as long as my writing isn't truly dreadful, this exposure that I am getting will almost certainly convince a publisher to buy a book written by me."

"Undoubtedly, and you need to be quick. Can you get it finished in a couple of months?"

"I think so, I have about forty thousand words so far, so almost halfway." Her sleep is back to erratic patterns and she's been grabbing a few hours here and there to write.

"How long have the forty thousand words taken?"

"About a week." Elvira looks impressed. "You haven't read those words, Elvira, they might be rubbish!" Elvira laughs.

"True, but somehow, I doubt it. I read your script, remember?" Estella nods.

"Elvira, I'm shit with money. I need somebody to manage my money and make sure I pay my taxes. Make sure I don't spend everything in five minutes."

"I can put you in touch with a guy in London. He's reasonable and you can set limits for him to enforce."

"I suppose that it'd be pointless trying to reimburse Oscar for all the stuff he's paid for, like the hospital in Hereford?"

"Absolute waste of time, and, if you don't mind me saying, he should have paid for it. Posting that video of you was a rare error on his part. He's generally a careful person, but that was a stupid thing to have done. He lost you your job." Estella is shocked. She feels compelled to defend him.

"I haven't lost my job yet," she counters. "They have to investigate, and I'm being paid while they do that." Elvira smiles.

"The guy I'm putting you in touch with, in London, he can also find someone good to defend you. I don't think that your employer can justify suspending you. You went to a nightclub and danced. The people you were dancing with are all adults over the age of twenty-one. I think that you could sue your employer for defamation of character by inference." Estella is stunned.

"Really?"

"Yes, really." She pauses. "Estella, you could sue Oscar for posting that video without your consent." Estella sighs and shakes her head.

"No, Elvira, I couldn't."

"I assumed that you would say that." She almost looks disappointed, Estella thinks. What's that all about? Elvira sends a few emails on Estella's behalf to her London contacts, and they chat about the contracts they're signing that afternoon.

Elvira's housekeeper has cooked them a paella for lunch. It's delicious. Elvira's house is full of colour and she has an interesting collection of contemporary abstract art. She mentions no partner or spouse and doesn't speak about children. She talks passionately about the paintings in her collection and she tells Estella about her childhood in A Coruña in Galicia. Estella feels privileged and proud to know her. She feels safe and seen.

After a delectable homemade creme caramel, Elvira has a coffee and checks her watch.

"Oscar's driver will be here in about fifteen minutes." Estella looks at her sharply.

"Oscar's coming?"

"No, but he insisted on sending his car." Estella doesn't say anything. She had assumed that they would take a taxi. It seems a little over-protective to send his car. Then it occurs to her to ask, "Does he think I might not sign the contracts?" Elvira thinks for a moment; she seems to be really considering the question.

"I'm not sure, Estella. I think he knows that you want this contract. He can see that it will make a good difference to your life. It will give you more freedom, the chance to work less and play more. So, I don't think it's about that. I think it might be guilt and a kind of overprotectiveness. Or, maybe, it's just Oscar's desire to control everything down to the last details."

"Hmmm," says Estella. "He does like to be in charge, doesn't he?"

"Yes, he does. I'm going to quickly check my emails. It won't take a minute. If you'll excuse me?"

Estella leans back in the armchair and lets her eyes close. She feels sleep very close by and she's thinking about getting into a swimming pool and the magical moment that her body suddenly becomes weightless in the water. She imagines herself floating on the surface of a pool, sunshine on her face, cool water caressing her limbs. She floats and smiles. Floats and smiles.

Elvira's phone pings. Estella's eyes snap open.

"Apologies," says Elvira, "Rocio is here."

On the drive to the offices, Estella's phone pings and she finds a text from Oscar wishing her luck and a couple of e-mails from Elvira's contacts. She feels in such safe hands with this woman. Elvira's emotions don't seem to project onto her like other people's do. Elvira, like Igor, seems to be very careful about what she shares and with whom. She'd like to learn how to do that and wonders if the same technique would stop her from absorbing the emotions of others.

The contract signing takes fifteen minutes and then Nuria talks through a schedule of writers' meetings, starting in one month, when she expects to have the drafts of the first two episodes as outlined by Estella's plan. Estella is to return to Madrid once a month for meetings with the writing team so that they can collaborate in person for a few days. She talks about building a rapport with the writing team and ensuring continuity with the existing style of the show. Estella is wary of how the established team will feel about working with her, but it's something that she has no control over, so she shelves it for now. She's to be in Madrid from the start of filming in August until final wrap at the close of September. She has to ask the question that has been worrying her.

"When will Oscar find out about the storyline with Nito?" Nuria cocks her head and looks as sly as a fox.

"You haven't told him?"

"No, I suspect that he might not like it."

"Possibly, but it's dynamite. It's such an unconventional ending. It will make *Los Amores de Oscar* standout."

"So, we keep it from him?"

"Yes, until the last possible moment."

Estella catches Elvira smiling at this exchange. There's a story there. She can't work out what it is, but there's something that she knows about Oscar or that maybe happened with Oscar. She knows that Elvira will never tell her because Oscar is her client, but something about the discomfort that they all feel Oscar will have with this storyline gives Elvira pleasure.

Elvira drops her back at the Thompson. She says that her money will be with her in about a fortnight and that she'd like to meet with her when she returns to Madrid next month. Estella tells her that she has already heard from the lawyers in London and thanks her again for her help.

She writes for a couple of hours before showering and changing into an evening dress that she hasn't had the opportunity to wear for years. It's a heavy black satin with a raised textured pattern of bisected circles. It has cold shoulders, partial sleeves and the skirt is shaped and cut on the bias to give an asymmetric effect. She's always felt that it's very sophisticated.

Oscar is in a good mood. He takes her to a restaurant that he tells her Elvira introduced him to. When she sees the name, she understands why: Los Montes de Galicia. They feast on crispy cod fritters with roasted garlic aioli and accompanied by Avancia Godello. Then, they wait with bated breath for slow-cooked veal shank in its own juice. It melts in their mouths as they take sips of a Crianza from Carmelo Rodero. Finally, they can manage nothing more than a lemon sorbet made with Cava. Estella thinks that she will burst. So, when Oscar suggests walking back to her hotel, she agrees readily.

As they walk, Oscar starts speaking very calmly, taking her hand and looking at her to punctuate his words.

"Rafa, I want us to be a couple. I want to have a physical relationship with you. I'm in love with you." She feels his need and his wanting like a smothering blanket on a hot day. She's stifled by panic and fear. She feels the food inside her and her stomach writhing to eject it. She realises instantly that this will be the end of their comfortable friendship. Now that this has been said, there will be no chance of returning to how it was just moments ago. So much for learning to trust him. So much for being the mother he so desperately needs.

"So, from your silence, I can tell that you don't feel the same way. Not now, at least, but maybe with time you could come to love me?"

"I do love you, Oscar, but I'm not ***in*** love with you." She tries to take her hand back, but he won't let it go. "I'm not sure if I have the capacity to fall in love. I explained that other people's emotions take over mine. To be in love, I'd have to keep my feelings to know. I don't know how to do that."

They walk a little further and Estella concentrates on not being sick. He is still holding her hand. She can feel it sweating. She can feel sweat trickling down her back.

"Yesterday, you were talking about the life that you need to stop yourself from feeling bored and keep you stimulated. I can give you that life. We can travel. You can write. We can act. I can sing." His need is so strong, but it sounds like a business deal. She feels his desperation.

"Are you saying that I should have a relationship with you to get the life I want?"

"No!...Well, perhaps." He huffs a little in frustration. She feels the first lick of anger coming from him. "I mean that a relationship might help you to have the stability to live the life that you want."

"Oscar, I don't know how relationships work. I've never had a real one. I don't know if I'm able to keep enough of me to have one. I would just become you. I would absorb all of your emotions. I'm already suppressing most of who I really am, being with someone else I would just lose me completely. I thought that I'd explained that."

"Yes, but now that your life is more aligned to your needs, perhaps a relationship will be easier. We get on so well."

"Oscar, I love spending time with you. I'm enormously grateful to you for the world that you've opened up to me, but I'm a mess. After everything that I told you, after what you saw in Hereford, I can't understand how you could even think that having a relationship with me would be possible. You told me that when you went to the States, you met people that you felt comfortable with and that you fell in love. It sounded fun. My attempts at relationships aren't like that. I fall in love and lose myself in the process. I agree to anything that will let me be with that person. I told you; I've let people do terrible things to me. I'm soiled goods."

She sees him wince. She sees the prude in him revolted. He has to see this. He has to wake up from whatever fantasy he has of her. She feels his frustration and anger that things aren't going as planned. He looks her in the eye and pulls her hand even closer to him.

"All the more reason for you to finally have someone love you for the right reasons and care for you from a place of love."

"Are you trying to fix me, Oscar?"

"No, you don't need fixing. You're exactly as you should be." He's saying all the things that he thinks that she wants to hear. He's so earnest. He hasn't heard her. He didn't listen. He hasn't understood. She decides to take another route.

"Have you ever had sex with somebody of my age?" This takes him off guard and she sees the prude in him flush.

"No."

"I'm not toned and elastic, Oscar. My body is slack, sloppy and saggy. Have you considered what a physical relationship will be like?"

Suddenly he has grabbed her by the shoulders, and she feels his mouth meet hers as he slides one hand to the small of her back pulling her against him. The other hand is in her hair cupping the back of her skull. The kiss is passionate, and she finds that she is kissing him back with the same hunger and intensity. She feels his desire and need and it has become her own. She feels heat radiating from her groin. He manoeuvres her into a nearby shop doorway and when she is up against the wall, she feels his hand slip inside her coat and find her breast while the other drops from her waist to her bottom. The kissing continues. He pushes his crotch up into her abdomen and she feels his hardness. He stops kissing her and groans.

"See how much I want you?"

"Okay, Oscar, then have me." She says hungrily. "Let's go back to the hotel and you can scratch this itch."

"What does that mean?"

"I mean let's have sex so that you can stop fantasising about what it'll be like. Once you've done it, you can get past the idea that we are going to be some perfect couple and you can get on with finding the right person for you." He pushes away from her.

"This isn't about sex, Rafa. I want a life with you."

"Why?"

"Because I feel good when I'm with you. Because you're a good person and you make me want to be the best that I can be."

"So, why do we need to be a couple? Why can't we just stay friends?"

"Because..." He kisses her again and his desire surges through her.

She feels her own fear and despair somewhere smothered behind the heat of his feelings as she realises that it's all over now. She doesn't want to lose his friendship. There's the writing and the filming. How can she keep those and him for a bit longer? She feels the tears. She tries to hold them back, but it's all too much. Everything is being snatched away from her. He stops kissing her, looking straight into her face.

"Why're you crying? What did I do? Did I hurt you?"

She shakes her head. The tears are rolling down her cheeks now. Her legs are weak with the burden of his desire.

"This will be the end of us," she sobs. "It always is. As soon as we have sex, that'll be the end of our friendship. I'll lose you."

"But we'll be more than friends, Rafa. We'll have a new, closer relationship." She laughs then. A hard, bitter little laugh.

"Not in my experience, Oscar. Is that how your relationships have worked?" His face shows the first signs of uncertainty since this conversation started. "How long is your longest relationship?" He's still looking at her, but he's the one who looks close to tears now.

"I haven't had a relationship as such," he says. "I've hooked up with people a few times over a couple of weeks, maybe a month. I've never wanted to be with someone before. I've never wanted a relationship."

"Then, neither of us knows what we're doing," she states flatly. She is on her haunches now in the corner of the doorway. She's so tired that she could sleep right here, right now. "You've never wanted a relationship, and I've always found that as soon as I have sex with someone, I lose myself and they either use me or leave me. The blind leading the blind." She pulls herself up by grabbing his coat and suddenly starts walking; she feels like she should run, but she doesn't want to fall over. She needs to get away from his pushy desire. She hears him moving to catch up with her.

"But Rafa, the kiss. The kiss was good, wasn't it?" She sighs and glances at him as they continue to walk.

"I don't know. All I felt was your desire. I don't know what I felt. But that kiss didn't involve taking our clothes off or waking up in the morning being uncertain how to behave with each other. That's what a relationship is about. I have this script to write and then I'm going to be acting the role of your mother and all of that is going to be exciting, but also challenging. It'll be even more challenging if we're trying to work out what we are to each other, or if we wake up and realise it was a terrible mistake."

"But that won't..."

"Don't," she cuts him off, stopping abruptly. "You're not psychic; you have no idea what will happen. We don't really know each other. You haven't understood what I told you on Wednesday." They stand there looking at each other and anxiety eats away at her, she's not sure if it's hers or his. She starts to mentally prepare herself for this dream to be over. He gently takes her hand and starts walking again and she reluctantly lets herself be guided.

"I'm sorry, Rafa, I'm rushing you. You've only known me for a few weeks and here I am trying to convince you to spend the rest of your life with me." He raises her hand to his lips and kisses it. She wants to snatch it away. His reasonable tone is at odds with the curdle of anger and desire that's coming her way from him. "I feel very strongly about you. You're very special." He stops and turns to her. "Let me woo you. Give me the next six months to show you that you can trust me and that I'm serious about being with you. Let's finish the filming and then go away together." It's a reprieve. It doesn't dispel any of her concerns, but it gives her time to convince him of the truth of her and for him to lose interest. Hell, he might fall in love with someone else in six months.

"Okay," she agrees. "When filming's over, we can talk again."

"But I get to take you out to dinner, and we spend time together, right?"

"Yeah, of course."

A temporary relief begins to unknot her stomach and she feels how tight her neck is. They walk the rest of the way back to the hotel talking about when they will next meet. He has to be in London in a couple of weeks. He insists that he will take her to the airport the following day. He suggests that they have breakfast, but she says that she'd like to sleep in.

In the lobby, he kisses her forehead and watches until the lift doors close on her. When she finally gets into her room she closes and locks the door and collapses on the floor. She digs her thumb into the wound on her arm to stop her mind which is working on overdrive. She still feels his desire. She still feels his need. She still feels his anger. She wants rid of it. She feels as if she'll be suffocated by the strength of it.

Víctor

There is no chance of sleep now, despite the exhaustion. She cleans the wound and her thumb. She gets out her laptop and writes. It calms her, but as daylight breaks, she feels exhaustion and anxiety at the idea of seeing him again. Around 7 am she goes out to walk. She doesn't think about direction or destination; she needs action. She wishes that she could swim, but the hotel pool is open air and closed for the season. On her headphones she allows herself the reassurance of his voice. The same three songs over and over again as she strides. Sometimes she comes to the end of *I'm Just Divine* and she has to jump straight back to start it again. Every time the smile comes at the introduction and the recollection of his voice. She has a meme locked in her head of his expression, half amused and half terrified, and his hands as he made the gesture of explosion after Oscar's outburst at The Ned.

She's been walking like this for some time, the city is waking up around her and she's no idea where she is when she feels a hand on her shoulder and she feels the heat of an adrenaline rush. Fight, flight or freeze? She's so far into her fantasy world that it takes her a beat or two to realise that it's Víctor. She pulls off her headphones.

"Hey, Estella! How come you're in this part of town?" He asks, smiling and looking pleased to see her. He seems to be out jogging; AirPods in, slightly breathless and a little sweaty.

"Víctor!" She cries in genuine pleasure. They hug a moment and he kisses her on both cheeks.

"Are you visiting Oscar?"

"Does he live around here?" she asks in panic. He frowns.

"Not far from here," he says. "Aren't you staying with him?"

"No, I'm at the Thompson."

"That's the hotel the production company has on contract. Are you here on business?"

"I made a pitch to Nuria and the producers for the season three scenario. They've bought my idea."

"I didn't know that you were a writer."

"Well, neither did I. I've always wanted to be but never had an opportunity. I told Nuria at that party in London that I had ideas and teased a couple and then she invited me to come and talk about it. They liked what I suggested and I wrote some script that they enjoyed..."

"So, we'll be working together?" He asks with pleasure.

"Yes, we will."

It's almost 10 am and Víctor suggests getting some breakfast. She's in his neighbourhood and he takes her to a place he knows with great pastries and she has a delicious thick hot chocolate. When they're seated, comfortable and friendly, he falls quiet for a moment.

"Are you okay, Estella?" She doesn't hesitate.

"Not really, Víctor, but to be honest, that's nothing new. I haven't been okay for years. My mental health is very fragile."

"And then you met Oscar..." He says with a sarcastic lilt. She laughs.

"I can't blame him, Víctor." His brow furrows.

"Of course you can. You should. He posted a video of you without your permission."

They sit quietly for a minute.

"I could, but what would that achieve? Besides, if all of that hadn't happened, I wouldn't be having this opportunity now. I'm writing. I'm going to be acting too."

"You're going to be in season three?"

"Oscar's mum." He laughs.

"That's genius. They're really cashing in, aren't they?"

"Yeah." She hesitates. "But so am I."

"You need to, you lost your job."

"Well, not yet. I'm suspended. I'm going to take legal action against the company for suspending me. Oscar's lawyer's helping me." Victor fiddles with his coffee cup.

"I've seen the pictures of you two together this week. Are you a couple now?"

"No, Víctor."

"But he wants to be..." She sighs. She doesn't want to lie to him, she likes him.

"Yes, he does." He waits. He waits a bit longer.

"But you don't feel that way." It's a statement. She sighs with all the weight of the pressure she feels.

"I don't feel that way. I know he's handsome and kind," she glances up at Víctor, "at least to me, but I just don't feel that way about him. He thinks that I just need time."

"He won't take no for an answer?" She nods.

"I've bought some time by saying that we have to wait until the filming is done."

"He won't change his mind." She sees the pain in his eyes. "Él es terco."

Stubborn, she thinks, he's more than stubborn. He's pushy.

They exchange phone numbers. They hug. She feels that she has an ally. Just as they are about to part, he asks, "Are you worried about the age difference?" She flushes almost immediately.

"I think any relationship with that age gap is likely to be short-lived, but that's not the problem here. It's not the years that are holding me back, it's how I feel about him."

"Good, because that shouldn't be the reason."

He kisses her cheek and jogs away.

It's almost 11 am and Oscar will collect her at midday. She jumps in a taxi and races back to pack, shower and change. She feels a little lighter from the relief of talking about her situation.

Oscar arrives on the dot in what she thinks must be Tom Ford, a blue suede western jacket with linen trousers and green relaxed shoes. It's the weekend after all. He doesn't take her breath away, or rather, not in the usual way. She's still feeling uncomfortable from last night. Her discomfort, however, is displaced by the anger that reaches her across the lobby from him. Her stomach turns with tension.

"Good afternoon," he says tersely. "The car's waiting outside." He wheels the case through the lobby towards the door. It's not until he gets to the pavement that he realises that she is still sitting in the lobby, frozen in fear and apprehension at the force of his anger rushing through her veins. She considers her options. She has her hand luggage. She could run and give up her dresses. She's back in Mexico, where she was constantly looking for escape routes and waiting for the opportunity to run.

"Rafa?" He asks gently. He's back by her side. "Are you okay?" She stands and grabs her case and makes for the street. She's on the pavement and looking for a cab when he catches up with her.

"I'm sorry. Rafa, please look at me." She turns on him then.

"What have I done now? Why are you angry with me now? Why have you filled me with your anger?" He's taken aback. He hasn't seen this trapped, defensive animal before.

"Víctor," he says. "Someone took a picture of you and Víctor having breakfast. I didn't know that you were in contact with him. It was a shock."

"I wasn't in contact with him," she yells. She's so full of his anger that she feels like she might froth at the mouth. "I couldn't sleep last night because I felt so fucking stressed about what happened. I went out when it got light to try to walk off some fucking tension. He was jogging and saw me. I needed a friend. I needed a fucking friend!" Then the tears come. Between sobs, she says, "I'll take a taxi to the airport. I don't need this shit."

He tries to hug her, but she pushes him away.

"Get off me!" She shouts. "Leave me alone. I don't want your feelings."

She's beginning to sweat. She's so tired. "I don't need this shit," she says weakly. It occurs to her with horror that her heart is beating far too fast and that her head is pounding. She gasps for breath. She sees his mouth move, but all she can hear is a rushing in her ears.

...

She opens her eyes, the brightness jabs at her and she has to close them. Her stomach turns and she realises that she's going to be sick. She tries to turn but feels restricted. She puts her hands up to her mouth and tries to quell the nausea. People speak. She hears the sound of paper rustling and then feels a bag being put into her hand. She's sick into the bag, and it is taken away. She's crying. She's in the car; she can feel it moving.

"Rafa, I'm taking you to my apartment." Her eyes open at once, despite the pain.

"Airport. Take me to the airport."

"Rafa, you can't travel like this."

"Don't tell me what I can and can't do." She says with venom. His venom.

She finds her bag and finds tissues and WaterWipes. She cleans herself.

"We need to talk."

"Not now. I want to go home."

"Rafa, you need..."

"Don't tell me what I need, Oscar. I want to go home and get away from your anger and your manipulation. You don't listen to me. You believe you know better than me. You're a bully."

He tells Rocio to take them to the airport. He calls British Airways. The tone of his voice is calm and slightly distant.

"The flight's delayed; you'll be able to join it, or they can bump you to the next flight."

"Igor will be waiting."

"The next flight is only two hours later. Igor will be fine." She wants to yell at him that it isn't fair to keep him waiting, but she hasn't the energy. They sit in silence. She hates him a little now for his moods and his desire to be in charge. She hates him for not listening and understanding. She feels bullied and belittled. When they arrive at the airport, she gets out and thanks Rocio, taking her case from her.

He moves to walk with her, but she turns and looks him in the eye, "Leave me alone. Two weeks on Monday in London. I'll speak to you then." He's pale and tense; his anger is debilitating. Finally, he nods his agreement.

As she walks into the airport to check in, the further she gets from him the better she feels; her muscles begin to relax and the pain in her head subsides. She's exhausted, but she feels that she has won a small victory. She makes the delayed flight and has a couple of glasses of champagne that help her to relax a little more.

A Fortnight

"I told you," says Igor, "he take all of your energy. You got to protect yourself."

This he says as soon as they are seated in the car. As she exited arrivals and he caught sight of her, he frowned and looked cross. She nods at him in the rearview mirror. She's close to tears with gratitude for his reassuring presence and care.

"You sleep now."

She does sleep. She sleeps like she's dead. She knows nothing until he wakes her. He gets her into the house, switches on the heating and makes a hot drink. He talks to the cats and gives them some treats. She sits on the sofa and stares into space. He carries her case up to the bedroom and comes back to the living-room.

"Igor, Thank you. I don't know what I would do without you. I have to go back to Madrid next month, can I book you for the airport run?"

"Of course. Text me details."

"And Igor," she looks directly at him, "don't take any bookings for me from Oscar. If I need you, I will contact you directly. Is that okay?"

"Good with me," he says and smiles.

He asks her about a picture that she has on the wall of her bedroom and she tells him about the fiestas in Menorca when there are dancing horses and the people let them come into their houses. She lends him a book about the island before he sets off to return to London.

Estella decides to go to bed. Despite sleeping in the car, she falls asleep instantly.

Waking on Sunday morning, Estella lies for a long time in bed thinking about the people who do not give her their emotions. She's realised since that day spent with Santi, Igor and Win that she doesn't feel any transfer of mood or feelings from any of those people or from Elvira. She's aware of their feelings, but they don't become her own. With Oscar, she feels his emotions, and sometimes they invade her like a virus. This happens with other people, too. She remembers the man in the front seat of the car driving down Insurgentes in Mexico City; it had been the same with him, but she hadn't understood at the time. She'd thought that the self-loathing was hers, but she sees more clearly now that it was his. He'd never expressed it, she wasn't even aware of it until much later, but she felt it from the moment she met him. No wonder he was so obsessed with her and wanted her with him all the time; she must have unburdened him of his disgust with himself. It had driven her insane. She remembers the drinking spree and the attempt at swallowing the sleeping pills he had got for her when he saw how little she slept. She remembers him tipping salt water into her mouth to make her sick and punching her in the stomach when it didn't work. The punch did the trick, but he wouldn't stop. After that, he'd stopped letting her go to work and kept her with him at all times until the night he had to go out to see his boss. She seized the opportunity, made her way to the airport and flew back to the UK with nothing but the clothes on her back, the passport and credit card that she had sewn into her jeans and a fist full of cash she had stolen from his bureau.

The cats make her get up and feed them, and when they are satisfied, she decides to make another list. She has a fortnight until she has to meet with him again, in London. She has work to do on the scripts for episodes one and two. She wants to swim every day and researches the private pools around

Hereford. She has a car and she can drive each day to one or other so that she can get exercise without having to walk there. She doesn't want to see people. Her students will want to ask her questions, and she's not sure what she wants people to know.

At Florian
scripts
swim
eat well
sleep better

She feels that a timetable is necessary if she's going to get everything that she needs to do done. The fortnight will be intense, but she also needs to be strong for when she meets Oscar again. She can't let him overwhelm her. She has to build a working relationship with him so that they can get through the next six months. She can't have him transferring all of his feelings onto her.

She takes a drive to a village not far from town and signs up to use the pool at a private leisure facility. She asks about the quietest times of day. It's busy, being a Sunday, so she decides to start swimming the following day, mid-morning. She plans the rhythm of the coming fortnight: up, breakfast, two and a half hours on scripts, swim, lunch, four hours on *At Florian*, supper, an hour and a half on scripts, try to sleep. Repeat fourteen times.

By Thursday morning, the plan is working like a dream, and she's achieving. She finds that if supper is very small or missed, she can sleep better. On Thursday, as she finishes her thirty lengths and floats on her back, she realises with alarm that someone is waving at her. She's wearing a swimming cap and goggles; she can't imagine that anyone could actually recognise her. Reluctantly, she flips onto her stomach and swims to the steps to get out of the pool. She removes the earplugs she wears and looks at the woman who waved at her. She doesn't look familiar. "Hi," she says without warmth in the hope of deterring the stranger.

"Hi, sorry for the interruption. I think I might be able to help you." Estella cocks her head to the side, wondering if she's misheard or if she's just been accosted by the village eccentric. "I know what you're thinking, but please listen for a moment." Estella wraps her towel around her and sits on one of the loungers by the pool. She takes off her goggles and then her swimming cap. The woman does a doubletake. "Oh," she says, "I didn't realise it was you. No wonder you don't want to listen to me. But, actually, all the more reason." She seats herself on the lounger opposite Estella.

"My name is Vera. No easy way to put it. I see auras. The energy field that surrounds your body."

"I know what an aura is."

"Great, that saves a lot of hassle. Your aura is in a bad way. Sorry to be blunt. I'm guessing something pretty bad has happened recently. Your energy is... well, it's low, but it's also blocked. I think that you might be holding onto a recent trauma. Maybe something happened and you're... hard to express this..."

"I'm defending myself," Estella says. "I'm just trying to keep the bad stuff out." Vera shakes her head.

"I see what you're trying to do, but you've got to release the bad stuff before you start defending yourself. You've trapped the recent crap inside. It's going to make you ill." Estella looks at the woman sitting opposite her with disbelief. How on earth does she know this? But then she thinks of all the things that she knows about people without them telling her. She lets herself really look at Vera and look into her. She knows that she can trust her.

"How do I do that, Vera?"

"I can help you to do it. I think you'll learn quite fast, but I think you're going to need to do it regularly. You feel a lot of emotions from other people, don't you?"

"Yes," Estella says.

"It's okay. I can help."

She lives in the village and Estella drives them the short distance to her house. Like her house, Vera's is full of colour and interesting objects. Not quite so many books, but there's a cat not dissimilar to her fat cat. Vera pours a glass of water for both of them from a lovely blue glass bottle and asks Estella to sit in a comfortable armchair in a warm conservatory. Estella feels very calm and relaxed, almost as if she might sleep. Vera asks her to close her eyes and listen to the sounds around them: there's a quiet ticking clock, the sound of the cat scratching, the distant sound of cars on the road outside at the front of the property and there are birds in the garden. Vera tells her that these sounds are there, but not important and asks her to look up at the sky and find a quiet place where she can look down on herself. "Do you feel any pain?" Vera asks. Estella nods. "Where is it?"

Suddenly, Estella feels the lump in her throat that presages tears and through the tight, thick, contorted voice of weeping, she hears herself say, "Everywhere."

"It's okay. You've got this, Estella. Let's start with the pain in your belly, shall we? I could see that at the pool." Estella's hands comfort the roll of fat below her belly button where she feels tightness and discomfort. "Where did this wound come from? Why does it hurt so bad, Estella?" The voices come quickly; so pleased that someone has asked.

"Nobody loves me," says Little Estella.

"Nobody understands me," says Stel.

"Nobody wants me," says Ella.

"Nobody supports me," says Esta.

"Nobody cares for me," says Sella.

"Nobody believes in me," says Stella.

"Nobody sees me," says Miss.

"We're so lonely," they say.

"Beautiful," says Vera. "You understand yourselves well. I want you to let go of this pain. I want you to let the sadness attached to it go. You think that holding this wound here is defending you, but it's holding you back. This wound is stopping your energy from regenerating. It's stopping you from feeling real joy. Understand that this wound is full of pain, but some of this pain isn't even yours. You're open to the emotions of others, and you absorb them and sometimes they get trapped inside you. The guilt that you feel, the sense of responsibility for all the people around you, it isn't your guilt or your responsibility. You're doing the best you can. Always. You are always doing the best that you can; nobody can ask more of you than that."

Estella is weeping. Huge tears of relief roll down her cheeks. Each tear takes a little of the pain away and eases the burden that she has been carrying for so long. She starts to regulate her breathing and expels pain on every controlled breath out. Colours come and go behind her eyes as she imagines the Aurora Borealis might be. The colours go from red to orange, yellow and green, then blue and purple and a blinding clear white light. Her mind seems to grow lighter and less conflicted with every release of breath. She feels a gentle vibration in her body so different from the usual sensation that her heart is beating a little too fast.

Vera explains that she's going to put headphones on Estella's head and asks her to hold onto a couple of rod crystals. Estella is so relaxed that she just accepts the crystals and does as she's told when Vera asks her to hold them against her belly. Through the headphones come the most exquisite angelic voices, strong, harmonious, a little like Gregorian chant but with soothing frequencies that ping and vibrate in the background.

Estella stands in a cool breeze on the steps of a temple at the top of a mountain. She looks out across the valley below and the surrounding peaks. The angelic chanting inhabits her being and red and orange hangings flap and stir in the light wind. She is filled with an overwhelming sense of possibility. The air lifts her hair and presses her robes against her, she senses her feet leaving the ground and feels no alarm, but rather, leans forward into the current of air and feels herself launch like a bird onto the wind. Then, she is flying. She is soaring through the valley, looking down on the yaks in the fields and the people looking up at her. She glances to her right as she wheels and sees the feathers of her wingtips tensing against the current and she lets out a high-pitched squeal of beady-eyed delight. She swoops and whoops with the sheer joy of freedom and release.

...

When she opens her eyes, she's alone in the conservatory. The headphones and the crystals are on a table beside her chair next to a MacBook and an odd silver box with a blue light on it. She picks up the water glass which has been refilled and hungrily drinks it down. She feels more relaxed than she can ever remember feeling. She watches a robin on the bird table in the garden and thinks about flying through that Tibetan valley. She wonders what she was; a sacred vulture, an eagle or maybe even a Garuda, but she doesn't think that her wings were golden.

"Estella, would you like some more water?"

"Vera, thank you, I would love a little more, please." Vera pours the water. "Thank you, Vera, that was incredible."

"You're welcome. It's only a start, but if you find it helpful, I am happy to teach you the techniques you need."

"Yes, please. Is this your business?"

"Yes."

"How much do I owe you?"

"Nothing for today. It was a pleasure to help you. If you want to come regularly and learn the techniques, then I can tell you about my charges. I think that you could really do with some help with the burden you're carrying." Estella looks Vera in the eye.

"Can you see it?"

"Your burden?"

"Yes."

"Sort of. The disruption to your aura shows me that something is off balance, but it's more something that I feel. I feel that you're carrying something that's far too heavy for you."

"Thank you for seeing me, Vera, and for the kindness you did me in talking to me."

"It was my pleasure." She hesitates. "You went somewhere, didn't you?" Estella smiles broadly.

"A mountain-top temple in Tibet."

"Lush!" Estella shakes her head.

"It gets better. I became a huge bird, and I flew over a valley. I could see the people looking up at me and the yaks in the fields."

"What kind of bird?"

"I don't know. I want to say eagle, but I think Tibetan eagles have golden wings and mine weren't golden."

"Eagles are about new chapters in life. They symbolise power and your inner strength. I know that you got suspended from your job, maybe it's about your next chapter. Maybe there's something new around the corner?"

Estella wants to tell her about what's happening for her, but she feels uncharacteristically reticent. She arranges to meet her again the following week and Vera warns her to take it easy for the rest of the day, drink lots of water and try to get an early night. Driving home she feels herself lighter, but enormously tired. It's only 2:30 pm when she closes her front door, but she has a light lunch and watches a couple of episodes of *Love Struck* and then goes to bed.

She wakes around 7 am feeling well-rested and with no headache. She doesn't remember getting up in the night. She works well on the scripts and realises that she has the general shape for both episodes already. She swims and comes home to lunch and as she sits down to start work on *At Florian*, she sees the sun coming out from behind the clouds and longs to see the sea.

She thinks of Aberdovey and the Trefeddian Hotel. She Googles their number and hunts for her credit card. She hid it a couple of years ago when she moved into this house in an attempt to kerb her propensity to live beyond her means. It hasn't. She just hasn't run out of savings just yet, but with money on its way, she feels that a couple of nights in Wales is hardly going to dent her credit card too badly, and she'll be able to pay it off by the end of the month. The credit card hunt takes rather longer than anticipated, but she does finally find it in one of a pair of uncomfortable shoes at the back of a wardrobe. She calls the hotel and books a superior double room with a sea view, calls the cat-sitter and hastily packs. The cat-sitter arrives to collect the keys just as she has loaded the car. At 3 pm she sets off on the well-worn path to the sea.

The drive from Hereford to Aberdovey goes through some spectacular countryside, most notably the valleys. The day is cold, but there has been sun, so a mist has been created that fills the lower parts of the valleys. As she drives up out of a valley the mist is suddenly left behind and she is above it amongst the sunset-streaked peaks and the mist below looks like a palpable sea of snow. As she hits the zenith and starts downward again, she meets a wall of mist and the day turns grey until having hit rock bottom, she rises again to be propelled back above the vapour and into the dying sunshine. It's like a cycle of life and death or hope and despair; it's inevitable and totally natural. She feels tears of joy and understanding. She feels as if she has, for the first time in a very long time, synchronised with the natural rhythm of life. Then, suddenly, the sea is there, and she feels the pull of it and the power that it gives; she rejoices for the beauty and majesty of the dying light on the water. She considers momentarily driving straight off the cliff and plunging into it, and letting it take her away to the place where nothing can hurt her anymore. *Not today*, the others tell her. *There's so much that we can still do. Think of the sand between our toes tomorrow morning on the beach. Don't forgo that!*

Win describes the Trefeddian as a sweet-smelling, upmarket old people's home. For Estella it has all the charm of a hotel that an Agatha Christie mystery might be set in complete with multiple lounges, a huge dining room and quirky staff. Estella has been here many times, but this is the first time that she has come alone. She stayed here with her mum and dad and other family members, and she and Win have been a couple of times. The beauty of it is the amazing views out across Cardigan Bay and the proximity of the beach, which can be reached on foot in ten minutes. The town is a good heart-pounding trudge along the beach or a gentle ramble by road, creating the perfect circuit to build up an appetite for the epic dinner experience.

Estella also loves the opportunity to dress for dinner.

Ella, Esta, Sella and even Stella travelled a lot and, for the most part, they travelled alone. They had a fantasy that, if Estella were being honest, she still harbours. They always behaved as if they were in a film that only they knew about. They were the mysterious single woman who arrives at the aeroplane/hotel /restaurant (delete as appropriate) and causes a flutter of interest; who is she? Why is she alone? Her distinctive way of dressing and the air of confidence conferred by playing out the fantasy of being filmed always lent her an air of mystery. Miss, however, had reached an age at which she had become invisible to many people, and her entrances and exits had become less impactful. Since her meeting with Vera, her energy and the balance of her mind are sharper and more magnetic. When she walks into the busy dining room that Friday evening in the cerise to pale orange dress from the night she met Santi, a cerise pashmina wrap draped across her shoulders, she feels the eyes of the room on her as she is shown to her table for one. She doesn't mind admitting that it feels good.

Previously, Estella would have eaten all five courses of the dinner and hardly given it a second thought. Food helped to deaden sensation and gave pleasure that she did not receive from other sources, but now that she's writing and she has the filming to consider, she becomes easily full. The menu, which changes daily, is superb, and she struggles to turn down some of the options that she would formerly have embraced with gusto. The waitress who comes to take her order pauses a moment before saying, "Miss Marks, it's nice to see you back at the Trefeddian. How are you?"

"I'm well, thank you. How are you, Maggie?"

"Well, thank you. I'm sorry to see your mum's not with you." Estella feels the lump in her throat, but battles through.

"Three years now, Maggie. How about your mum?"

"Six months," a break in her voice. Estella reaches out a hand and lays it lightly on Maggie's arm.

"It's too hard, isn't it?" Maggie nods tightly. "Thank you for remembering, Maggie. So few people talk about her now. Sometimes it feels as if she never existed at all." They both take a moment. Estella knows that Maggie is seeing her mum in her mind, just as she is picturing her own mum in her memories. She thinks of the last year of her mum's life when they were so very close. She smiles and a couple of tears fall. She breaks the moment and orders to help Maggie move on with her evening.

The last time Estella came here, her mum was still quite well. They had walked on the beach together. It was summer and it had been warm enough and calm enough for her mum to walk over the dune. Stella had carried a folding chair that she had placed in a sheltered nook of the dunes and her mum had sat whilst she paddled in the sea, collected shells and a couple of large pebbles. The pebbles are on a shelf at the house in Hereford. She always intended to paint them; one for her and another for her mum, but her mum's health declined and there wasn't time to paint pebbles.

In the morning, waking to the light that is peculiar to being at the coast, she pulls on trousers and a sweatshirt, and grabbing a scarf, pushes her feet into sliders and almost trips herself up in her eagerness to get outside and across the road to the beach. It's cold but not biting. She scrambles breathlessly up the dunes and half slides down the other side and runs, yes runs, to the sea. A few meters away, she kicks off the sliders, rolls up her trousers, and trots the rest of the way to the water.

She gasps with the cold sting of the water and laughs. She feels her feet being sucked into the sand as the water retreats and lets the sound of the sea sift through her brain and sanitise the self-doubt that can be lessened but never eradicated. She throws her arms wide and whoops with joy, a deep-throated cry for the power surging through her and excoriating the dis-ease and the disquiet. She feels her legs growing stronger and her breaths becoming deeper and more nourishing. She feels her life pulsing excitedly through her whole being. "I'm alive!" She shouts with tears of joy. "I'm alive!"

After a tasty full Welsh breakfast, she takes advantage of the dry weather and drives to the waterfall at Dolgoch. It's cold and it's off season and she finds she's the only person parked in the car park. She's wearing her sliders again, which makes the going harder and rather precarious, but she gets up to the main fall and plants her bare feet on the mossy rocks beside the cascade and feels the pulse and vibration of the water. She closes her eyes and lets her body regulate to the beat of the land below her feet. She is mesmerised. She feels peace and contentment and her breathing deepens. She sees Oscar somewhere far off, a safe distance away, and feels his pain. So much pain. She makes sure that it cannot reach her; that it cannot hurt her. She sees him as a child and the strange life that he led often away from home and the poor relationship with his mother, the loss of his sister's presence, working all the time; she feels compassion for him. She sees him as an adult and his need to control everything including the people in his life. She sees how solitary he is and remembers how he had to be drawn into the conversation at the restaurant with his friends. She still feels compassion for him, but she also feels how lost and lonely he is and how she must seem like a lifeline for him. She remembers thinking in those first few days that she seemed to be his talisman. His desire for her, she doesn't understand. That doesn't make sense at all. When she touches on this, she feels her connection to the rocks and the water faltering. Something feels off-kilter when she explores this. She knows that there is nothing positive that can come from the two of them becoming intimate; nothing positive for either of them. She senses danger in that eventuality. The more she asserts this feeling, she feels the return of the connection with the rocks and water. Message received.

When she opens her eyes again, it's overcast and she can feel spots of rain beginning to fall. She feels the refreshment that the rain brings. She carefully manoeuvres into her sliders and back onto the path making her way back to the car park. She's grateful for the warmth of socks and shoes before she makes her way back to the hotel driving through increasingly heavy rain. She's calm and grounded with a sense of optimism that she hasn't experienced for years.

The lounges at the Trefeddian have enormous picture windows and they offer a safe space to observe the drama of the weather. Estella spends the afternoon writing, seated on a sofa facing a picture window of lashing rain. She works steadily and feels the story of *At Florian* flowing through her onto the page. A couple of hours before dinner she goes up to her room, showers, reads, changes and goes to make her entrance. She is restored and vibrant in a bubble dress of watercolour stripes.

On Sunday she goes down to the beach before breakfast again despite the rain and paddles and whoops. She has to shower and change before breakfasting. At 11 am she drives back towards Hereford, but stops on a rainy mountainside to climb a little in the drizzle and plant her bare feet in the muddy ground. She's wearing a waterproof over her clothes and head, but she lets the rain wash her face and waits for the sense of completion that comes when her pulse has regulated to that of the mountain.

Her energy is bright and light and seems to carry her swiftly as if her feet are not quite touching the ground. She does all the things that she usually does: dinner with Win, script work, swimming, *At Florian*, cooking, washing and even some cleaning, but none of it seems to exhaust her and yet she sleeps so much better at night.

She meets with Vera on Thursday, when she identifies a pain in her right knee that she has been aware of for years, but never really paid any attention to. Vera helps her to focus on the pain in her right knee and she feels the catch in her throat again as she reaches the centre of the issue and Vera asks, "Where did this pain come from, Estella?"

"They disapproved of me," cries Little Estella.

"They tried to control me," says Stel.

"They were disappointed in me," says Ella.

"They thought I was a fool," says Esta.

"They relied on me for everything," says Sella.

"They needed me to care for them," says Stella.

"They left me," says Miss.

"They couldn't love us the way we needed them to," they say.

There was always a burden, Estella realises. The burden of their disapproval and the discomfort of their control. Then there was the weight of their disappointment and the humiliation of their embarrassment at her gullibility over Armando. Then, when she came back to Hereford, she became their social life and it was hard to do things without the sense of responsibility to include them in everything she did. She was happy and willing to care for them, but it was hard. She knew that neither of them would fare well in institutions, so she kept them from that until the end. She failed with both of them to fulfil their wishes to die at home, but that was all due to circumstances beyond her control; she sees now that she has been carrying the burden of guilt over that. Finally, she feels the weight of grief and what she can only describe as what felt like abandonment after living so intimately with them, after feeling their pain and the humiliation of their aging and physical deterioration. Her life had been so full of them and their needs and then she was completely alone. Suddenly. No amount of anticipation could have lessened the blow.

The headphones bring her modulating harmonies that ebb and flow like the water that she feels supporting her. She hears drops of water falling into the pool that she is floating in. As she lets the water caress her, lying on her back she can hear a gentle rumble of thunder and a light rain falls as bells jingle, Tibetan bowls vibrate and somewhere in the distance she hears the glass pendants of a windchime grazing and striking one another. She's at peace as the energy of the water pulses through her and she's content as she feels this gentle electricity enter and leave her body in a flow of deliverance and purification. She flips herself onto her belly and there is a delightful flurry of fish swimming with and around her and it's as if they are playing with the force flowing through her. She giggles at the delicious tickle of their bodies around her and the pleasure of being so close to other living things.

When she wakes, she is smiling and refreshed. She drinks the water Vera has poured for her and takes the crystals out from beneath her knee. She feels brand new.

The Metropolis

On Sunday afternoon, she takes a train to London. It's one of the now rare trains that goes directly from Hereford to London Paddington via a plethora of beautifully named stations. The train is quiet and she's able to work on *At Florian* while she glides through the countryside heading south. Earlier that day she sent the first drafts of the scripts for episodes one and two. This is two weeks before the due date, but she doesn't feel that she can do any more until she gets feedback from the Spanish writing team. She has booked a serviced apartment near The Ned for the five nights she's planning to be in London. She doesn't know where Oscar will be staying because he has respected her request and left her alone since they parted in Madrid. They are due to meet tomorrow night for dinner. She liked the location of the apartment because she has several meetings in that area in the morning and the price is a fraction of the cost of a hotel.

Stepping down from the train at Paddington and hefting her case onto the platform, she feels the rush of energy and confusion that characterises a large station full of anxious travellers. She acknowledges the energy but concentrates on her breathing and listens to waves on her headphones as she makes her way to the taxi rank, making sure not to give in to the temptation to rush. The streets are quiet on an early Sunday evening, and she enjoys the run through Hyde Park and the sightseeing going past Buck House, The Mall and Trafalgar Square. The driver takes her along the river passing Somerset House and on to Blackfriars before turning up into the City to Queen Victoria Street and finally onto Cannon Street. At 7:30 pm, she is inside her apartment and unpacking. She is almost entirely unscathed by her journey. It feels like a miracle.

She sleeps well and has a productive series of meetings through the morning and early afternoon. She's left fifty-five thousand words of *At Florian* with the lawyer who is going to get it assessed and get back to her. The financial advisor has opened her eyes about tax and deductible expenses, and she has engaged him since her bank account is now the healthiest it has ever been with the first payment received through Elvira. She's also engaged a different lawyer to challenge her employer over her suspension on a 'no win, no fee' basis. The last meeting had been over a light lunch at Leon which was busy and noisy, so she was glad to be so close to her digs.

She's been lying down and feeling the tension building in her belly about seeing Oscar. He messaged mid-morning to say that he's staying in Holborn but hasn't told her where. He's asked permission to send Igor to bring her to dinner, but didn't ask where she's staying. She's agreed to Igor collecting her because she feels that seeing him will steady her nerves before dinner with Oscar. She follows the process that Vera uses with her and finds the quiet space where she can look down on herself from above, and then she asks her body where the tension in her belly is coming from. She feels the catch in her throat.

"He's a bully," says Little Estella.

"He didn't listen," says Stel.

"He was rough," says Ella.

"He's controlling," says Esta.

"He's manipulative," says Sella.

"He's fucked up," says Stella.

"He's lost," says Miss.

"We can't trust him," they say.

She feels the tension easing with the acknowledgment of what they know about him and the knowledge that they're stronger now. They're stronger than they've ever been. She feels her power and she isn't going to give any of it away to anyone. She still feels compassion and empathy for Oscar, he's had a difficult journey, but she's not about to let his insecurities impact on her. She will spend time with him, but on her terms.

Getting into the back of Igor's car she's so happy to see him that she feels a few tears of joy. She's wearing a Japanese-inspired Ralston dress with floating pockets in black and white drapey linen. She's dressed her eyes and lips too and as it's still cold at night she has the ubiquitous black velvet coat and a bright orange pashmina.

"Good evening, Igor. How lovely to see you. How are you?"

"Wow!" Says Igor. "What happen to you? You're different."

"I'm feeling stronger, Igor."

"You look dynamite, Estella."

"How about you, Igor? How are things?"

"Busy. This is good. I'm good."

"I'm pleased to hear it."

"You have dinner with Oscar tonight?"

"Yes, I haven't seen him for a couple of weeks. Not since you picked me up from Heathrow."

"Remember what I say you?"

"Yes, Igor. He will take all my energy if I let him. I'm not going to let him."

"Good." He nods, "But you have more energy now, I think." She laughs. It's such a pleasure to be seen.

"Yes, you noticed, thank you. I have more energy than I've had for a long time. I'm planning on keeping it that way."

"There is light coming from you." Igor smiles with genuine pleasure.

The journey is short so there isn't much time to talk. He drops her outside a classy-looking hotel and restaurant and as she gets out of the car she's struck by the name in neon above the entrance: L'oscar. She's transfixed.

"I know, it's very embarrassing!" She'd forgotten the timbre of his voice and the gentle kindness that he usually uses when he addresses her. She lets her eyes drop from the sign and she takes him in. Tall, slim, olive skin, slightly wayward hair, facial symmetry, immaculate Hugo Boss suit and proper lace-up shoes. She sees his nerves and feels them.

"They're putting me up for free," he blurts. "My Insta is all about #Oscar@L'oscar. Everyone thinks it's cute, but I knew you'd see it differently."

"Oscar, it's cool. Kudos to their marketing people for thinking it up."

"It's funny though, don't you think?"

"Yeah, but funny ha-ha, not funny peculiar." He fiddles with his tie. "¿Come estas, Oscar?"

"Nervioso, de verdad. ¿Rafa, discúlpeme? ¿Por favor?"

"Oscar, I'll forgive you, but only on the condition that you treat me fairly. If there's something that I do that troubles you, then you need to talk to me about it. I don't want to be subjected to moods and conjecture."

"Yes, I understand, Rafa. I haven't had a lot of friends. I haven't had a lot of practice. I will do better. I promise."

"Okay, then let's have dinner, shall we?"

The restaurant has a bar that's illuminated from the inside, which makes it look like molten lava; she adores it. She's seated on a banquette, thinking about the day they met in Fischer's. She thinks about the pain he was dealing with and the fear that he had of going back to Parker Grove's house. He was in a very vulnerable condition and seemed so lost, and yet within weeks, he was trying to organise her life and start a relationship with her. His need to be in control is the least attractive thing about him, and the intensity of this need sets off alarm bells. She'll need to be vigilant with him; there will not be any more intimate confessions or casual tactile contact. This will make things different between them, and she is certain that he won't like it.

"You look different, Rafa. You look really well."

"Thank you," she smiles. "I am really well. I feel great. I'm enjoying the writing immensely." Then it's his turn to smile.

"I'm so pleased." The smile fades. "I was very worried when we parted so badly." She lets him hang. He's apologised and she's conditionally accepted his apology; there's no need to keep going over this.

"These cocktails look good. I think I'd like to try the *Do You St Tropez*." There's only a minimal pause.

"Yeah, let's try that. It sounds refreshing."

"I rather like things with violet flavour," she chats. "There are these beautiful chocolates called violet cremes. They're made with bitter dark chocolate but with these painfully sweet violet flavoured fondant centres. They're divine." He's not sure how to behave. He's not somebody who has a lot of conversation, she realises. The evening on the terrace at The Ned, when she thinks about it was mostly her telling him things, asking questions and him responding.

"So, what brought you to London this time, Oscar?" She opens.

"I have a photoshoot on Wednesday for Paul Smith for the autumn collection," he says. "I have to do some stuff for Selfridges too for their Christmas campaign; that's on Friday. How long are you in town for?" She considers cutting the trip short, but decides that seeing some culture will do her good. The apartment is comfortable, so she can write there. She might as well have a change of scenery.

"I leave on Friday," she tells him, watching as he battles the impulse to persuade her to stay longer and wins.

"Are you free for some exploration tomorrow?"

"What d'you have in mind?"

"There's an exhibition by a Spanish artist I know at a gallery in south London. A place called Limehouse?"

"Wow, Limehouse! That's a very interesting part of the city. Historically very poor, but in modern times regenerated. There's a fascinating church by Hawksmoor."

"Maybe we could check that out too," he says without enthusiasm. They agree to meet at 10 am the following day to take a trip to Limehouse.

They start their meal with L'oscar's mezze to share and a beautifully cold bottle of Sancerre. Oscar chooses black cod miso for his main and she goes for the Cornish monkfish, but they both try each other's dishes. Almost defeated, they just manage to share the crème brûlée until they have to stop before they explode. Estella misses her appetite. She used to be able to eat so much more. When the food and wine have been finished, she feels tired from keeping up the conversation and as she relaxes, the flow dries up, and they're seated in silence for some minutes before Oscar shifts uncomfortably and clears his throat.

"I wanted to explain about the... difficulty before we left for the Netflix party." She regards him with compassion but doesn't say anything. She waits while he literally squirms in his seat. "I don't have the best relationship with some of my fellow cast members. I don't make friends easily. I don't have a lot in common with any of the people I work with." He stops. She wonders what he wants her to say. She can't think of anything that would be helpful. She just wants to say, *you're not kidding*.

"I particularly have a problem with Víctor," he announces, without further explanation. She takes pity on him.

"In what way?"

"I've known Víctor for years. We worked together as teenagers. We fell out... I've never really felt comfortable with him since. It was a shock when I found we'd be working together again in this show. I try to be polite, but it's hard."

"What did you fall out about?"

"I don't really remember," he lies.

"Then, surely, if you can't remember, it's time to forgive and forget."

"What he did was unforgiveable," he says with warmth.

"But you just said that you didn't remember what he did..." She sees the tension in his jaw and feels the anger rising in him, her hands instinctively go to her belly to shield it, but she doesn't say anything more. She continues to look at him and offer empathy, but she doesn't say anything. She isn't sure how long it takes; it feels like hours, but she knows that it isn't. Finally, he releases a long sigh.

"He kissed me," he says with disgust. "I didn't ask him to do that. I didn't give him permission to do that." She's transported back to the night in Madrid when he did the same thing to her and the fear and confusion that she felt. "I thought he was my friend." That too resonates with her.

"You felt betrayed."

"Exactly," he says with fervour, "you get it." She'd like to point out that she does get it, that she feels the same about what he did, but she hasn't the heart when he's opening up to her like this.

"That was hard. Did he apologise?"

"Of course he apologised, but what good does that do? The relationship was never going to be the same again. I couldn't ever trust him again."

"Yes," she says, "I can see that you'd feel that way."

"I haven't really had friends since then. I get along with the people that I work with. I sometimes hang out with them, but it's not like when Víctor and I were friends. We did everything together."

"How old were you?"

"Sixteen."

"This happened ten years ago?"

"Yes, and then he turns up on *Los Amores de Oscar*. I couldn't believe it. I try to be polite and friendly, but it... Sometimes it chokes me that I have to work with him. Worse, I have to act being in love with him. I bet he gets a huge kick out it." She measures his mood before she decides that she has nothing to lose.

"I've met Víctor. I don't think he's getting a kick out of anything. I think he misses your friendship just as much as you miss his."

"Then he should have thought that through before he kissed me."

"Do sixteen-year-olds have the capacity to think through their actions? Aren't they just a mess of hormones?"

"Fourteen. He's two years younger than me." She wonders if that added to Oscar's outrage, the fact that Víctor, younger than him had made the first move. What if Oscar had chosen to kiss Víctor?

"Has he ever tried to kiss you again?"

"Of course not!" He sounds shocked by the suggestion. Estella tries hard to maintain her empathy, but the intensity of Oscar's disgust seems absurdly over-blown. She tries very hard not to ask him, but she knows that it's inevitable that she will.

"Did you like the kiss?" Oscar's outrage reaches supersonic proportions.

"Rafa!" He's almost spitting feathers. "Whose side are you on?" She's very good. She could easily burst into laughter at this point. She remains calm and maintains her empathy.

"It's not about sides, Oscar. I understand that the experience was traumatic, but it occurs to me that it would've been even more traumatic if you'd liked kissing him."

"I didn't kiss him. He kissed me!" She looks straight into his eyes.

"You didn't respond to the kiss? You didn't kiss him back?" He can't hold her gaze. His hands which have been gesticulating his outrage, are suddenly clasped together as he crosses his legs. He is literally tying himself in knots.

"I'd never considered kissing a boy. I hadn't realised that I had... those feelings. I did kiss him back and it disgusted me that I liked it. If he hadn't kissed me, I might never have found out that I'm bi."

"Then that's a small thing to be grateful for, isn't it?" She can see what he thinks of that logic. "But, Oscar, I know that you said that you are a prude, but surely you don't disapprove of your own sexuality?"

"I try not to think about my sexuality." She wants to tell him that *she* also tries not to think about his sexuality because the more he tells her, the more mystifying his feelings for her are. "Víctor's presence tends to send me into a panic. That's what happened the night of the party when I was so rough with you. I wanted you to understand that Víctor's a trigger for me. That's why I was so upset when I saw that you'd been hanging out with him."

She nods at him.

"Thank you for sharing this with me, Oscar. I'm sorry that you feel this way. I'm also sorry that you can't forgive Víctor. Víctor's a lovely person and I think he'd be a great friend, if you'd let him." He shakes his head.

"I'll never trust him again." She feels deeply sad for Víctor, but even more so for Oscar. She wants to explain the phrase 'to cut one's nose off to spite one's face' to him, but it's pointless.

"Okay, I understand. Thank you for trusting me with this."

She lets a little time pass. She watches his body begin to relax. He uncrosses his legs, eases his neck and leans his elbows on the table.

"Have you seen any of the collection that you'll be modelling on Wednesday?"

"No," he says, much more relaxed. "It's top secret. It's a closed set, or I would've brought you along."

The tension seems to have been broken and he chats, quite loquaciously for him, for another forty minutes. Around 10:30 pm she says that she needs to get some sleep and messages Igor to come and collect her. Oscar walks her out to the car and kisses her cheek. She catches camera flashes from the corner of her eye. She resigns herself to the inevitable.

Igor is fat again after another meal cooked by his friend's wife. They chat easily on the short journey back to her apartment. Oscar, he tells her, has booked him for their excursion in the morning and they bid each other goodnight.

Limehouse

In the mid-1980s, when Estella was a teenager new to London, she explored the city relentlessly and one of the areas she fell in love with was seedy, derelict Limehouse. She watched that relict of the Victorian era of London's dynamic past undergo sanitisation and regeneration, and she felt the loss of authenticity. Coming back after so many years and seeing the bustling businesses and the towers of Canary Wharf she sees the point of it, but can't help mourning the loss of the communities that were shipped out to allow for the renewal.

The chic warehouse apartments and basin developments appeal to Oscar and Igor drops them near Limehouse Basin in front of a rather bland-looking, glass-fronted commercial space. The gallery appears to be a pop-up, the space being more suited to an estate agent than a gallery. Oscar pushes open the rather wobbly large glass door and lets Estella step inside first. A painfully slim young person smiles and offers her welcome from behind a startlingly white desk on which there is a large pink Stanley flask and a MacBook. A couple is examining a painting and discussing it with animation, and a man is sitting on the uncomfortable-looking moulded plastic sofa in the middle of the space. When Oscar follows her in, the young person shoots to their feet and looks excited.

"Mr Pérez, welcome. We were told that we might see you today. Thank you so much for your visit."

"My pleasure," says Oscar, fiddling with the buttons on the front of the forest-green, double-breasted Ralph Lauren suit that he is airing today. It's the colour of Estella's eyes and she loves the way his well-tailored rear slightly elevates the double vent. "This is Miss Marks. Is Chico here today?"

"Nice to meet you, Miss Marks." Estella sees the penny drop. "Chico should be here shortly, he had a flat on his bike, but I think he's managed to repair it. Please take a look around. There are quite a few new pieces since the Amsterdam show."

The paintings are not large. Mostly they measure only thirty or forty centimetres either way, but they're full of detail and intense colour. The subject matter is diverse, and she's surprised to see that this artist is equally adept at people, landscapes and buildings. She gasps at the colours and vibrancy of a canvas showing La Casa de los Azulejos in Mexico City and wonders at the blind man that Chico has portrayed tapping his way along the pavement outside.

"Where's that?" Oscar asks. "It looks like Lisbon."

"¡Hombre!" She exclaims. "It's DF. You must've been there as a kid. It's a Sanborns."

"Is there a mural with a fountain and a... pavo real?"

"Yeah, that's right. A peacock sitting on a balustrade with its tail draped down. Actually, there are lots of birds in that mural."

"Yeah, mom used to take us there sometimes if we were shopping in the city centre."

"Is Chico Mexican?"

"No, he's from Madrid."

"Why d'you think he put that blindman there?" Oscar tilts forward.

"I didn't notice that. You can ask him when he gets here."

There's another picture from Mexico, a barge on a canal in Xochimilco Park with a drunken party in full swing inside. In the forefront is the tired gondolier with his pole, sweat stains at the armpits of his white t-shirt. It's disturbing. She goes back to the previous picture.

"Viste el ciego, ¿verdad?" A gravelly Spanish voice comes from a tall, broad-chested, rather unkempt man around her age.

"Sí," she takes in the smell of tobacco, the paint-stained fingers and the once good but now rather crumpled suit. As he takes in her face, there's an odd moment that looks like recognition and a slight confusion. She smiles in encouragement. "Qué quieres decir con él?" She continues. "¿Qué somos ciegos a la belleza que nos rodea? ¿O qué no todas tienen acceso a cosas hermosas?"

He smiles broadly. The confusion is gone.

"You aren't Spanish," he says. "I was sure that you were Spanish in that dress." She laughs.

"Is my Spanish really that bad? And, for your information, this dress is Italian."

"Disculpa, hablas muy bien, pero tienes un poco de acento. ¿Sabes?"

"Yeah, I don't get as much practice as I'd like."

"The dress might be Italian, señorita, but my point was that it's not the sort of dress that an English woman would wear. I mean," he looks at her appraisingly, "it's cerise and you wear a purple scarf with it!" She touches the purple scarf. "Es magnifica." He adds quietly. She smiles but doesn't respond.

"¡Chico!" Oscar calls from across the room and strides over with his hand extended. "¿Qué tal? ¿Todo bien con la bicicleta?"

"Sí, hijo, todo bien," he says, pulling an embarrassed Oscar into a bear hug.

"Well, I see," he says rather flustered, "that you've met Estella." Chico looks back at her and then at Oscar, and she sees him realise who she must be.

"Encantado, Estella."

"The pleasure is all mine," she responds. "Do you mind if I keep looking at the pictures? I'm thoroughly enjoying the show." Chico extends his arm in welcome, and she walks away to leave Oscar to catch up with his friend.

The rest of the show is just as interesting as the pictures of Mexico City. Estella approaches the young person at the gleaming white desk about buying one particular piece showcasing a flight of stone steps down to a harbour. Many years ago, in Stel's day, she and a friend were driven down those steps on a motorbike by a young man with a broken leg. The memory of it remains as vivid as the moment in which it happened because Stel learnt something true and important which she constantly reminds the others of; taking risks and grasping opportunities offered to you can lead to the deepest joy and the most profound satisfaction.

"I'm very sorry, Miss Marks," says the young person, blushing intensely, "I sold that picture this morning and I haven't yet put the sold dot on it. I'm so sorry."

"What happened, Xris?" Asks Chico with a furrowed brow.

"Miss Marks wants to buy a picture, but I've already sold it. I need to put a dot on it, but I forgot. I'm so sorry."

"Don't worry, Xris." Estella tells them. "These things happen. I was surprised to see that it wasn't sold."

"Which one was it?"

"Steps to the harbour," says Xris.

"Mahon," Estella interjects. Chico smiles at her.

"You know Mahon?" She smiles back and nods.

"Those steps are very dear to my heart." She can see Oscar engaged in conversation with the couple that has been viewing the show. She's safe. "When I was fourteen, I went to Menorca for the first time on my own. I'd always been with my family before. My dad had a friend there, and mum was friends with his wife, and we kids were friends with their kids. My friend in the family was a couple of years older than me. One morning, around five o'clock on our way back from partying all night at a fiesta, my friend's boyfriend, who had one leg in plaster, drove his motorbike down that flight of steps with me and my friend clinging onto the back. It was the single most exciting thing that I'd ever done in my life up to that point. It was magical." Chico seems entranced and then suddenly glances out of the front of the gallery into the street. Estella follows his gaze and sees that he's looking at an enormous motorbike parked outside. She suddenly laughs.

"¿La bicicleta?" He nods and laughs.

"I'm so sorry that the painting is sold, Estella!"

"Don't worry, Chico," she smiles, "it's all up here." She taps the side of her temple and they smile at one another.

"Thanks for sharing the story," he says quietly.

She buys the picture of La Casa de los Azulejos instead and as she's finalising the purchase Oscar joins her at the desk.

"Which one are you buying?"

"La Casa de los Azulejos."

"Great choice." Then to the gallery assistant, "Can I get twenty-four? The one of the teenagers drinking in the square." She looks at him. She feels compassion flood through her.

"The youth you never had." He kisses her cheek.

"You always get it, Rafa."

Chico demands that they have lunch with him. He walks them around the Limehouse Basin and down a couple of older streets, which Estella enjoys visibly, until they reach The Bread Street Kitchen on Narrow Street. Inside, it's busy and a little noisy, but the staff seem to know Chico and they are shown to a table in the conservatory looking out across the water. The men take pains to make sure that she has the best view. She excuses herself, and Oscar makes the usual joke about the lavatory and explains to Chico in Spanish about this word that he finds so amusing.

As she returns to the table, a waitress is setting up an ice bucket and opening a bottle of Perrier-Jouet Grand Brut, and she smiles broadly.

"Oscar says that you like champagne. I, too, am a fan."

"What a treat! I haven't had Perrier-Jouet very often, but I once had a glass of their Belle Epoque and that is not a moment that I'll ever forget."

When they all have a glass, they pause for a moment.

"To your talent, Chico." Proposes Estella and Oscar raises his glass.

"No," laughs Chico. "To living life to the max!" Estella hoots and raises her glass even higher. Oscar drinks. Estella closes her eyes and smells the wine, as she opens them to take a sip, she sees Chico doing the same. They smile, but not at each other.

"Nectar," Estella announces.

The conversation is easy, at least between Chico and Estella, who is careful to keep drawing Oscar in by asking him questions or his opinion of something. Chico also makes an effort to get Oscar to join in, but for both of them, it's a bit of a chore. They have fish and chips and exclaim at how good they are. They're sitting debating dessert when Oscar's phone rings and he goes outside to take the call. Estella takes the opportunity to asks Chico how he met Oscar.

"About fifteen years ago, when I was still an art teacher, Oscar's mother hired me to give lessons to his sister, who was quite talented at painting. I used to go to the apartment in Salamanca. I didn't see much of him; he was almost always away working, but when he was there, he seemed to enjoy having a man in the house." He sips his champagne. "After about three years, my career started to take off, finally! I started to get solo shows and I gave up tuition. I lost sight of him for a while. I knew he was doing well. I saw him on TV from time to time and he was always touring with his singing career. Then there was a lot of stuff in the newspapers about him and his mum and the money. It didn't come as any surprise to me." He seems to consider what he wants to say. He looks her in the eye. "His mum isn't a very nice person. She's not warm or caring. She has the air of being constantly dissatisfied."

"Well, that explains a lot," she offers, and he nods in agreement.

"Anyway, shortly after the dispute with his mum, he turned up at a private view for a show of mine in Madrid. The papers all said that he'd bought this amazing apartment in Retiro, and he bought a picture saying it was for his new place. He often buys a picture and he comes to a lot of my shows. I have to say, I think he's added to my success. Having Oscar Pérez at your private views can do wonders." She nods.

"The Oscar Factor should never be underestimated!" He laughs and nods his head.

"You know, Estella..." but he doesn't get to finish. Oscar is back.

"Are we getting dessert?" She tries and fails to eat a sticky toffee pudding, but Oscar finishes it for her after eating a massive ice-cream sundae. Chico receives a call as they are ordering coffee and has to return to the gallery and Estella's sad to see him leave. He's a good conversationalist and she knows that she's safe with him. When she and Oscar finally leave, they find that Chico has paid the bill.

"So, where is this church of yours?"

"It's about a ten-minute walk from here." He crooks his arm, and she takes it. They walk slowly through the grey day across a small bridge and down the small, sanitised streets of light-coloured brick buildings. They go through a neat park with no sense of the power of nature, and by a canal until they leave the park and cross Newell Street into St Anne's Passage. At the end of the passage, the church stands massive and classical. They pass through the gate and walk towards the steps to the front door.

"It won't be open," she tells him.

"We can't get in?" He stops walking.

"No, but I didn't come for the inside. What I want to say hello to is in the graveyard." She guides him round to the left. Beside a tree is the pyramid that has fascinated Estella ever since she first saw it in 1987. She shows Oscar the carving and the inscriptions and explains what is conjectured about it. He actually seems to be interested. As they're standing there talking, Igor appears on the other side of the pyramid.

"Hi," he says. "Sorry, did not know that you were here. I read about pyramid and think to come and look." Oscar shows him the carving and gets Estella to explain it to him. They all discuss it on the way back to the car on Three Colt Street. Igor drives them back towards the city, and Estella can feel tiredness beginning to tense her muscles. She's looking forward to lying down. It's only three thirty in the afternoon, but she's ready to sleep for a bit. She lets her head rest back and closes her eyes, careful to keep her hands out of Oscar's reach. It's been a pleasurable day. She'd like to rest for a while and then perhaps write for an hour or so.

Oscar arranges to see her on Thursday morning. She doesn't ask what the plan is but rather leaves it as a surprise for herself. She bids him goodbye avoiding physical contact and thanks Igor for his services. As she's letting herself into the apartment building, her phone rings. It happens so rarely that she's surprised and fumbles slightly. She doesn't recognise the number and answers somewhat hesitantly.

"Hello?"

"Hi, is that Estella?"

"Yes."

"Hi Estella, my name's Rosie, I work for Peter Dunbar. I understand that you met with him yesterday about your manuscript."

"Oh, yes, I did, Rosie."

"Estella, I've just finished reading it. Have you written any more?"

"Erm, I think you have about fifty-five thousand words, don't you?"

"Yeah, that's right."

"I think there's about twenty thousand more, so far. Should I stop writing? Is it not very good?"

"No! I'm desperate to see what happens next."

"So, you think that you can sell it?"

"Well, not me, I do the assessments, but yes, my colleagues in sales will have no problem." Estella smiles and something inside that she didn't know was tense releases.

"That's great news. I better get it finished."

"Yes, please! I want to read the rest of it." Estella laughs.

"Okay, give me a couple of weeks. Is that alright?"

"Great. My colleagues will start to drum up interest with what we have so far, and we'll let you know what kind of offers we get. Keep writing, please."

"Thanks, Rosie."

"No, Thank you, Estella."

She makes her way to her apartment feeling wonderfully light and hopeful. Praise for something that she has written is a pleasure that she hasn't experienced since education. It feels so good. Inside, she locks the door and lies down and goes happily to sleep.

Treehouse and Mughals

The previous night, after her nap, Estella wrote for several hours and then slept again. She writes for a couple of hours on Wednesday morning before Igor collects her. They pick Anna up for lunch at the Treehouse Hotel in their Mexican restaurant which has a stunning view out over central London. Anna is stronger today, apart from being a little pale and some puffiness in her face, she's her usual suave and sophisticated self. In the car, she looks at Estella carefully.

"You're different." Estella nods. "I wasn't expecting to see you looking..."

"So sane?" Estella asks, laughingly.

"Well, yeah. To be brutal."

"I know. It's a bit of a shocker, isn't it?"

"In fact," shaking her head slightly and exhaling cigarette smoke through Igor's open rear window, "I'm not sure I've ever seen you look quite this sane..." Estella laughs, throwing her head back.

"I don't suppose I've ever been this sane before."

"What happened?"

"Anna, if I told you, you wouldn't believe me."

"So, it's not Oscar Pérez?" Estella's mood drops at the idea.

"No, nothing to do with him." Igor catches her eye in the rearview mirror.

"Shame," Anna says briefly. "Come on, try me. What happened." Estella wonders if she could explain to Anna.

"I afraid that you're likely to think it's all metaphysical woo woo."

"Probably, but I still want to hear about it. I promise not to be scathing."

They arrive at Treehouse, and Igor offers a small, encouraging smile as they thank him and enter to take the lift up to Madera. Over Dom Pérignon, calamari and guacamole, Estella explains what happened at the swimming pool and Vera's guided release of pain and blocked energy. She talks about the frequency soundscapes on the headphones and the crystals. The crystals will almost certainly be a step too far, she thinks.

While they share chicken enchiladas and flambe king prawns marinated in tequila and garlic, Anna asks questions about the visions that Estella had whilst listening to the soundscapes. She asks a lot of questions, too, about how she identified where the pain was and what she means by releasing it. She thinks deeply about everything that she's told and takes on the alert, bright-eyed intensity that Estella loves so much about her.

The staff let Anna go up to the terrace around the Nest upstairs to smoke. As Estella waits, she sips her champagne and opens her e-mail. A message from Nuria tells her that the writing team are happy with the scripts and looking forward to meeting her the week after next. She asks if the same hotel will be okay, along with her preferences for her flight times, arriving Sunday and leaving Saturday. She responds, texts Igor the dates and times and finds a text from Win.

Win

FYI, old thing. Bloke came into the shop asking questions about you. Think he might be a journalist? Obviously said I didn't know you. Just thought that you should know. Also, as you are still a technological troglodyte, you should be aware that you are all over Oscar's fans' feeds in various places around London including some weird pyramid thing. You really are a weirdo! 💋 ! XXX

WTAF! I didn't even see anyone filming us in Limehouse. I know they caught us outside L'oscar!

Moments later:

Win

Having a nice time with Anna at Treehouse?

????

Win

You're hot property on TikTok, you freak.

😮 !

Win

Dinner Sunday?

Fuck off! You just called me a freak!

7: 30 pm?

Win

Perf with Surf.

Anna returns, looking refreshed and they finish the second bottle of champagne in a gentle haze of inebriation. They talk about school friends, London in the 1980s and recent books read. Estella hesitates, but she wants someone to know and as she can choose, Anna is the best person to tell.

"I'm writing a novel."

"Excellent, about time. What part of your *interesting* life are you plundering for material?"

"Something that happened in Venice. We weren't in contact at that time, so you don't know the story."

"How far have you got with it? It's not as if life's been uneventful recently."

"About eighty thousand words now. It's reaching the dénouement." Anna gawps at her.

"That's a lot in a short time!"

"It feels like the story's always been there," she explains, "I just have to write it down and edit it. Actually, I have to pace myself or I end up sitting writing for hours and hours."

"You've always written, haven't you? Am I remembering poetry?" Estella nods and smiles.

"Yeah, I used to write a lot of poetry, especially when we were at school, but for years afterwards, too. I still write it from time to time, but less frequently than before. This is the first novel, though."

"Wow. Do I get to read it?"

"Of course. I'm just in the process of selling it. Once the deal's done and it's finished, I'll get the manuscript to you."

"You already have a buyer?"

"I'm cashing in on this notoriety that I have from Oscar's attentions."

"I see. Makes sense, I suppose."

"Actually, I'm also writing scripts for the next season of *Oscar Loves*...and..." Anna shakes her head as if her mind is boggled.

"And..."

"You can't tell anyone yet." She feels absurd. She waves her hand as if to erase what she's said. "I know that you won't want to tell anyone. It's hardly earth-shattering information!"

"What?!"

"I'm going to be in the third season, acting." Anna laughs deeply.

"That's wonderful! Drama school finally pays off! You've come full circle. Who are you playing?"

"Oscar's mum. I don't know if you know the plot line." Anna scoffs.

"After you started appearing on Instagram with him and I wasn't well, I binge-watched on my laptop in hospital." She hesitates. "It's appalling crap, Stel!" Estella laughs heartily.

"I know! Pure soap opera."

"I can see that you're going to add a bit of class to the show." Estella frowns and bites her lip.

"That's what Oscar said. That's why he wants me to do it."

"That and keeping you close. He's after you, isn't he?" Estella nods tightly and sighs, her mood dropping despite the Champagne haze.

"I'm sorry about what I said last time. You seemed so well, and I thought that it'd be fun for you. I should've respected your reservations."

"None of us was in possession of the full facts."

"He's respecting your refusal?" Estella shakes her head.

"He's giving me time and space to reconsider." Anna widens her eyes.

"Tell him to fuck off!"

"I'm about to fulfil two of my life's dreams; being a published author and being paid to act. None of that will or would have come about without him. I think he'll lose interest."

Anna doesn't respond to this and Estella can see that she's starting to get tired.

"Shall I call Igor?"

"If you don't mind, Stel."

While Anna goes for another cigarette, Estella calls Igor and pays the bill. In the car on the way back to Anna's house, she's quiet and looks unhappy. Estella feels the sadness, tinged with a little bitterness and wonders if her friend is considering how much time is left to her. There had been talk of a bucket list, but that would involve money, and Estella knows better than most how difficult that can be. She walks Anna to her door and they say goodbye, planning to meet again in a month when Estella will be back in London.

"Good person," says Igor, as she gets back into the car. She nods. He has a way of cutting to the important information. She smiles at him

"You're amazing, Igor. I'm so pleased that I met you." He smiles at her in the rearview mirror.

"I feel same." He leaves a beat. "Where to?"

"Actually, Igor, could you just drop me at the V&A? There's a special exhibition that I'd like to see there. Then I'm going to take a walk. I need some thinking time. I think well when I walk."

The Mughals are one of Estella's obsessions. About fifteen years ago she watched an extraordinary biopic of Akbar, the Mughal general and emperor, played by the unfeasibly attractive Hrithik Roshan and with an exquisite soundtrack by A.R. Rahman. She must have watched it ten times and she read history books, Googled and finally took a trip to India to see the Red Forts, Taj Mahal and Fatehpur Sikri. It's not that the culture appeals to her, all those brothers and fathers killing each other and keeping harems of unhappy women, but more the art and architecture that they left behind. After years of adoration of the Moorish architecture and art in Spain, it was as if she had discovered the criterion from which these Spanish imitations had been born.

It's almost four o'clock when she buys her ticket, and the dim exhibition rooms aren't as crowded as they might've been. She's grateful for this. The items on display are small and highly detailed. She adores the sophisticated portraits and pictures that, in their vibrancy and precision, might have been laser printed just a moment ago. Instead, as she looks at them, she can sense the men hunched over their work with brushes so fine that every strand of hair seems to be discernible and blending colours that leap off the page even now, four hundred years later. The opulence of their subjects' attire, the enormity of their jewels, the intricacy of their headwear and the beauty of their intelligent, calculating, murderous and misogynistic faces is intoxicating. She has no illusions, but she also appreciates the extraordinary achievement that is these works of art and the civilisation that produced them. The flower of culture cultivated from the blood and bones of the servants, the women and the defeated. The lotus that blooms from the mud. It's exhausting in a highly satisfying way.

From the V&A she walks down the Brompton Road, pacing herself in order not to damage her equilibrium on what will be a long walk. She has a slight headache from the champagne and stops to buy a bottle of water. She enjoys the sights as she walks and thinks. She's considering the two possible endings to *At Florian* and which she should write.

She passes Harrods and Harvey Nichols. She makes it to Hyde Park Corner and sits for a while in Green Park. She knows that if she'd let Ella take charge, they would have had no chance to stop. She cuts through by St James's Palace onto Pall Mall and calls into Berry Brothers and Rudd to buy Win a treat.

Back along Pall Mall, she eyes the gentlemen's clubs with mistrust and navigates the pedestrian crossings to pass in front of the National Gallery and St Martin-in-the-Fields before crossing the Strand and walking down Villiers Street, through Embankment Gardens and finally reaching the Victoria Embankment. She stops at the last bench of the gardens and tries to recall a poem that she wrote about them, but memory stumps her.

She looks across at the Southbank and the Royal Festival Hall and remembers the night that she got a stand-by ticket for a performance of Joaquín Rodrigo's uplifting *Concierto Heroico* and found that she was sitting only five seats away from the composer himself. She laughs as the hilarious performance of *A Midsummer Night's Dream* at the National comes to mind, when the whole stage turned into a mud bath and the actors slid around during the scene of confusion.

In a life where every opportunity has been seized, there is much to revel in, and it has been a long time since she allowed herself to review any of the highlights.

She walks steadily, but leisurely, along the Embankment enjoying being beside the water, finally bidding it a good evening as she cuts up White Lion Hill, along Queen Victoria Street and finally back to Cannon Street. Once she gets into her little apartment, she locks the door, drinks water and goes to bed. As sleep embraces her, she considers what a superb day it has been; she also knows how *At Florian* will end.

Memory Lane

Waking at daybreak after her early night, Estella writes for almost four hours before it's time to get ready to meet Oscar. She's very close to finishing now, and the closer she gets, the more apprehensive she feels. Whilst writing *At Florian* she's been inhabiting that world, and finishing the story means that, inevitably, she'll have to leave the world she's created. She doesn't want to do that. She doesn't want to say goodbye to the characters either. She's enjoyed immersing herself in the streets of Venice, building the relationship between the protagonists and telling their back stories. She feels simultaneously the urge to complete and release the story to be enjoyed by others and the desire to keep this world to herself for her own selfish escapism. She has to remind herself of Rosie and her desire to find out what happens next.

When she goes outside, she finds herself bathed in crisp sunshine. A welcome change from the recent grey days. When the car pulls up to the kerb, she finds that Igor is alone.

"He have something to do at Selfridges. We collect him there."

"Okay. How are you today, Igor?"

"Okay. Little sad with news from home."

They discuss the war and his fears for his country, but he quickly ends this conversation. Estella has noticed that he tries to be as positive as he can, at all times. She finds this admirable and endearing. She finds him interesting, compassionate and intuitive. He asks her why she's going back to Madrid, and she realises that she hasn't explained what's going to happen. She was in such a bad way when she arrived from Madrid that she just slept in the car. She tells him all about *Los Amores de Oscar,* and then she tells him about the novel.

"Oscar doesn't know about the novel, Igor. Please, would you not tell him?"

"No problem. I never chat with Oscar. I am driver to him. Nothing more. We are not friends like you and me." Her eyes prick with tears. She smiles at his reflection. She feels enormous gratitude.

"I think you are good writer. You see and feel much."

"Thank you, Igor."

Oscar rushes out of the side entrance from the food court and jumps into the car next to Estella. Today he's wearing jeans and loafers, a white shirt and a brown leather jacket. She can't discern any brands. He also has a baseball cap in his hand. Incognito, she thinks. Interesting!

"Sorry," he says. "One of my brands has a release today, so I thought I'd kill two birds with one stone and do the post at Selfridges. So, all done for now."

She smiles at him but doesn't know what to say. Oscar always says that money isn't a thing for him, but he spends so much time working on his socials. She wonders if it's a way to be busy. She's never seen him with a book. He doesn't seem to have any friends. She knows that he must go to the gym and maybe jogs, but otherwise she hasn't the faintest idea what he does all day other than post stuff. The idea is quite depressing to her.

She realises that quite a silence has just occurred since she didn't know what to say. She gives him an encouraging smile.

"Anyway, to celebrate the great weather, I thought we would go up to Hampstead. Have you ever been?"

Oh, bloody hell, she thinks. Do I pretend that I've never been there, or do I tell him that I know it well? She's getting tired of walking on eggshells.

"Yes, I know it quite well. I had a part-time job there when I was at drama school." He looks a bit shocked.

"You went to drama school?"

"Yeah. Didn't you Google me?"

"No. I knew that you didn't have any social media, but I never thought to Google you."

"Nuria did. That's how she knew that I'd acted before."

"She never said anything about it to me."

"Who first suggested that I play your mother?"

"Nuria."

"You never wondered if I could do it?" He looks nonplussed.

"The very first day that I met you, you pretended to be a Netflix employee, and when you discovered you were having dinner with four twenty-something Netflix stars, you became some sort of... sophisticated socialite. Sometimes you just become someone else for a bit. I didn't realise that it was acting skill; I thought it was just your personality." She laughs with sheer joy.

"You saw them all? You saw all the different people?" He laughs too.

"Well, yeah! Sometimes they were all there at once. That was scary. Mostly, though, they come one by one." He pauses. "Not so much recently." He looks at her and furrows his brow by way of a question.

"They're still here." She touches her belly. "But I don't trust them as much as I used to. I listen to them, but I don't let them take charge anymore."

That seems to make perfect sense to him. She finds herself reevaluating their relationship. For a man with almost no conversation and a crippling inability to make friends, he's now stunned her more than once with his powers of observation. He's inconsistent. She wants to say something friendly, but she has to consider his intentions towards her, so she just gives him a warm smile.

Igor drops them on Hampstead Lane, and they walk along the path to Kenwood House.

"My Mum and Dad used to bring me here when I was a child." She tells him. "We used to come to London to visit my Dad's sister, Florence. She lived in Highgate," she points back that way. "She was rather eccentric. I don't think my dad liked her very much, but he liked being able to bring his family to London to stay for free in her house. I liked her; she always told the truth, even if it meant being rude." He smiles. She understands that when it comes to family, he doesn't have a lot to contribute to a conversation, so she asks him where he'd like to go.

"I think there's a garden with a pergola. Do you know how to get there?"

"Sure," she says, and decides to make him walk the long way. It's lovely being out and about and after yesterday's walk, she feels limber and ready to stroll for hours. She's been missing her swims.

He loves the Hill Garden and the pergola, and they start to name all the films that it's appeared in. He asks her permission to post a selfie of them by one of the niches, and she agrees because Nuria has asked her to let herself be seen with him officially. When filming starts, they'll be teasing her part in the series, and she needs to start to get used to this posting malarky. By the time he's put on filters and posted the bloody thing, she feels quite bored with the whole process. She gets them onto Heath Road and then Heath Street.

"Did you have somewhere in mind for lunch?"

"No. Do you know somewhere?"

"There's Heath Street Kitchen; they have a good reputation."

"Do you think we can get a table without a reservation?"

"Not sure. We can try."

They're squeezed onto a table towards the back of the restaurant by a helpful young person who almost certainly knows who Oscar is. They order sparkling water, she feels dehydrated, and Oscar gets a beer. They share four small plates: pumpkin ravioli, baked goats' cheese, seared scallops and in honour of their first meeting, chicken schnitzel. It's tasty and the atmosphere is nice. She suggests that he posts something, and there's a lot of faff getting the shot right, and she regrets initiating it, but he seems so pleased.

When they're ready to go, she asks if he minds if they just take a short walk to where she used to work. She knows that the shop isn't there anymore, but to be so close and not to visit seems wrong. They cut down Oriel Place to Hampstead High Street and cross over and up to Flask Walk. The first part of this road is pedestrianised and lined with Georgian shopfronts. The history of the place is palpable, which is why she loved working here so much. She worked at a bookshop at the very end opposite The Flask pub, but the first shop on the left from the High Street had been the most glorious treasure house of secondhand and antiquarian books as well as maps and prints. The elderly owner had been encouraging and interested in her. The whole street had been a little down at heel in those days and now it is very smart and chi-chi. It takes the shine off it, rather.

She dutifully points out where she worked, but she doesn't talk about the antiquarian bookshop because he'd confuse it with the one that's there now, which is a whole other world. They buy gelato from Oddono's. She has stracciatella and he gets pistachio. They wander down the High Street, and when the gelato is finished, she goes into the bookshop and wonders what it will feel like when her book is there.

"I haven't read a book for years," he tells her. "Do you read?"

"Usually, I read quite a bit, but when I'm... not well, I find it hard to concentrate on reading."

"Rafa, you're really well now." He says, with emotion in his voice. "You should get yourself a book." It's a sweet thing to have said. She sees Tracy Chevalier's *The Glass Maker*. She's read the reviews; she's already a huge fan, and when *At Florian* is finished, it'll be fun to read something. Especially something about Venice. She takes it to the counter and buys it. It feels significant. It feels positive. She's moving forward.

When Igor pulls up in front of her apartment block, she keeps their farewell brief. She's going to see him again in ten days. She thanks him for a lovely day. Wishes him a good day tomorrow and says she'll see him in ten days' time. She thanks Igor. Just as she thinks that she's got away with it and is turning to open the door, he gently pulls her back towards him and tries to kiss her on the lips. She turns her head and puts up a hand to make a barrier. She sees the hurt in his eyes, but mostly she feels his restrained anger.

"Sorry," he says tightly.

"I'll see you next week," she says and climbs out of the car.

Not all of the anger is his.

The End and The Beginning

Back in Hereford, she finishes *At Florian* in a sleepless flurry on Friday night through to Saturday morning and then, without feeling the need to go to bed, during the rest of Saturday rereads and edits; all the while tears streaming down her face. Tears for the story and tears for finishing this exercise that's brought her such enjoyment and peace.

Once the editing is finished and she's almost desiccated from the constant tears, she sends the file to Rosie. She drinks water and makes herself eat something. The cats stare at her as if she's insane. She showers and crawls into bed. She's warm and hollowed out and sleeps deeply. She's soaring on the air currents above that Tibetan valley and looking down on the yaks and people, feeling the heat of the sun on her back and squealing with the pure joy of being alive. She's wheeling, gliding, swooping and whooping.

When she wakes, she feels wonderfully refreshed. The cats sit on the rug by her bed, staring. She says hello to them, but they don't respond. She doesn't blame them. She switches on her phone to find out what day it is, what time it is almost to find out who she is.

It's Sunday, 10 am. She has a few emails and messages. She can't remember when she last looked at her phone. She switched it off when she went to bed on Thursday night. Did she switch it on when she got up? Surely, she did. She remembers waking on Friday and writing. Suddenly seeing the time on the laptop, she'd hastily bundled everything together and gone down to Cannon Street to hail a cab to Paddington. When she got to Paddington, the direct train was already on the board. Once settled, she'd opened her laptop to write. When she got home, she opened her laptop again. She's seen the emails, but the text messages have been there for a while. She vows to do better.

SATURDAY 10:06 AM

Win:

Are you back, old bean? Still on for dinner tomorrow?

FRIDAY 6:17 AM

Oscar:

Rafa, I'm so sorry. We had such a lovely day. I ruined it. Please forgive me.

FRIDAY 1:24 PM

Oscar:

Rafa, please.

FRIDAY 9:02 PM

Oscar:

Are you okay, Rafa?

SATURDAY 1:42 AM

Oscar:

Rafa?

SATURDAY 12:38 PM

Oscar:

Rafa, I'm getting worried.

SATURDAY 9:44 PM

Oscar:

Rafa, just text me, please.

SUNDAY 2:18 AM

Oscar:
Rafa. Please.

SUNDAY 8:01 AM

Oscar:
Rafa?

Some of the sense of wellbeing dissipates, but she makes the effort to maintain what she can. She leads the cats downstairs and feeds them. She sorts out their litter trays. She texts Win.

Sorry for rude lateness of reply! Offer still open? 7:30 pm?

Win
I've had a better offer. You can bugger off!

😟

Win
😂 See you later!

Maybe. Maybe not...

Win
🙄

7:30 pm. I come bearing a gift.

Win
Just the one?!!!!

Greedy! CUL8R.

She responds to Oscar.

I forgot to turn my phone on when I got up on Friday. I just turned it on and have seen your messages. I wasn't ignoring you. I have to remember to turn the phone on in the morning. Looking forward to seeing you next week.

Within seconds.

Oscar:
You're okay?

All good. Busy.

Oscar:
Good. Why so busy?

She feels her irritation building. The only person she texts is Win and there's always a purpose to their exchanges. When people want to chat to her on text, she feels it's an intrusion. If they called her to chat, she'd make a decision about whether she wanted to speak to them or not. She'd have the option to put the call to voicemail, but she feels honour bound to respond to a text message. She knows that it isn't rational, but she seems bound to this code.

Washing, cleaning, cooking. I've been away for a while. Stuff to catch up with.

Oscar
Okay, I understand. I'll let you get on.

She dithers.

Thanks. Have a lovely day.

Oscar
Gracias, Rafa.

She imagines him at a loose end in Madrid, wondering what to do with his day. She wants to text him to phone Víctor, but she knows that Víctor crossed a line ten years ago. She has to consider how she felt when Oscar kissed her, but there's a difference; Oscar liked Víctor's kiss. She responded to Oscar's kiss, but can't honestly say that she enjoyed it. She remembers how she felt when he embraced her the night of the party in the foyer of The Ned; that she really enjoyed. She enjoyed it so much that she'd felt real shame. His kiss in Madrid had triggered anxiety. She knows that she responded, but that had been his desire flowing into her and responding to his own kiss. It wasn't her desire.

She just can't help feeling that Víctor's the right person for Oscar.

After that Sunday, Oscar takes to texting her once a day. She's pleased that it's just the once so responds cheerfully. He sometimes sends her pictures of what he's doing. She imagines they're the same as the pictures on his social media feeds. He always looks perfect and curated.

On Monday she starts swimming again and realises instantly how much she's missed it. She sends an email to Nuria and asks if there's any chance of getting a hotel with a swimming pool in Madrid. She feels listless now that *At Florian* is with Rosie, so she starts to work on scripts three and four so that she doesn't get maudlin. It's while she's working with these on Tuesday morning that her phone rings, showing Rosie's number.

"Hi Rosie, how are you?"

"Oh my God, Estella! I did not see that coming." Estella laughs.

"You just finished it?"

"Yeah. I'm still reeling."

"Did you enjoy it?"

"So much! I can't believe it's over."

"Me too! I'm feeling bereft."

"I can see that you would. I'm going to send my assessment to Peter. I know that the sales team already have a few people interested. With my synopsis and some excerpts, they can start to get some bids in."

"What about editing?"

"Minimal. Speed is of the essence here. We're going to need to get some photos for the sales package. When are you free for a photoshoot?" Estella senses the panic inching into her lungs, but breathes through it.

"I don't live in London."

"Okay, when can you come?"

"Does this need to be done quickly?"

"This week would be ideal. Next week would be tolerable."

"I'm leaving for Madrid on Sunday for the week. I suppose I could come on Thursday."

"You don't sound very excited, Estella."

"I'm excited for the book, but less so for the photoshoot. I also just got back from a trip to London."

"Estella, you're going to have to get used to being photographed. Besides, you're already all over social media with Oscar Pérez. When the book comes out, there'll be travel for readings, signings and guest appearances to boost sales. You're going to be okay with that, right?" The panic turns into more of a tingle of excitement. A life less boring.

"Yes, sorry Rosie. Would Thursday work?"

"Great. Let me call the photographer and check availability; I'll call you back this afternoon."

After her swim, Estella makes an appointment for the following day at the hairdresser and then walks for the first time since she came out of hospital into the centre of Hereford. It's a Tuesday afternoon in March, and she tries to take the less frequented streets. It's quite sunny, so she wears a pair of sunglasses and puts her headphones on. She practically sidles down East Street to get to Church Street and to her objective. Estella can't remember a time before Robes graced the pedestrianised street leading up to the glorious cathedral. Its large display windows with their effortlessly attractive displays have always been a draw for her. Here in Hereford, she can buy the best names in women's ready to wear dresses. She opens the door with the excitement that she always feels and steps up into the light and airy space. The poised proprietress, Jacqui, smiles at her warmly and welcomes her as she drops the catch on the door and flips the sign to closed.

"Well, Estella," she purrs, "tell me all about it!" They go through to the changing rooms and Estella tells her the story of meeting Oscar, getting suspended and the exciting new opportunities in her life.

"What do you need?"

"Probably three or four dresses for daytime and I need a couple of outfits for evening. You know, dinner or drinks."

"Or a club?" A cheeky smile met by Estella's rolled eyes.

"Perhaps some skirts, trousers and tops, if you have the bubble type trousers?"

It's fun. It always is, but she's never been able to do this without a budget before. Jacqui knows what she likes and what suits her; Estella simply spends the time in the dressing room in her slip trying on different outfits. She finds that she's buying clothes a size smaller than she usually does and puts that down to the swimming. In the end, there's so much stuff that they have to call a taxi to pick her up and get all the bags back to her house. She feels prepared. When she has the right clothes, she feels capable of anything.

One of the many outfits that she bought at Robes is a Vetono skirt and jacket in lime green with a floral drapey top that goes underneath. On Thursday, for the photo shoot, she's paired the outfit with powder blue shoes, a matching scarf and her hair, cut a little shorter than usual, looks shiny and smart. She's made up her eyes and used her lipstick. The session is more fun than she'd anticipated. The photographer's studio is in Mile End, which feels significant since she's been so close by in Limehouse so recently. The photographer is a lovely young woman, and she makes the shoot enjoyable. Estella declines the opportunity to look at the photos, but Mary encourages her, and they don't look anywhere near as bad as she had thought that they would.

As the day is dry, she decides to walk down to Bread Street Kitchen for a meal before she returns to the station to go back to Hereford. As she's walking there, a huge motorcycle growls past her, brakes and returns.

"Estella?" He kisses her on both cheeks.

"Chico, ¿qué tal?" Blushing.

"How come you're here?"

"I had an appointment in Mile End. I thought I'd get something to eat at Bread Street. It was so good last week."

"I can't believe it. I'm on my way to a business meeting, or I'd come with you. Are you free tonight?"

"Sorry, Chico, I'm going back to Hereford this afternoon. I'm just here for the day." She feels flattered that he looks so regretful.

"When will you come again to London?"

"Not sure, at the moment. I leave for Madrid on Sunday for a week. Maybe a couple of weeks after that?"

"The show will finish before that. Will you be coming to Madrid again soon?"

"I think so. I'm doing some writing for *Los Amores de Oscar,* and I have a small part in season three." He looks a little surprised at that, but smiles.

"We shall see each other there?"

"I'd like that."

"I'm so sorry, I must go." Two more hasty cheek kisses and the machine growls away.

When she sits in Vera's conservatory the next day after her swim, the woman smiles at her.

"You've been practising, haven't you?"

"Yes." In fact, she had practised on the train back to Hereford the previous afternoon.

"Your aura is so much better. I'm surprised that you've achieved so much in such a short time."

"Oh, there's still a lot to release, Vera, but I do feel that there's hope; I feel so relieved to be letting go of feelings that have been bothering me for so long. Letting go of other people's feelings that I've been carrying around for decades."

"What are we working on today?"

"My back, please." Vera gets her into the quiet place where she can listen to her body, and she asks her to focus on the pain in her back. Estella begins to realise that there are a number of discomforts that she can now itemise. There's the tightness in her neck first, then an ache across the muscles around her shoulder blades and between them. Then there is the odd sense of disjointedness in her lower back that sometimes shoots down into her thighs. She decides to focus on the shoulder blades and between them.

She asks her body where this pain came from. She feels a small catch in her throat, and they start to speak for her.

"Other people's feelings are so heavy," says Little Estella.

"Other people's disapproval weighs me down," complains Stel.

"Other people's disappointment is such a burden," sighs Ella.

"Other people's scepticism is pulling me down," groans Esta.

"My dissatisfaction is a constant encumbrance," growls Sella.

"My self-loathing is an endless oppression," moans Stella.

"My boredom is dragging me under," whispers Miss.

"We are struggling with the weight of our thoughts," they realise.

Then come a few tears, and she breathes with purpose, letting go of the self-limiting beliefs that she's carried for so long and which have caused her back to bend and ache under their weight. She releases the judgments of others that she took so deeply to heart that they became a part of her. There's so much of it, so many moments where she felt disapproval, dissatisfaction, disaffection, discomfort...

"It's okay, Estella, you've got this. There's a lot to process here. We won't be able to discharge it all at once. You may need to revisit this a few times. Let go of what you can."

The headphones bring her the Gregorian-like chant, and Vera puts the crystals between her shoulder blades and the chair cushion. Estella leans back and lets the music take her. She stands on a mountain, her bare feet planted on the earth, her arms raised above her head, hands open and her head thrown back. She can feel the energy of the earth moving through her and being transmitted into the air above her. She feels the warmth of the sun and the caress of a breeze. The energy moving through her is drawing out her self-limiting beliefs and burning them up until they become pure energy that leaves through her hands and goes out into the atmosphere to give power to others. She says the same thing over and over again: I love you, I'm sorry, please forgive me, thank you. I love you, I'm sorry, please forgive me, thank you. I love you, I'm sorry, please forgive me, thank you. I love you, I'm sorry, please forgive me, thank you. I love you, I'm sorry, please forgive me, thank you.

Tears of relief and joy stream down her upturned face.

...

Her face is still wet when she opens her eyes. Vera sits opposite her with her eyes closed and her arms stretched out, hands splayed. A smile plays around her mouth. She opens her eyes and gives Estella a brilliant smile.

"Thank you, that was incredible."

"You felt the energy?"

"I drew on it. I'm fully charged. Where was it coming from?"

"A mountain."

"Lush!"

"Was I speaking?"

"Ho'oponopono."

"I'd forgotten all about it."

"You hadn't. It was just waiting until it was needed."

"I'm cleansed." Another huge smile.

"So am I."

It feels like the week has vaporised and when Igor arrives on Sunday to take her to the airport, she has so much to tell him that they're still chatting as he pulls up at the terminal. He's cross that she didn't call him for the Thursday photoshoot, but she's still worried about money because she doesn't yet know what they will pay for the novel. She knows it won't be a huge amount, but it will be another buffer of cash between her and needing to go back to a nine-to-five job. She's not sure that she could do that anymore.

On the journey to the airport, she tells Igor about Vera and the technique for releasing blocked energy. Igor listens to her intently and asks questions from time to time.

"This is religious, no?"

"I find it spiritual. I feel uncomfortable with the idea of religion because, for me, it suggests a limitation of beliefs and a fixed way of looking at the world. I think humanity's strength is that it can adapt, accept and embrace the changes that happen in society. Organised religion stops us from doing that. Religion is about saying that people are allowed to do one thing but not allowed to do another."

"Yes, yes, I understand. So, this is spiritual. Yes, it is of spirit. It is something cannot be seen, just feel."

"Yes, that's it."

"I want try."

"Great. You can stay at my house. I can arrange for you to try it."

Estella Marks: Writer

Meeting the script writing team is nerve-wracking for Estella. She feels like she has stepped on their toes massively coming along with her ideas for season three. On Monday morning, as she travels in a taxi to meet with them, she is sweating and nervous. There are four of them. Two young men, one young woman and a man who looks about forty. Nuria introduces Estella to them, tells them all that the scripts for episodes one and two need to be done by Friday and leaves.

The older man, Francisco, smiles at Estella.

"Well, thanks to you, Estella, that's not going to be hard!" His Spanish is beautifully enunciated.

"Are you annoyed that they brought me in?" She blurts. All four look surprised.

"Not at all," says the young woman, Marijose. "Why would we be annoyed?"

"Isn't *Los Amores de Oscar* your baby? You developed the scripts for the other two seasons." The four of them glance at one another in amusement.

"You know, Estella, that this was not our concept?" Francisco asks.

"They just give us an outline," says the young man with glasses, Javi. "We just write the dialogue to the specifications we get given."

"Occasionally they accept a suggestion or an idea from us," says the fourth member of the team, Alejandro, "but, mostly, we just join the dots."

"What do you think of seasons one and two, Estella?" Asks Francisco. She hesitates and looks around at their amused faces.

"They're okay," she says, and they all start laughing. The tension is broken and from that moment she knows that it's all going to be fine. In fact, they all work well together, which makes the experience much more enjoyable. They go out for long lunches together in fabulous local restaurants with set lunch menus that are delicious and a steal. She meets their partners and their dogs. They fall into a relaxed familiarity.

Evenings are more complicated and harder work with Oscar, but she's staying at a hotel with a pool, and she gets at least one swim a day, sometimes two. One evening, she tells Oscar she's unavailable and has a wonderfully boozy dinner with Elvira. They laugh quite a bit and talk about their lives. Elvira tells her that she was married, but explains in detail all the reasons why it didn't work. They laugh even more at that. They arrange to meet up next time Estella's in town. The week goes absurdly fast, and before she has time to think, she's on her way back to the UK.

The following week, she's working on scripts when Peter Dunbar calls her to say that he's got offers for *At Florian* and sends her a summary of what's on the table. She measures the offers in terms of how long they will keep her from having to go back to a nine to five job. The upfront offers for the rights to the book are all much of a muchness, but the royalties vary, as do the promotional packages and what involvement the publisher wants from her. She works through it all with Peter's guidance and picks the deal that has the best promotional package and an upfront payment that translates into ten months of not having to work. She is slowly financing the just over nine years that she has until she can start to draw her pension.

The decision on the publisher requires another trip to London to sign documents, meet her editor and set the schedule. There's also the matter of the case against her employer, who has decided to settle out of court and has agreed to pay her the equivalent of two years' salary in compensation. The lawyer has paperwork to sign. The financial adviser also wants to meet to discuss an investment opportunity. She knows that she's going to have to be in London for a few days, and she decides that she really can't do without a pool for a whole week. She books into The Dilly.

Weeks become months. There's a sort of rhythm. When she's going to London or to the airport, Igor (who she has discovered is a deductible business expense) comes to stay. He arrives the day before and has a session with Vera. He sleeps in Estella's spare room, and they make their journey the following day. The time in Madrid is divided between working with the writers, evenings with Oscar and a night out with Elvira. Twice she accedes to Oscar's entreaty to stay for the Saturday, and they take day trips to Toledo and Segovia. He doesn't try to kiss her again, and she feels that he's beginning to lose interest.

She feels guilty about her cats being left behind with only the ministrations of the cat sitter, also a deductible business expense, and she notices how much needier they are when she comes home. They're getting older and she worries for them, but she's living her best life. She continues to work with Vera and invests in the computer programme, silver box and crystals Vera uses in their sessions together. She takes these with her on her travels with huge benefits to her wellbeing. She enjoys her Sunday night dinner with Win whenever she's in Hereford.

The eight scripts are finalised in excellent time and the filming, on an extremely tight schedule is set for August and September at a studio on the outskirts of Madrid with a few outdoor locations in the suburbs. *At Florian* is being released in mid-October and a tour of bookshops for readings and signing sessions has been set. She'll be on radio a couple of times, too.

She can hear Esta complaining that they aren't booked for any TV chat shows and that makes her giggle.

She manages to see Anna a couple of times and they further explore the culinary delights of the metropolis together. One evening in June, Oscar takes her to a private gallery viewing in Madrid and she sees Chico but hardly has the opportunity to speak with him. They go out for dinner after the opening and Chico is part of the party, but they get seated at opposite ends of the table from each other. They exchange looks. Oscar never lets her get very far from him. He calls her his talisman. She feels like an inmate of his harem.

The date for departure for the full two months in Madrid is suddenly here. Igor has stayed the night following a session with Vera and they are getting ready to leave the house. The cat sitter is booked, but Win, sensing her disquiet has also agreed to pop in to see them from time to time. Estella's packed two huge suitcases and has a substantial bag for the cabin with her electronics. Elvira's found a flat for her in a building with a pool and the production company has agreed to put her up there for the two months of the shooting. It's going to be sixty days of intense work for Oscar and the regular cast. Each episode has been scheduled one week of filming. Monday is always a table read, discussion, rewrite, rehearsal, sometimes filming and then they shoot from Tuesday to Sunday. The script for the next episode being given to the actors every Sunday prior to the Monday table read. It's regimented and relentless.

Oscar also has a relentless schedule of posts and appearances to raise excitement over the forthcoming season three. He needs to include Estella in some of his posts and the *Los Amores de Oscar* official social media feeds are all set to introduce her as a guest cast member without revealing her role. She understands the importance and she knows that it's going to support the pre-publication hype for *At Florian*, but she finds it tedious. Her publisher's social media team is curating a feed on an account that they have set up for her. She's been trained to take photos, but usually she just gets Oscar's photos and sends them onto the team.

Oscar realises that this account in her name has appeared during the filming of episode one and he doesn't hold back in telling her how hurt he is that she hadn't told him what she was doing. He isn't hurt. He's angry and she can feel it. She tells him, lightly, that she doesn't see why she should have told him as he isn't a reader and secrecy around the book had been essential. She experiences another moment, as at The Ned, when she thinks he's going to shout at her. Almost like a cartoon character, he seems to go dark around the eyes and his fists clench, and she feels a cold trickle of fear.

Whenever filming finishes before dark, she and Oscar go out for dinner, to the theatre, the opera or a gallery opening and encourage the press to photograph them. It's near the end of filming on episode four when they return to Los Montes de Galicia for dinner. Oscar seems unusually tense. As they are preparing to leave the restaurant, he tells her that tomorrow is his mother's birthday.

"Are you going to visit?" He nods.

"Would you come with me?"

It feels too intimate, but what's she going to do? He's alone. She knows that part of that is the result of his choices, but she's felt the pain of the relationship with his mother and that compels her to agree to go with him. They agree to go as soon as filming finishes the following day.

It's around 7 pm when they approach the apartment block in Salamanca, which is a traditional, old-fashioned, palace-style building with small windows and no terraces. The moment she sees it, she thinks of dark interior rooms around a central courtyard and close interior corridors. She has experience of apartments like this and the idea of it makes her feel claustrophobic. Memories flicker like a cinefilm in the back of her mind, but she chooses to ignore them. The living room and dining room are probably relatively light and airy, but she suspects that there will be dark wood panelling and heavy dark wooden furniture with dust-capturing finials and lace curtains. Images flash and bubble, demanding her attention, but she fights them. She regulates her breathing. He has a key to the main entry door. The passageways to navigate inside the building are wide and faced with cooling marble to fight the heat of a Madrid summer, but they're dim and musty. They take a shabby lift to the fourth floor, Oscar's jaw working with tension, his face paling the closer they get to their destination. She's tempted to take his hand to show friendly support, but she has to be careful, knowing what he thinks he wants from her.

The fourth-floor corridor is dimmer than the ground floor and there are smells of fried food and the sound of televisions behind the doors. Oscar moves slowly towards the last door on the left. He stands in front of it. He rings the bell and looks fixedly at the spy hole with what looks to her like defiance. He looks very young as he stands there, his shoulders a little too high, his fists clenched. She hears footsteps tap quickly to the door, and then there is a pause before they move more slowly away again. He sighs, and she feels his anger as he starts to walk slowly back towards the lift. She's about to follow him when she hears another set of footsteps behind the door, slower and heavier this time. She looks up at the spy hole with calm steadiness and doesn't move away until the footsteps shuffle a muffled retreat. She thinks that both the inhabitants have had a look at her now.

She decides not to tell him.

On the street, he appears completely normal, but she's aware that he's both confused and angry, possibly even a bit relieved. She remembers that during his confession at the Darwin, he said that if they opened the door, he wasn't sure what he'd do.

"Please, can we get a drink?" She asks. He nods. They get back into the car, and he tells Rocio to take them to Salmon Guru. It's a bar they've been to before with great cocktails. It's busy, and every other person wants to take a selfie with him, some with both of them. The back of her neck prickles with discomfort when this happens as Oscar takes the opportunity to pull her closer to him. Finally, they get taken to a booth towards the back of the bar where there aren't so many people, and a curtain keeps them safe from being bothered.

"What did you send today?"

"Flowers, a card and a bottle of champagne. She's fifty today."

She can't speak. She's going to be fifty-eight in a few weeks. She feels herself get hot with discomfort and alarm. He doesn't notice.

"I thought that today... she might have decided to open the door. She must be having a celebration of some kind."

A waiter arrives opportunely. She has a little longer to recover.

"Salmon Sherbert?" She nods. She feels herself cooling and able to speak again.

"Perhaps it's time to stop making these visits, Oscar. It's giving you too much pain. Every time you do this, you have the build-up, the anticipation, and then the anxiety of standing there waiting to see if the door opens. The worst is the aftermath. You're angry, hurt, disappointed, maybe even relieved. You've just put yourself through hell."

His jaw works. His anger is pushing at her stomach, and she puts her hands there to protect herself. She waits for the explosion. She breathes deeply and makes an effort not to tense up; she sends compassion across the table. She is working on unconditional positive regard when he speaks again.

"This is the ninth year." He says tightly. "I'll do this for ten years. I'm not giving up on them easily. I'm demonstrating my commitment to them."

She understands his plan, but she wants to tell him that the look of defiance on his face and his body language at the door are never going to encourage any person behind that door to open it. She would think twice about opening a door to someone looking like that. She considers telling him, but her gut tells her that it's a waste of time. She thinks that perhaps he shows that face to ensure that they don't open the door, and he can complete his ten years of commitment and prove he's the better person.

She realises that she has started to feel more than a little frightened of him.

As they are leaving, they have to perform again in the circus of celebrity for the Salmon Guru's clients, and as they are being photographed with a teenage girl between them, she catches Chico watching her. She tries to convey to him in a single look the conflict that she feels about what she's doing. Something must get through, because he smiles at her and rolls his eyes slightly. She darts her eyes to Oscar subtly and then slightly rolls hers. He smiles sadly. He doesn't approach them, and Oscar doesn't see him, so they leave without speaking to him.

The relentless filming continues, and she's surprised by what a difference the new style of script and the deeper storyline are making on the show. She's also impressed that the cast has also stepped up their game. Oscar's father, in particular, is a fine actor. Víctor is superb and she's excited for the twist that he doesn't yet know about. She appears for the first time in episode seven. Oscar meets her in the final scene. She's nervous and excited, but mostly she just wants to do it. She notices that a number of the producers are on set as they're setting up for the first take. Her only worry is Chico's comment about her accent; she doesn't want to sound British while she delivers the lines in Spanish.

Take One:

A street in the suburbs of Madrid. A down-at-heel community. Oscar waits by the door to a supermarket. A woman walks out with a bag of shopping.

"Excuse me," Oscar says to her, "are you Isabela Sánchez Rodrigo?" She looks terrified and tries to run away. Not a lot of acting required for that these days with Oscar. He gently catches her and stops her from running. They look into each other's eyes. She conveys sadness and conflict.

"Mum?" He asks her. She starts to cry. She puts her hands on either side of his handsome face.

"Yes, son." She tells him.

The shot is held for a moment and then they'll roll the credits to end episode seven. As soon as the director calls cut, Oscar crushes her to him and there's a ripple of applause. She pushes away from Oscar and looks bemusedly at the people on the set. Nuria approaches.

"It's okay," she says. "It's relief. The gamble paid off; you really can act."

The Shit Hits the Fan

On the Sunday night that episode seven wraps, Oscar is pounding on the door of Estella's apartment. The script for the final episode has been given out. The plot twist is out of the bag and Oscar is furious. Having foreseen this eventuality, Estella is not at home. A couple of nights earlier, during a conversation with Elvira, Estella had told Elvira her concerns over sounding like a Brit speaking Spanish because of Chico's comment. Elvira, with her interest in art, knew who Chico was and told Estella that the artist was in the process of hanging a show of new work at a gallery in Salamanca. The private viewing is on Monday, so Estella is pretty sure that Chico will be there on Sunday until late, so she's taking a chance and knocking on the door of the gallery.

A young person opens the door and is almost certainly about to tell her that they're closed when they realise who they're talking to. Estella apologises for the inconvenience of her visit, but nonetheless explains that she'd like to speak quickly to Chico. He appears very soon after looking crumpled and exhausted.

"Chico, I'm so sorry, I won't take much of your time. I don't think I'll get to see the show and I'm leaving Madrid as soon as we wrap at the end of this week or early next. I think it'll be a while before I get to return to Madrid. I want to tell you something. I'm not sure if it's important to you or not, but it's important for me that you know." Chico looks at her sadly.

"You're leaving?"

"Yes, I have to. I have a novel being published in a few weeks and I need to be in the UK to promote it. Also, I have to get away from him. I've been holding him at arm's length for too long. It's starting to get dangerous. He's starting to scare me."

"You aren't with him?"

"No, I've never been with him. Back in February he tried to persuade me into a relationship, but I told him that it wasn't what I wanted. But..."

"He wouldn't take no for an answer." She nods.

"I should have run then or, at the very least, been emphatic about it. But I'd just signed the contract for the scripts for *Los Amores de Oscar* and the small role that I play. I couldn't see how I could do all of that if he turned against me. I was weak." He is listening very intently.

"If the coverage on social media was right, Estella, you weren't in a very good state of mind at that time. Hadn't you just had a... breakdown?" She nods. "Besides, you said no, didn't you?"

"I made it clear that I didn't think it was a good idea. I did everything I could to persuade him it wasn't a good idea. I told him that I wanted to be friends." He nods. "I've done something to the storyline in season three, which is going to make him even angrier. I think the coming week of filming is going to be really hard and I'm a little frightened of what he might say and do. In February, I foolishly agreed to revisit the idea of a relationship after filming ends. It was a very poor decision." Chico steps closer to her.

"Thank you for telling me this. Knowing this is important to me. But your situation is perilous; I see this. Let me have your number?"

They exchange numbers. He talks about meeting when the book has been launched. He suggests Menorca, where he has friends that he visits regularly.

"Estella, there's something that I wanted to tell you in London, and I think that it's really important that you know this. I should have found a way to tell you before. It's about Oscar's mother." He pauses, looking confused and uncomfortable. "Estella, you look very similar to her; like you could be sisters. It's uncanny."

Estella goes cold. She breathes deeply. She rejects the hurt that she feels as pure vanity. She had been right all along. She had said it to Santi. She's a surrogate mother to him. If that's right though, why does he want a physical relationship with her? Freud? It feels disturbing.

"Estella, the way he treats you, it's not as if he thinks of you as a mother. I think, maybe, he hasn't realised the physical similarity. In reality, he doesn't know his mother very well. He didn't spend much time with her after the age of eight and he hasn't seen her for almost nine years."

"Chico, thank you for trying to normalise it, but he knows what his mum looks like." He shrugs an apology.

"I know. Sorry. It's just such a..." he hesitates, "creepy idea. No?" She nods.

"What time is it, Chico?"

"Almost half past eight."

"The apartment isn't far from here, is it?"

"You're going to try and meet her?" She nods. "She's a recluse, Estella. I don't think she's left the apartment in years. After the press coverage and her cancer, she stopped socialising."

"I think she'll see me," Estella tells him. "I went with Oscar a few weeks ago to stand outside the door and not be let in. It was her fiftieth birthday. I think they both saw me through the spy hole. I heard two sets of footsteps come to the door and retreat. If I look like her, I bet she's just as keen to meet me as I am to meet her." He shrugs and makes an appraising face suggesting that she might be right. They hold each other's gaze. She steps forward and he opens his arms. They stand holding one another for a few minutes feeling the electricity weaving through them, into the other and back again. They take strength from it. She steps away holding his gaze and his hands.

"See you in Menorca." They smile, and he nods and lets her out of the gallery door.

She finds the apartment block easily. She rings the bell for the apartment and a young woman's voice, overly bright, almost excited, asks who it is.

"It's Estella."

There's a long silence, a muffling of the handset, murmured conversation and then the front door buzzes open. She retraces the journey of a few weeks ago, pacing herself and watching her breathing, regulating her feelings of anxiety and alarm as she goes. She realises, as she approaches the door, that Oscar has never mentioned his sister's name. She's about to ring the bell, when the door opens and a stunning woman in her late twenties smiles at her girlishly. She's so like Oscar that Estella almost gasps.

"Hola, soy Adela." She awkwardly holds out a tentative hand and Estella gently shakes it.

"Mucho gusto, Adela."

Estella follows her down the dim, claustrophobic corridor with a lingering smell of a recent meal. They pass the doors leading to the interior rooms and Adela shows her into a brightly lit room with windows giving onto the street.

"Le presento a mi madre, Herminia."

Herminia doesn't stand. She remains seated, appraising Estella with something close to a sneer on her face. It's unnerving. For quite a while, they simply look at each other. Estella recognises herself, but a paler, slimmer and less animated version. When she speaks, she has the lisping, lilting cadence that takes Estella straight back to Mexico City. She points emphatically at the chair opposite hers commanding Estella to sit.

"Who told you?" Her tone cold and slightly mocking.

"Chico."

"I miss Chico," says Adela. Her voice is as girlish as her smile. "He was always so lovely to me." Estella has worked with young people for a long time. Why had Oscar never mentioned that his sister has a learning difference? Why hadn't Chico?

"He's a lovely person, isn't he?"

"He's fun."

"Yeah." She and Adela smile at one another. "Do you still paint, Adela?" She nods emphatically.

"Can I show her, mamá?"

"Yes, cariño, but in a little while. Estella and I would like to talk for a bit." Herminia's voice is entirely different as she addresses her daughter. Soft and almost cooing. Adela nods her assent and sits patiently.

"How are you, Herminia? He told me that you had cancer."

"That was some years ago now, thanks to God, that has passed and I have been well for five years now." She crosses herself. Her tone is bored and matter of fact. "Does he treat you well?" The question takes Estella by surprise and then she wonders how to answer. Does he treat her well?

"Generally, yes, he's ... caring."

"But, if he doesn't get his own way?" Herminia smiles maliciously. Estella blushes. Herminia barks a laugh.

"He's always been that way. From the day he started speaking. I'm afraid I don't like my son. I never have." It ought to be shocking, but Estella isn't surprised. "There are reasons. So many reasons." She looks significantly at Adela and back to Estella. "Adela, cariño, would you please go and make some camomile tea?"

"Of course, mamá," she says leaping up and smiling at Estella. She practically skips from the room.

"How much did he tell you about DF?" She sounds deeply bored.

"He told me that your husband, his father, was a violent man. He said that he hit you." Herminia frowns, then shrugs.

"That's what I told him, but that isn't the real reason my marriage broke up." She continues in a dull tone, but Estella can feel Herminia's anger rising. "My husband was very disappointed when our first child was a girl. I got pregnant again after a year or so. I thought for a while that the stress would stop me from falling pregnant again. To my relief, a boy." She holds up her arms in a mocking gesture of success.

"Nacho was over the moon. Oscar became his whole world. Adela loved her little brother too and she always wanted to help to look after him, but she was too little. Her father, once he had Oscar, ignored her at best, but when she craved attention or tried to play with Oscar, he could be quite rough with her." Herminia's eyes darken with the recollection. "He drank quite a bit and a couple of times I caught him slapping her. Finally, one night when Oscar was sick, just a temperature. She was trying to cradle him. He was four at the time and she a little over six. Nacho lost his rag with her and belted her hard across the face, she fell backwards and smacked her head. I've never seen so much blood."

Estella regulates her breath. She stays still and quiet and sends empathy across the room to her doppelgänger. Herminia wants none of it. She continues as if she's telling her about a boring day.

"It was touch and go. The skull was fractured. There were operations. She recovered physically, but as you see, she never reached mental maturity." She meets Estella's eyes and seems surprised at the empathy. She looks contemptuous. "Nacho was arrested. His family was furious with me. They were an old DF family with status and power. I was just the middle-class gold-digger who had tricked their son into marriage. We had to hide for a while; a friend from college days, a Spaniard, helped us out. Nacho didn't go to jail, but a lawyer friend of my family managed to get an injunction taken out against him, but I knew that we needed to get away. I considered giving Oscar to him, but I still loved him in those days. That was my mistake; I should have left him with his father."

Adela comes back into the room carrying a tray with exaggerated care, the tip of her tongue slightly protruding from between her pursed lips. She smiles with the joy of her achievement as she places the tray safely on the table by her mother.

"Gracias, Adela. You've done very well, my daughter." Herminia serves Estella and herself some camomile tea with a little honey. "Adela, would you like to make some Cola Cao for yourself?" Adela looks thrilled at the idea, nods and bounces back out of the room.

"We came to Madrid thanks to the help of the Spanish college friend. He helped us for as long as he could, but he was getting married and he had very little spare cash. I took a job in an office, but the cost of having someone look after Adela meant that most of what I earned was spent on care for her, and I worried about the quality of the care she got. We hadn't been here long enough to be entitled to any support from the government. And there was Oscar." She sighs heavily and sips some of her camomile tea.

"He always wanted something. A toy, a chocolate bar, a new pair of shoes... As soon as something looked less than perfect or used or got broken, he would fly into a rage about it and demand a replacement. If things didn't go the way that he wanted them to go, like a test at school or he went to a birthday party and the food wasn't to his taste, he'd have a tantrum. He had the voice of an angel, and his teachers recommended that he have singing lessons. I couldn't afford that. He was furious that I denied him the lessons. So, when I saw the auditions for the talent show on TV, I couldn't resist."

Alarm bells are ringing in Estella's head. She's maintaining empathy for Herminia's difficult situation, but suddenly behaviours and attitudes are starting to make sense, and she's beginning to think that she might understand what lies below the surface of Oscar's perfectly regulated life. Much of the rest of the story aligns with what Oscar has told her, apart from, of course, the whole issue of Herminia's biggest worry.

What will happen to Adela when her mother dies? If she's to avoid being placed in a state institution for the rest of her life, where the quality of her care will be dependent on the culture of the institution and the character of the people delivering her care, a great deal of money will be required to keep her safe and stimulated.

Adela returns with her glass of chocolate milk held carefully in both hands. A satisfied smile on her face as she sits. She smiles at her mother and then at Estella and starts to suck the brown liquid up through the paper straw she has put into the glass. The older women both smile back at her.

She can't help it. She tries not to, but it's inevitable. She has to ask.

"Did you ever get Oscar screened for learning differences? Did he ever speak to a psychologist?" Herminia looks non-plussed.

"I beg your pardon?"

"It's just that, I'm a teacher. What you're describing sounds exactly like TDAH." Does Oscar have ADHD (TDAH in Spanish)? Oscar's sudden rages, his need to be in control of the schedule and the way that things are done. The habits and ceremonies that seem to help him feel safe. The sudden affection for her. The occasional violent outbursts. The lack of understanding at times and hyper-focus at others. She thinks of all the ADHD students she has worked with and their struggles with the unexpected.

"What is that?" Asks Herminia.

"It's a learning difference. Don't worry about it. I was just interested."

They chat a little more. Herminia isn't a warm person, apart from with her daughter. Making conversation with her is almost as hard as making conversation with her son. Her whole life is caring for Adela, the child that her husband damaged. It's a necessary obsession for her. The fact that Oscar has never mentioned his sister's situation is baffling to Estella, but then she wonders if he understands.

"Did you ever tell Oscar what happened?" She looks significantly at Adela and then back at Herminia.

"No. He didn't need to know that. My explanation meant that he didn't ask about his father or want to see him, which kept us safe."

"Did he understand that her life was always going to be different?"

"I doubt it," says his mother, scoffingly, "he was very self-obsessed. What he loved about his sister was the endless affection that she gave him and the fact that she always obeyed him. She would have jumped out of the window, if he'd asked her to."

"Did she miss him?" Herminia's expression darkens.

"Of course. She still does. Every time he comes and rings the bell; she pleads for me to let him in. He's causing trouble, still, after all these years." Adela doesn't seem to realise that they're speaking about her. She keeps sucking up the chocolate milk even though it's been finished for some time.

"You won't open the door, will you?"

"Never. I can't bear the idea of him coming back here."

"He's planning to keep it up for ten years. Then he says that he'll stop."

"Good, he'll stop coming soon, then."

They're quiet for a while, both looking at the beautiful, contented Adela. Estella is watching her so intently that she doesn't notice that Herminia is looking at her. She's surprised to find the woman scrutinising her when she speaks again.

"Do you think that we're related?" She asks blandly, trying to hide her interest, which Estella can feel. Estella shrugs.

"I don't see how we can be. I don't have any Mexican relatives."

"My grandmother was British. I don't remember her family name, though." Estella laughs.

"Perhaps we are then!"

"Now, mamá?" Asks Adela.

"Yes, my daughter, now."

Adela takes Estella's hand and leads her back into the dim corridor and takes her a little deeper into the apartment to her bedroom. Despite the lack of natural light, the room is pretty and bright; full of flounces, bows and stuffed toys. Adela pulls out folder after folder of pictures and paintings. They're a Naive style with excellent use of colour and bold subjects. There are recurring themes of flowers, cats and perfect symmetrical houses surrounded by regimented gardens. Estella's careful to spend proper time looking at the pictures and asks Adela about what materials she used and which ones she likes best. There are many, many pictures, but when Estella sees that Adela is growing bored, she thanks her for letting her look and gets up. She's almost out of the door when Adela taps her shoulder.

"For you!" She says, holding out a particularly vibrant picture of flowers.

"Thank you, Adela; I love it." She says with genuine pleasure. Back in the living room, she takes the script folder out of her handbag and puts the picture carefully into it for safekeeping and smiles her thanks again to Adela.

"I'd better get going," says Estella, rising from her seat again.

"I hope he does the right thing and marries you," she says crossing herself.

"Oh Herminia, no, the relationship's not like that. We're friends."

"Maybe, Estella, but he won't let you go, you're far too kind and giving; you understand that, don't you?" She smirks. A shiver goes through her, and Herminia sees it.

"Best of luck, Estella." Still smirking. Herminia nods at Adela, who is waiting to take her back to the front door.

At the front door, after Adela has opened it, she looks back down the corridor and then tries to whisper to Estella, but it comes out rather loudly.

"Please tell Oscar that I miss him, Estella. Tell him that I love him." She promises to do this and places a consoling hand on the younger woman's arm.

"I promise," she repeats.

The Wrath of Oscar

It's past eleven when she finally arrives back at her flat, exhausted; her mind working on all of the new information that she now has. As she had expected, Oscar's there, slumped by the front door. She's been rehearsing this conversation for months and she's played it dozens of different ways. She isn't sure which part of the final episode is going to piss Oscar off the most, but she has a feeling that it will be the part where he has to kiss Nito, played by Víctor. Her suspicions turn out to be right.

"How could you betray me like this, Rafa?" he has the now battered script in his hand and he brandishes it as he speaks. "I trusted you!"

"You kiss him, Oscar, but you reject him. I thought that it would be closure for you." She has taken the wind out of his sails. He hasn't thought beyond the necessity to kiss Víctor. He hasn't considered the fact that the story lets him reject his former friend.

In episode eight, Estella has the straight best friend, Nito, realise that he has feelings for Oscar. Nito realises that he's bi and that he loves Oscar as more than a friend. He invites Oscar to the school prom as his date. Oscar is ecstatic. They go together, Oscar sings a song to Nito and as they're walking home, they kiss. Nito's in seventh heaven, but Oscar realises from this kiss that they've shared that Nito isn't the person he wants. The kiss isn't right for him. Nito isn't right for him. Why, he asks, is the kiss never right? Nito is devastated and season three ends with Oscar setting out on a tour with his band, leaving the door open for a further season if Netflix wants it.

He stands there a little longer. Speechless and vibrating with tension. She protects herself and doesn't allow herself to take in any of the confusion and anger that he's exuding. She gives him time.

"So, you were trying to help me put Víctor in his place?"

"No, Oscar. It's a great storyline for the show. It has nothing to do with Víctor, it's about Nito. It's about the show, not about your life and anything that might have happened between you and Víctor. It leaves the door open for another season, but without the tension between Oscar and Nito. Nito won't have any hold over Oscar anymore."

He nods his head as he absorbs it all. She knows that this won't be the last of it. When they get to the filming of the kiss, he's likely to kick back again, but his professionalism will carry him through.

They're still standing in the passageway. There's no way that she's allowing him into the flat. A few minutes later, he seems to come to himself and properly looks at her. It's as if he can't quite understand where he is and why.

"It's late, Oscar, you need to get home and sleep. I'll see you at the table read in the morning, okay?"

He nods, furls the script like a baton and starts off down the corridor. She lets herself into the flat and locks the door. She takes a long shower and then lies down with her headphones. The crystals are tucked inside her waistband against her stomach. She allows the chanting to carry her away. She is walking down an elegant staircase that she recognises from a stately home that she's visited. The further she descends the closer she gets to the sea, which is lapping at the foot of the stairs. On the bottom step, she raises her arms above her head and dives into the sea and swims strongly towards the horizon. She realises after a while that she doesn't need to raise her head to take a breath. She's a fish. She laughs and feels the sensation of bubbles around her gills.

At some point in the night, she must have removed the headphones and crystals; she wakes under the covers and feeling relaxed. The table read goes well and that afternoon she and Oscar rehearse their big scene preparing to shoot it that evening. Whilst she's relaxing in her trailer waiting for the evening shoot, she receives a visit from Víctor.

"How are you, Víctor?"

"It's an amazing storyline, Estella, but did you have to write in the kiss?"

"Víctor, you're an actor. There'll be dozens of people on the set. Both of you will want it to be over as quickly as possible. You're professionals. It'll be a dynamite scene."

"You're right, but the anticipation is horrible. Do you think he'll behave?"

"No, probably not, but he's a professional. He's getting paid, so he'll do it." He nods.

"How about you, Estella? How are you doing?" She smiles.

"Thank you for asking, Víctor. You're a kind person. I'm well, thanks. I'm tired though. These two months have been intense."

"Yeah, you haven't experienced this before, have you? It's hard work and the sitting around waiting for scenes to be set up can be just as exhausting as the filming."

"You're excellent in this season," she tells him.

"Because I have the best lines I've ever been given for this show. Your ideas and the style that you've written it in have changed the whole feel of the thing... For the better, I mean."

"That's a kind thing to say. Thank you."

"Is it true that you have to leave at the end of the week?"

"Yeah, exciting times in the world of Estella Marks! My book comes out in a few weeks."

"Is Oscar in it?" She laughs.

"No. It's a novel."

"Yeah, but have you based a character on him?"

"No," she says again, puzzled.

"He'll be furious." She thinks for a moment and sees what he's saying.

"Oh, my goodness, he will, won't he? You're right." She feels a little tension at the thought, but then she giggles a bit. "I don't think he'll be speaking to me by the end of the week, though. Besides, he doesn't read. I don't suppose he'll read it."

"Why won't he be speaking to you?" She feels real tension now. "Because I'm supposed to be starting a relationship with him once the season wraps."

"He's still expecting that to happen?" She considers this for a moment.

"I think so, yes. He hasn't told me that he's changed his mind. I think that if he had, he would have felt honour bound to say something."

"Yeah," says Víctor, "he would. Like when he texted me to say that we were no longer friends and that he was blocking my number. Like I hadn't got that message loud and clear already!"

"Víctor, I think he might have ADHD. What do you think?"

"I don't really know much about it."

"It would explain a lot."

"I see. I'll Google it."

They talk about the rest of the cast and how hot the weather still is in Madrid. The time comes for the shoot, and it goes well. She wrote the lines and it's so close to her heart that it takes only three takes to get it done. Her two scenes are complete. She just has to do the dubbing into English with Oscar at the end of the week and work with the team on any changes that need to be made to the script over the next few days of filming. It's almost done.

On Friday, they're filming the kiss. Oscar and Víctor are both tense. They look gorgeous in the dinner jackets that they've worn to prom. Nito's bowtie is loosened, but Oscar still looks characteristically immaculate. They walk hand in hand, talking and laughing. At the third lamppost, they stop and kiss.

"Cut!" The director trots over to the lamppost. He says it discreetly, but she hears it, nonetheless.

"Oscar, you're not supposed to enjoy it. It doesn't feel right to you." She sees him blush.

The next take he acts disgusted, and he's asked to tone it down. The next he looks too indifferent. The director calls for a ten-minute reset and asks make-up to come in. She pulls Oscar to one side.

"You go in for the kiss of your life, but it isn't what you thought it would be. It feels wrong. You pull back. It's as if your whole life has just crashed to the ground around you."

"This is a kiss that you've experienced?"

"Yeah. Hold the stages in your mind: excitement, confusion, understanding, devastation."

He mouths the words. Takes a steadying breath. Turns back.

"Take four!"

Finally, they get a take that works. There are some applause. Oscar turns to her and smiles his thanks.

They're in the dubbing studio on Saturday evening. She's tired. She can't wait to get home and see the cats for a while before the book promotion starts. Her flight leaves in the morning. She's on edge about how they will part. She knows that there's going to be a scene. For the time being, she focuses on the job in hand. She watches herself on the screen and says the words that she wrote.

"But mum, why did you leave me?" Oscar asks.

"It was very hard, son, very hard. I was suffering from post-natal depression. I didn't know that at the time. I didn't know that sometimes women feel very low after they give birth because their hormones change. I was so tired all the time."

"You didn't love me?"

"I did love you. I loved you so much, Oscar, but your dad just kept telling me that it was bad for me to be around you. He told me that my depression would affect you, that I would make you sick."

"Dad? Dad said that to you?"

"Yes, son, I think he was worried for you. He thought that you being alone with me all the time would affect your development. I didn't know how long the depression would last."

"Alone with you? But he would have been at home in the evenings and at weekends..."

"Oscar, he didn't live with us. Didn't you know that? He left when I was six-months pregnant. He moved in with your step-mum."

"He never told me that."

"Oscar, I'm sorry, I thought that you knew."

"Mum, I'm so glad that you are back in my life. Please don't disappear on me again."

"Oscar, I love you. I've watched you growing up all these years and becoming the amazing young man that you are, but your father was right. After I gave you to him to care for, my depression became deeper and deeper. I've struggled with my mental health ever since you were born. There are times that I can't get out of bed. There are days that I simply can't stop crying. There are times when I can't work for weeks on end. I'm unreliable. You can't count on me."

"Were you ever depressed before I was born, mum?"

"Maybe a little, when your father left, but I was excited for your arrival. The affair had been going on for a long time. He kept saying he would stop it, that's why I got pregnant. He said he'd stop the affair if we had a child. I so wanted him to come back."

"But before you gave birth to me, you were fine. There was no depression."

"No, not before, son."

"And after you gave me to dad, did you miss me?"

"Every day, son. Every day."

"I'm not going to lose you again, mum. I'm not going to let you be alone anymore."

"Your father won't like it, Oscar."

"I don't care, mum. He's kept us apart for too long."

She quite enjoys the work. Using her voice and working on the timbre and intonation is interesting. Synching the words with the film is also a stimulating challenge and seeing how differently mouths move in different languages.

He takes her out for dinner after they've finished. She's on edge. His original suggestion was that they would go away together when the filming wrapped. He knows that she's leaving in the morning; he has a couple of scenes to finish on set tomorrow and then he'll be dubbing for a week. Since he found out about the novel, he hasn't asked her anything about it. He hasn't asked to read it. He hasn't asked if he's in it. The only thing he's asked about are the details of when she'll be leaving.

He takes her to a small, relaxed, family-run restaurant that they've visited a couple of times before. After the initial flurry of selfies, they are able to sit back and enjoy a beautiful homecooked meal of croquetas, followed by a delicious herby roast chicken with roast potatoes and salad, with a very drinkable Verdejo. They even indulge in a crème caramel each. The conversation is neutral around the plot twist, the excitement of the season three premiere, which will be at the end of November and the chance to relax after the intense period of filming. As they sit, stupefied with food, she begins to release the tension that has been building for her since the confrontation on Sunday night outside her apartment.

"You aren't going to give me a chance, are you?" She's taken completely off guard and the tension snaps back painfully, creating a hot prickly sensation around her head and neck.

"Isn't that what I've been doing, Oscar? You asked me to let you woo me. I've done that, haven't I?"

"And I've failed?" She winces at the edge in his voice.

"It's not a case of failure on anyone's side. We're not really very well suited. Don't you agree?" She feels breathless and lightheaded and concentrates on trying to lengthen her breaths.

"We get on really well," he says earnestly, leaning forward, placing his forearms on the table.

"Oscar," she tries to keep the wobble of fear from her voice, "you don't really know anything about me." He looks at her incredulously.

"You're a teacher;" he starts to enumerate on his fingers, "you're fifty-seven; you live in Hereford; your best friend is called Win; you like to wear dresses; you like to dance; your happy place is Menorca...you're kind and thoughtful."

"Tell me about my parents and my siblings." He looks confused.

"We've never talked about them!"

"You've never asked about them, Oscar. Have I ever been married?" He throws his hands up.

"You never said that you had, so I assume not."

"You never asked, Oscar. I told you that I've had some really bad relationships, but you weren't interested in why they were bad. You never asked me what went wrong."

"I assumed," he snaps back, "it was due to your mental health problems." That comes like a slap to her. She feels herself slipping into the role of victim. She senses her desire to show how hurtful his comment is by letting tears come and getting up and running away from him.

"Oscar, if you thought that my previous relationships failed due to my poor mental health, what did you think would be different between **us**?" The hands fly up again in incomprehension.

"Because we make such a great team!"

"In what way are we a team? What do we do together as a team?"

"We...we..." He cannot find anything to say. She sees him searching his memories and trying to find something that they have done together as a team. She lets him think for a good period of time. The waitress comes and clears the table. Estella asks for the bill. She keeps looking at him. His mind is still working. He's stunned. She pays the bill.

"Oscar, let's get you home."

He seems to come into focus enough to stand. She prompts him to smile and to say thank-you and goodbye. He responds to the prompts as if on autopilot. Rocio is parked nearby. She gets him into the car and asks the driver to take them to his apartment. Estella's never been there. Rocio pulls up outside a glass and chrome tower and points out the door for her. She asks if she should wait, but Estella tells her to go, it's already after ten. She can get a taxi to her own flat.

In the lobby, a concierge jumps up at the sight of Oscar being shepherded through the door. She helps Estella get him into the lift and goes up to Oscar's floor with her and lets them into Oscar's apartment. Estella tells her that Oscar is feeling unwell and that she'll let her know if they need anything. The door opens into a living-room space and Estella moves Oscar towards the sofa prompting him to sit. The place is huge and furnished minimally, like a show apartment. Everything is immaculate and much of it is white. The living-room is like a huge glass box with a living area and a dining area with a huge glass table and leather chairs. The glass walls, on two sides, give a panoramic view of the city lights below. On the internal white walls are huge abstract paintings that might have been produced in a factory with a spray paint gun. It's the polar opposite of his mother's home.

She finds a door that leads to a huge marble panelled guest toilet with a shower. There's a long white corridor with doors going off on either side and a glass wall at the end. She finds a gym on the left before she gets to the kitchen, opposite, where she is dazzled by immaculate marble work surfaces, a central island and another dining area beside the glass wall and its vertiginous view of the city. She finds a bottle of water in the huge fridge and heads back to the living room.

He's still sitting on the sofa, but the glazed expression has changed. He looks sad as he takes the bottle of water from her with a tight smile.

"I always dreamt that you'd come here, but not like this."

"It's very classy," she says.

"It's not your style, is it?" He says dully. "Your house is so..." She laughs quietly.

"Old, unfinished, cluttered, colourful, dirty..." He huffs out a laugh.

"Yeah! All the stuff and the bright colours kind of gave me a headache." She laughs properly.

"I can understand that. I have a lot of stuff, but so much of it is from my mum and dad and it makes me feel like they're still here. I miss them all the time."

"They're both dead?"

"Yeah." She sees and feels his shock. "It's normal at my age, Oscar. It's part of life."

"Why did they die?" She finds the question odd. She wants to say, because we all have to, but she's beginning to understand how his mind works.

"My father had cancer for many years and that's why he died. My mum died of old age. Her body wore out. She was ready to die. Life wasn't much fun for her for the last year. I gave up work to look after her and I saw how hard each day got." She sees the fear in his face. She shouldn't have talked about her mum. She feels like she's just poked the open wound that is his relationship, or lack of it, with his mother. She scrabbles for something to break the moment.

"Where's the picture that you bought from Chico?"

"I have lots of Chico's pictures," he says, getting up from the sofa. "I'll show you."

She follows him down the white passageway past the doors to the gym and the kitchen. There are two more doors. One on either side. He turns into the one on the right. It's a bedroom. Hard to say if it's his. The glass wall gives the ubiquitous view out over the lights of the nighttime city. There's a door into a walk-in wardrobe and another into a bathroom. The bed projects from one wall and opposite is a riot of colour against the uniform white. A mosaic of Chico's paintings. Maybe twenty of them. They're imaginatively hung. Not in regimented rows, but as if the hanger has tried to jigsaw them together. The shape seems to have grown organically and there is space for more to be added.

"How wonderful!" She exclaims and turns a smiling face towards him. She's brought up short. He's close to tears. "Oscar, what is it?"

"I met Chico because he used to come to the apartment in Salamanca and give lessons to my sister. She was good at painting. Her pictures were full of colour. I wish I had some of *her* pictures."

She isn't sure what to do. She promised Adela. She senses that she shouldn't talk about this with him. She's almost certain that her visit to his old home will make him angry, but she really wants to try and help him. She wants him to know that Adela still thinks of him. She also wants to know if he understands that she has a learning difference. She tries to stop herself. Adela would never know if she didn't tell him. She tries not to say anything, but it's inevitable. She's incapable of stopping herself.

"Wait a moment," she says and goes back to the living-room to get her bag. She takes out the script folder and finds the picture. She hands it to him. He looks at the picture and then at her. She gives him a small smile, almost apologetic.

"Oscar, I went back to the apartment."

"What?"

"Last week. I heard something and I needed to find out if it was true." He's rigid and staring at her. The picture in his hand is crumpling. "Oscar, the picture, be careful!"

"What did you hear?" She's transfixed by the picture which is beginning to crease and spoil.

"That I look like your mother." He looks confused. "Oscar, please, the picture!"

"Why would that be interesting?" She can't see how to explain her interest without touching on things that will offend the prude in him. She falters. She's still looking for the words, when he speaks again.

"Anyway, they wouldn't let you in." He says it as if that's the end of the conversation, but then he looks down at the picture in his hand. He stares at her with a mixture of anger and incredulity

"She let you in?" It's almost a hiss. She nods, trying to evade his gaze. "She let ***you*** in?" Louder now. He grabs her by the shoulders. The picture crushes against her. He makes her look at him.

"And?" Fear works its way through her gut and up into her lungs. Her voice is breathless when she replies.

"Your mother and I look very alike. We could be sisters." She tries to take a deeper breath. "Adela misses you. She asked me to tell you that she misses you and loves you. That's one of her pictures." It's as if it doesn't matter.

"What did my mother say?" Shaking her slightly.

"She's very busy caring for Adela. Obviously, Adela can't be left alone. It must be hard for her. I think she's very worried about what will happen to Adela when she dies." He shakes her properly now.

"What did she say about me?" He yells. "Why won't she open the door?" She feels his pain, but she's angry that he isn't thinking about Adela and *her* situation. She's angry that he's destroying Adela's picture. Her fear for herself is overridden by a sense of outrage that he's never once used his sister's name.

"I don't think she has time for you, Oscar." She says cruelly, but truthfully. She rarely speaks so bluntly to people. "Have you ever thought about how hard your mum's life is? Caring for a person who will never grow up. Worrying every day about their safety." He pushes her away and she falls backwards. The air is forced out of her as she hits the ground. Panic starts to take hold. Fight or flight? She battles to control her breathing. Adela's picture has fallen to the floor with her, half screwed up. She tries to reach out to the poor abused painting.

"It's always all about ***her***," he rants. "Adela this. Adela, that. *We have to do this because it's important for Adela. Adela needs this. I can't come on tour with you, I have to stay with Adela.* Adela spoilt everything." He turns on her as she's getting off the floor, the picture in her hand. "You're just the same. You have to spoil everything too, don't you? Why can't you just do what I say? Huh? Why can't you just love me, you stupid bitch?"

She freezes. This has gone too far. She tries to take a breath. She wants to move. She needs to run. She can't. She is frozen.

He grabs her again and forces his mouth onto hers. He holds her head between his hands and forces his tongue inside her mouth. She can't close her mouth because she's fighting to get air into her lungs. She feels her grasp on the painting loosen and she feels it slip away. Finally, she starts to hit him with her fists. She's feeling lightheaded. She's desperate to take a breath. He lets go of her.

"Bitch!" Before she can breathe or try to run, he wallops her with the back of his hand. Her head snaps to the left. She falls towards the bed. A laugh.

"Whore!" She tries to breathe. Tries to get up. To crawl. To do something. The painting!

"Ugly bitch!" She's yanked up. Dropped onto the bed. Her dress is ripped. She fights to breathe. Her underwear is pulled.

"Dirty whore!" She tries to sit up. She lashes out. He hits her again. Fighting for breath. He's on top of her. Tries to scratch his face.

"Puta!" Can't breathe. Pinioned. Scratches arm. His weight suddenly gone.

"Fuck you, bitch!" She pushes up. Breathe! He catches her. Turns her. Forces her down. Face against duvet. Hand on back of her neck. Too little air. No chance.

Don't.

Don't.

Don't...

END OF PART TWO

PART THREE: THE POWER OF THE NUMBER EIGHT

The Wake-Up Call

He wakes and yawns. He frowns as he realises that the lights are on. He turns his head to look out of the glass wall and sees the darkness outside. He's confused. He realises that he's clothed, or partly. He sits up and sees his trousers are open. Then he sees the smears of blood on the duvet cover.

He remembers.

He's on his feet. He's stuffing himself back into his shorts and trousers. He's sweating and breathless. He rubs his hand, which aches and he sees her head snapping to the side and her body falling. He's burning. Every cell in his body is burning. He sees the scratches on his arm and remembers flipping her over and holding her down. The images are so clear and vivid that he closes his eyes to erase them, but they're even clearer there, behind his eyelids. He whimpers. As he runs out of the bedroom, he recalls stabbing into her as hard as he could. There was no resistance. He doesn't recall any fight after he flipped her over. She must have passed out.

In seconds he's searched the whole apartment. He's checked every room, every closet and under the beds. She isn't here. Her bag isn't here. He ripped her dress! How could she have left like that? The concierge!

His breathing is ragged now. Two thoughts are battling in his head.

Is she okay?

What will she do?

He wants to plead her forgiveness, but he's also mortally afraid that she's going to go to the police. This could end him. He runs back to the bedroom, strips off his clothes and showers. He dresses hastily. He bundles his clothes into the duvet and stuffs it all into a hold-all he's never used. He grabs his keys and travels down to the foyer in the lift.

As he steps out of the lift, it pings and the concierge looks up from her desk. She looks terrified. She's seen the hold-all. He's frozen by the fear in her eyes and the implication of that look. She's seen Rafa. He steps back into the lift and goes back to the apartment. He's shaking now. He's crying.

If he's been divorced from his emotions before this moment, he's now so aware of every feeling that he's vibrating with them. He needs to lie down. He's struggling with the weight of the constant stream of sensations. He can't go back to his bedroom. He goes to the guest bedroom and crawls into the bed, covering himself with the duvet. The emotions keep coming; wave after wave of feeling and tears that he never knew he had to shed. He's paralysed with the effort of processing everything.

He keeps coming back to the same searing thought. The realisation is blinding and impossible to get past.

I'm a shitty person.

He feels ashamed. He feels more ashamed than when his mother refused to talk about the money he'd made because they had to think about Adela's future. He feels more ashamed than when he first realised that some of his friends were, in fact, more interested in his wealth and fame than in him as an individual. He feels more ashamed than when Victor kissed him, and he wanted him more than he'd wanted anything else before in his life. He feels more ashamed than when his mother told him to leave because she had to put his sister first. He feels more ashamed than when the woman he dated in Los Angeles told him that they were sexually incompatible when he was rough with her. He feels more ashamed than when he started pissing razorblades after picking up a male prostitute on a disastrous holiday in the Caribbean. He feels so ashamed of the way he edited everything that he told her. The pain of his shame is endless and crashes over him in waves that at their low points are merely self-disgust, but at their highs bring insights into how he has manipulated people in his life and made others miserable simply because he didn't get what he wanted.

He writhes in his discomfort until he finally feels hollowed out. As the waves subside to more manageable tides that are more predictable, he remembers with clarity what Rafa told him on their trip to Ávila. He groans as he realises that she described exactly what he's feeling. For fuck's sake, he thinks, how does she cope with this? He thinks of the thing that he and Igor found wrapped in her duvet and understands why it would happen. He suddenly feels a wave of despair that isn't his own. He sees her bruised face and the self-inflicted wound, he sees her plunging her thumb into it and he doesn't just see it, he feels it and he cries out with the pain and the horror of it all.

He feels Rafa's pain.

It's unbearable.

He feels the impulse to hurt himself.

Fear floods his body with heat and he shivers with cold. She told him about this. She told him that she felt what other people felt and sometimes it stayed with her, and he didn't believe her. He dismissed her as hysterical. He thought that she was mentally ill. He didn't listen. He didn't fucking listen.

Too late.

He's destroyed everything.

He's destroyed himself.

He sleeps. He's exhausted. He dreams of Rafa and her lovely eyes taking in his pain and unhappiness as he spoke to her in that café on the first day they met. He dreams of the gift she gave him that day by simply being there and loving him as he told her what he chose to tell her. In the dream he's back in the warmth of her positive regard and secure in the knowledge of her outrage at what had happened to him. He tries to let that empathy heal him, but in the dream, although she's still giving him the love and warmth that he remembers, he can't receive it. He feels it, but he can't absorb it because he knows that he no longer deserves it. His shame is blocking her love.

In the dream, as the truth that he is unable to receive Rafa's love anymore becomes clear to him, he feels the customary anger rising inside him. The dream becomes a nightmare as he stands and, leaning across the table, backhands her across the face, snapping her head to the side. When she looks back at him in hurt, shock and horror, he finds that he's looking at Víctor. He wakes, gasping for breath and bathed in sweat.

Are the police coming for him?

He thinks that he will never be able to sleep again. He finds his phone and sees that it's only five in the morning. He decides to work out, changes into sweatpants and a t-shirt, and goes into his gym. He can't touch the punchbag, but he runs on the treadmill and uses the cross-trainer. Shortly after six he takes another shower and dresses. He makes his usual vegetable smoothie and tries to drink it with very little success.

Are the police coming for him?

When he goes down to his car at seven to go to the set, the concierge has been replaced by the day shift member and he's greeted with the usual professional courtesy. He remains on edge. Rocio is as silent as always, but this morning the silence feels like a reproach. The image of Rafa's head snapping to the side keeps replaying in his head. He feels sweat break out again.

On set, everything is business as usual. The director has a quick word with him asking if they can try to get everything done today, if possible. He wants to try to maximise post-production time. It suits Oscar, who wants to be as busy and distracted as possible. He hyper-focuses. He does his professional best. The scene he has with Víctor is hard, but he's a professional. When he's not needed, he's in his trailer lifting hand weights or doing press-ups.

When the final scene wraps the crew applauds, he's handed some flowers and a bottle of wine and he goes back to his trailer to change. The door of the trailer is open and as he climbs the steps, he recognises Elvira's perfume before he sees her. He can't speak.

"You need to find new legal representation. I've emailed you a list of recommendations. Let me know who you choose, and I'll ensure that all the records that I hold for you are transferred to them. Please close the door and sit down."

He does as he's asked.

"Estella will not denounce you on the understanding that you meet a number of conditions. Please be aware that we have photographs of the crime scene, including a photograph of yourself asleep at the crime scene." He flinches at the repetition of the words. "Estella went to a medical facility last night for treatment, but she has also submitted to an examination which has been documented. Samples were taken of semen from the anal cavity and skin from beneath her fingernails." He swallows and involuntarily touches the scratches on his arm. "These samples are collateral against the eventuality that you do not agree to her conditions. Do you understand?" He nods.

"Yes. I understand."

"You are to make an appointment with this psychiatrist." She hands him the details. "I have also e-mailed these details to you. Failure to do this within two weeks of today will trigger the release of evidence and a denunciation for aggravated sexual assault and actual bodily harm. You will remain under the care of this psychiatrist, or another practitioner agreed through your lawyer contacting me, for a period of no less than two years. During those two years, you will meet with the psychiatrist at least once a week. Do you understand?"

"Yes, I understand."

"Failure to comply with this condition..."

"I understand. I'll be denounced." Elvira nods.

"The second condition is that you will never touch Estella Marks again and you will never refer to her as anything other than Estella. Do you understand?"

"I understand." His anger is rising, but his shame is still strong and it overpowers his anger.

"At press junkets, you may stand close to her if absolutely required for photos, but you will never intentionally touch her with any part of your body." His mind is flooded with recollections of him pushing, shaking and hitting her. He feels lightheaded with shame.

"I understand." He's close to tears now.

"Next, you will provide the money for a trust fund for your sister, Adela. We are currently taking advice on the sum required for this trust fund. The fund will be administered by a firm of lawyers who will work with Adela's mother to set out the terms and requirements of the trust. The sole purpose of the trust is to ensure that Adela's future is secure in the event of her mother's death. As she has never known any life without the constant care of her mother, the trust will need to offer the financial security to allow Adela one-to-one care when the time comes that her mother can no longer care for her. The trust will ensure that she does not have to move into an institution."

"I understand." He nods. "I understand completely. Whatever she needs."

"Finally," Elvira takes an envelope out of her briefcase, "I am to observe you read this." She hands the envelope to him. He recognises Ra... Estella's handwriting and he traces his name with his fingertips.

"Is she okay?"

"I'm not at liberty to say. I've been instructed to tell you nothing." A flash of anger quickly doused by shame. He nods. He takes a deep breath. He opens the envelope.

From a conversation with your mother, I learnt the following:

Your father was disappointed when his first child was a girl. Luckily, the second child was a boy. He was very pleased to have you and started to ignore Adela. When Adela tried to help with your care, he got cross and started to get rough with her. One day, when she tried to pick you up, he hit her. She fell and struck her head. There was a brain injury. That's why your sister is how she is. That's why she never grew up. Your father didn't hit your mother. She told you that he did so that you wouldn't want to see him again.

Your mother isn't very nice and she hasn't always treated you with love, but the burden she bears with caring for Adela is huge. You were not an easy child. You are not an easy person. She put you into that competition because you were so angry that she couldn't afford singing classes for you. She was trying to solve the problem of your dissatisfaction.

If you have any sense, you will take the opportunity of speaking to a psychiatrist to try and understand who you are.

Tears.

"You have understood the contents of the letter?" He nods.

"I understand."

"Inform me in the next 72 hours of your new legal representation."

"I will." She walks to the door. "Elvira, thank-you for everything that you've done for me."

"If I had been in possession of all the facts, I don't think I would ever have represented you." He hears the door open and close. The tears are still falling.

The New Normal

Estella's conditions are almost universally acceptable to Oscar. It almost feels that from beyond the end of their relationship she's still caring for him. Whilst, on the surface, he remains the same person that he's always been, his social media still buzzing with his carefully chosen brands and partners, he thinks more about the financial benefits of each of his partnerships. His success and the effectiveness of his social media are more important than ever now; he's newly motivated by the need to make money for the trust fund that's being set up for Adela. He continues to curate his image and appears, as always, immaculately turned out and on point. He's still in high demand for photoshoots and guest appearances. However, there are days that Oscar is not available and certain appointments that he cannot be flexible about. He doesn't want to be flexible about them. Mostly, he sees Robert Marshall once a week at his office in Malasaña. Sometimes he sees him twice a week. This is one of those weeks.

"How are you feeling, Oscar? Why did you want an extra meeting this week?"

"Next week is the premiere."

"I see."

"I have to be there, and I suppose that... Estella will be there too. I'm very excited to see her, but I'm also terrified to see her." He keeps unbuckling and re-buckling his watch strap. "After what I did, I shouldn't be allowed near her." The silence stretches. He knows that he's expecting some form of support. He recognises his need for validation, and he recognises that he doesn't deserve it. He feels his anger start to burn. He breathes deeply. "I want it all to go away. I want everyone to pretend that it never happened. I want everything to be as it was before."

"Before what?"

"Before I kissed her."

"Not before you raped her?" He winces.

"No, it was already wrong before that. It was wrong from the moment that I tried to get her to love me. No, not love me. She ***did*** love me. I mean before I tried to get her to be ***in*** love with me." He rubs his face. "Before I tried to control her."

More silence.

"I've had a message form her lawyer." He takes his phone out as if he's going to show the message to Robert. He looks at it, then puts the phone back in his pocket. "The message says that Estella understands that we'll need to talk and appear friendly, but it also reinforces the condition that I don't touch her at any point. I think that's going to be hard for me." He thinks about the hundreds of times that he's kissed her cheek, her forehead, held her hand, placed his hand at the small of her back. The image of his hand walloping her across the face arrests him and he burns with guilt and shame. He can't speak. He closes his eyes and pinches the bridge of his nose.

"Have you thought about how Estella might be feeling about seeing you?" Oscar's head turns quickly to look directly at Robert. How is it possible that he hasn't considered this before? He's so fucking self-obsessed! He opens his mind to consider how she might be feeling. He feels panic rising into his lungs and gasps. He feels a prickle of heat and anxiety. They aren't his feelings.

"She's very anxious. She's panicking. She's worried that she's going to have a panic attack." He puts his head in his hands and rocks slightly. He starts to bang his hands against his head. It's not his head. They're not his hands.

"Deep breaths, Oscar. Deep breaths."

These moments when he knows what she's feeling come and go. Sometimes he gets the same transfer of feelings from another person. Recently, during a promotional photoshoot for *Los Amores de Oscar* with Víctor, he became overwhelmed briefly by regret and a sense of futility. He knew that these were not his emotions. He's had to reconsider his estimation of Víctor. He knows that Estella tried to get him to see this before. Víctor's a good person, far too good for Oscar. Recently, after conversations with Robert, Oscar has been rerunning Víctor's apology a decade ago and wishing that he'd been less of a controlling shit. They might still be friends. They might've been lovers. He has to stop himself from these useless endless thought loops. This one and the one where he doesn't try to get Ra... Estella to be his lover.

Estella's kindness has continued even though she's made herself inaccessible. Her book tour, which he followed on social media, was made sensational by her bruised face and cut lip. *An unfortunate fall at the swimming pool* was her cover story and she played it so well that nobody questioned it. She spoke so frankly about her struggles with her mental health on the tour that she was invited to appear on UK national breakfast television discussing support for people who self-harm and, as a result, promoting the book.

He's read *At Florian*. He didn't understand all of it; he's not a big reader and the book's in English. He speaks English well, but he rarely reads or writes it. The story takes place over seven years in Venice and has something to do with a dead aunt, but the time periods go back and forth and he got confused. He doesn't recognise himself in any of the characters, or Estella, but the book is dedicated to him. *For Oscar, without whom I should still be bored stiff.* He remembers Ávila and how she told him that he'd offered her the best opportunity of her life. He tries to hold on to the good feeling that this gives him without the memory of his assault on her neutralising it.

There's a trend on social media to be critical of Estella. Oscar has noticed it among his fan base. The critics claim that Estella just used Oscar in order to launch a career for herself. He's been fretting about how to refute this. The difficulty is that a confession of his guilt means disclosing her experience. He can't do that. He's starting to understand how his actions impact on other people, but his impulsivity is still something that he battles to control.

On the Saturday night before the week of the premiere, Estella appears on a popular UK chat show and Oscar's able to stream it live. When Estella's introduced and walks out to the audience's applause, he doesn't recognise the woman who emerges. Her hair is cut short at the sides and is longer and floppy on top. She wears a beautifully tailored woman's dinner suit in black velvet with sequinned lapels. Her face seems bonier, her body less voluptuous and he has never seen her wear trousers before. It isn't until the camera zooms in on her face that, with a sharp intake of breath, he recognises her eyes.

The timbre of her voice is different, but it's still full of kindness and humour. She speaks, as always, with integrity and passion about the themes of mental health and about her book. Then the host turns the conversation to the forthcoming third season of *Oscar Loves*. She talks animatedly about how much fun it was to work on the project and how exciting the opportunity to act has been, all of which she is careful to accredit Oscar with.

"Now, Estella," the host interjects with a change in tone and tempo. "You've received a bit of criticism on social media about your relationship with Oscar Pérez. Some people are saying that you used his friendship to launch your own career and since that's taken off, you've had no time for him." He holds his breath. He sees her take a deep breath, sigh and then she says.

"I think that I have to admit that there's some truth in the criticism." She nods thoughtfully. "Shortly after meeting Oscar, completely by chance, I found myself in a difficult situation. A video of me dancing in a London nightclub with some young people was posted on the internet and I was suspended from work."

"I see. Why did that happen?"

"I used to be a teacher. My employer was uncomfortable with the image that the video portrayed. Everyone in the image was over twenty-one, but they didn't like the implications about my lifestyle. When I thought I'd lose my job, I became quite unwell with the stress. That too was shown on social media." She makes a tight little smile.

"Yes, there was some quite intrusive coverage, if I remember rightly."

"I have to admit that after that I was pretty worried about my financial situation and trying to ensure that I had enough income to keep my head above water. I would never have been able to publish this book without the notoriety that Oscar's friendship gave me. So, yes, I suppose I have to plead guilty to those criticisms. I haven't been prioritising our friendship during the promotion of the book."

Oscar doesn't hear any more.

How can she allow them to accuse her? Surely, she must be furious that these strangers are judging her, accusing her, disparaging her. He looks back at the television screen and sees Estella laughing along with other guests on the sofa of the chat show. She seems calm and relaxed, but he feels her hurt. She's not immune to the injustice of the accusation, but she's also still grateful to him for what their relationship brought her. He marvels at the delicate balance that she's maintaining between her pain and her gratitude. She chose not to point out that it was him that posted the video of her dancing at the club. He feels honour bound to tell the world what a shit he's been. He feels the need to post a confession on his socials. Robert frequently talks to him about not acting on impulse. He has to consider how his actions will impact on others. He has to fight the need to confess. He goes to his gym and works out. He still can't use the punch bag. He runs. He uses the cross-trainer. He starts to strain. He showers. He takes a sleeping pill. The dreams still come if he doesn't take a pill. He'd relive what he did to her every night without the pill.

The next three days are scheduled to the last second to allow for no free moment. The premiere is on Tuesday night at 8 pm. That's when he'll see her. They'll be expected to be on the red carpet with the other cast members, there'll be interviews, the first episode will be screened along with excerpts and teasers for the rest of the series. Then there'll be a Q&A session. He's anxious, but he's also aware of *her* anxiety and her fear, which is intensifying. He starts the useless cycle of wishing that he could take it all back to just before he told her that he was in love with her. His instincts tell him that if he'd kept quiet, things would have been very different. The regret is a palpable ache in his chest.

On Sunday morning, as he's working out again, his new lawyer calls him. He's a little older than Oscar with a similar penchant for good suits and a serious demeanour. He wonders if this is partly the knowledge of what Oscar has done, because he confessed everything the first time they met, or if the man just has a professional persona.

"Fernando, everything okay? Surely you don't work on a Sunday."

"Good morning, Oscar. Not usually, but this is a time sensitive matter. Miss Marks' lawyer has contacted me asking if you would agree to a meeting with Miss Marks tomorrow under the supervision of Robert Marshall." Oscar's stunned. His breathing, already slightly ragged from working out, begins to catch irregularly. "I know this must come as a surprise, Oscar. You're within your rights to refuse."

"No," he gasps. Then breathlessly, "This is precisely what I've been hoping for. Please tell Elvira that I agree."

Menorca

Elvira calls Estella to let her know that the meeting is agreed for the following afternoon.

"Are you really sure that you want to do this, Estella?"

"Yes, it's the only way. I realised last night that I can't see him for the first time on the red carpet; it would be a disaster. No amount of prohibiting him to touch me is going to help me feel safe. I need to confront him. I need to tell him how I feel."

"You sound tense."

"It was an absurd decision to go to London for just a day to do that chat show. I'm exhausted. I only got back here in the small hours. I'm also terrified, Elvira, but I can't spend the rest of my life in fear of seeing him."

"When it happened, you were so... organised. You seemed untouched by it all. When you arrived at my house in such a terrible state, I thought that you would fall apart, but you were almost clinical. Was that all a front?" A sigh.

"No, I was angry then. Anger can hold you together. I was so determined that he pay for what he'd done. When I came to and saw him there sleeping, it was all I could do not to go and get a knife from his pristine bloody kitchen and stab him with it." She takes a calming breath. "He was smiling in his goddam sleep with his dick hanging out of his trousers and looking utterly harmless. There's me, bloody, bruised and buggered and Adela's painting crushed and disregarded, when that was what he'd said that he wanted." She feels the anger rising and breathes it down again. "My bag was in the room and I just took out my phone and started photographing everything. I think I was half hoping that he'd wake up. The idea was part satisfying and part terrifying."

"You weren't in your right mind." A laugh.

"Elvira, I rarely am! But in the lobby, that poor concierge, I started to think a bit more rationally. I was going to call the police, but I was still fixated on Adela's picture. I realised that I had leverage. Then, in the taxi that the poor concierge called for me, on my way to you, the plan just materialised. As if someone far more intelligent just placed it in my mind fully formed."

"It was a good plan, but you've been too kind to him."

"Can you be too kind to people, Elvira? What would I have gained by denouncing him?"

"Closure? Justice?" Elvira is indignant.

"That's what tomorrow is for. That's why I have to meet him."

She can hear Elvira fighting back her objections and she gives her the space to do it.

"What about the book tour and the radio and TV appearances? You were still angry then? You seemed entirely in control."

"No, that wasn't me." Silence.

"What do you mean?" A small cough of a laugh.

"I don't think you'd believe me."

"You could try..."

Estella explains to Elvira about the Magnificent Seven. She tells her that during the book launch Esta has mostly been in charge with the occasional assistance of Stel and Sella, but that she is beginning to realise that there's a new member of the team. She's emerging bit by bit; first the haircut, a move towards a different style of clothing, something in her voice too. She realises that Miss has had to retreat since the night at Oscar's apartment. Miss's concerns for Adela, her instinct to protect the vulnerable, lays them open to too much danger. The new version, the eighth, is there to get the balance right.

Elvira's silent for a long time. Estella lets her process the information.

"The Netflix party in London?"

"Esta."

"The breakdown?"

"Miss blamed them for getting her into that whole situation with Oscar. The self-harm, the ambivalence about life, that was all Miss. She's been like that since mum died. She mostly feels like it would be better to just die and get it all over and done with. The self-harm helped her to shut the others up. She tried to do without them for a while, but we can't function without each other."

"Who am I talking to right now?" Estella has to pause a moment to think.

"It's the new one. I'm the new one."

"Estella, are you schizophrenic?" A genuine laugh.

"No Elvira, that's a common misunderstanding. Schizophrenia doesn't involve multiple personalities. Besides, these aren't personalities, they're just me at different stages in my life." She sighs again, a little sadly. "There's a condition called Multiple Personality Disorder. I Googled it. But in that, you have blanks when the other personalities take over. I just find myself in a situation I can't cope with, so I ask someone else to take charge. It's usually Esta; we were probably at our prime when she was top of the pile. She was very beautiful, which gave her confidence, and she was in the longest relationship we've ever had."

"Okay."

"Elvira, do I need to find another lawyer?"

"No, you don't. I think I understand. Besides, I know you, I believe in you." Estella feels the catch in her throat and speaks through the coming tears.

"Thank you. I feel the same way about you."

"I'll collect you from the airport tomorrow morning."

"Okay, thanks."

Estella glances out of the window at the miraculous sea. She feels the same every day that she looks out at it. She feels the power, the majesty and the energy. This is day ten. The six weeks of the book tour were intense, but exciting. Esta, Sella, Stel and the new girl did the most amazing job. They referred back to Miss's emotional intelligence from time to time, but they shielded her from the turmoil of having to speak about Oscar in rational and sane terms. Vera and the techniques have been a boon and that's how she's come to the point where she needs to be in the same room with him. She's released all the negative energy and her body is healed. She knows that it will take longer to release all her feelings. She now has to release herself from the fear that she has of him. She can only do that by being in the same room with him.

She knows that he's been going to the psychodynamic therapist that she recommended. She'd heard about him a few years before when she was researching her own issues. An American settled in Madrid with a reputation for working right back to the roots of childhood trauma and behaviour. Despite the progress they've made and the considerable healing that's happened, they can't help feeling frightened of seeing Oscar again. The new girl asks them to consider if it is pure fear or if there is also a seed of excitement. That shakes them up. They have to admit that since releasing the anger and letting the healing start, they have missed the excitement of life with Oscar. The restaurants, the bars, the theatre, the gallery openings... the book tour was sometimes lonely.

She walks out onto the terrace, where Chico is reading the Sunday papers and smoking a cigar. Chico's friends in Menorca are friends with Estella's friends in Menorca. It's hardly surprising; it's a small island and they're all much the same age, but that doesn't stop it from feeling fortuitous. She drapes her arms around him from behind and kisses his neck. He grabs an arm with the cigar-free hand.

"Mercy!" He begs, laughing. "Don't get me going again before lunch!" She pulls away languorously and takes the seat opposite him. "Querida, are you really sure about this?" She nods.

"Absolutely. I need to do this. I won't let the memory of him raping me fester and disease me. I need to show him that he has no power over me. I need to face my fear of him."

"Fuck!" He exhales. "I love you, Estrella, but you scare the shit out of me sometimes."

"Sorry, Chiquito, I don't mean to do that." He holds up his hands to bat the apology away.

"No apology required, it's good for me. You wake up parts of me that've been sleeping for a long time. That's profoundly positive." He stubs out his cigar, roughly folds his scrunched-up newspaper and leans forward to put his hands on her knees. "Are you really not going to let me come with you tomorrow?" She leans forward and kisses him.

"Really," she says affectionately. "I suspect that you might punch him and that would be counterproductive."

"You make an excellent point, Estrellita!" He kisses her. "Lunch at Trébol?"

"Always!"

The Phoenix Rises

Oscar is already there. She's in the waiting room. She knows he's in the room on the other side of the door that she's looking at. The receptionist has told her that he's there. The receptionist doesn't hurry her; he stands a couple of meters from her and remains calm. She's regulating her breathing, but panic is rising. She wishes that there was someone that she could have brought here with her to wait outside for her. She's never had anyone that she could rely on like that. She wonders if anyone does. She knows that Chico wanted to be here, but however wonderful the last ten days have been, he doesn't really know her. Win knows her. She knows the best of her and the worst of her and she's still there any Sunday evening that they're both free in Hereford, but Win was so horrified when she told her what happened. Her hand had flown to her mouth and tears came to her eyes. She expressed her regret for suggesting that it was a good idea to get involved with him. Oscar knows her too. He was there when she was at her worst and he was still there afterwards. They'd only known each other for a few days, but he felt responsible for what had happened; there was a reason why ***he*** stayed.

Estrella, the new one, is losing her patience. Esta's also keen to get this started. Not one of them doubts that it's going to be carnage, but they all agree that it has to be done. They can't move forward without this. Estrella steps forward, gives them all the heads up, turns the door handle and steps into the room.

He's sitting on the edge of the seat of an armchair rocking slightly. His hands, palms together, lodged between his thighs so that his shoulders are hunched up around his ears. His hair is more unruly than usual and he's wearing a white T-shirt and a pair of dark jeans. He's wearing running shoes. He's not looking at her so, she gets to really look at him. She sees his pain and feels the turmoil of his feelings. Robert sits in another armchair. He nods as she comes in but doesn't say anything.

She sees the armchair that's intended for her. It's too close to him and too far from the door. She drags it so that it's near the door and sits down, holding her stomach and focusing on her breathing. The tears just won't be denied. She doesn't want to cry, but the thought of what he did to her is overwhelming.

"Estella," Robert says. "You may leave at any time. Please don't feel obliged to stay if you're too distressed." She nods and continues to cry quietly. The silence lengthens and she supposes that, as always, if they're to speak, she'll have to find the way to start this conversation. She's trying to find the breath and the courage, when he speaks.

"Estella, I'm sorry. I wish that I could go back to the night that we went to Los Montes de Galicia, and I would never tell you that I was in love with you. I think that's where it all started to go wrong. If I hadn't said that, I think we would have been good friends, don't you? You're so kind and empathetic, you never stopped trying to be my friend even when I made it so difficult to like me."

She thinks of the panic and fear that she felt that night and the instant knowledge that it would never be the same again between them. She nods.

"Do you hate me now?" She nods again. She hears him crying and that seems to light the touchpaper.

"I did everything that you wanted," she spits. "I cared for you. I listened to you. I spent so much time with you. I tried to be a good friend to you. You wanted me to be in the show; I did it. Then you attacked me. YOU RAPED ME!" As she yells the last words, she loses all control. She hears her gulps for breath and whimpers of injury, and she holds herself because there's never been anyone else to hold her. She's in the pit now, but she's determined not to stay there. She wrestles her way to the side and starts to pull herself up out of the darkness. She masters her breathing. She brushes away the tears. In a thick voice of barely controlled despair, she starts to speak her truth.

"You are just the most recent in a depressingly long line of men who have felt the need to take my power away from me. It's not even as if I have ever had that much power to take, but what little I've had over the years seems to have been an affront to the men in my life. All the things that are most important to me: love, compassion, empathy and kindness have been met with violence, derision, cruelty and disregard."

"I felt your love, Estella. It made all the difference to me." He pleads.

"AND THEN YOU RAPED ME!" He whimpers and rocks at the force of her shouting. "How am I supposed to continue to share the gifts that I have, when they're met with violence? Where do I find the strength to continue to be a good human being after what you did to me?"

"I'm sorry," he whispers. "I'm so sorry. I'm trying to change. Telling me to come here. You did me a kindness. A kindness that I don't deserve. I'm trying to be a better person."

"What about me?" She cries. "Who's going to do me a kindness? Who's going to help me?"

She realises that she has reached the real wound. All these years caring for other people. All this time worrying about how she speaks to others and being so careful to be fair and supportive. A lifetime of putting everyone else before herself. The loneliness of taking responsibility for everything and everyone. She is lost. She has been lost her whole life; Little Estella knew it at seven years of age, and nothing has changed through the long years. The long, lonely years.

Then she feels them. Stel wraps her arms around Little Estella. Ella embraces Stel. Esta throws her arms around Ella. Sella pulls Esta into a bear hug. Stella holds Sella tightly. Miss clasps Stella to her, and Estrella clutches them all to her heart with a depth of unconditional positive regard that none of them has ever known before.

Estrella takes a deep breath and feels the length and breadth of love that nests inside her and knows that there is no end to this love. This love is unassailable. And the power that this love gives her is untouchable and indestructible. She feels her outrage wither in the face of it. Her pain diminishes to a memory. The rape was something that happened to her body, but which the sisterhood inside her will not allow to touch her spirit. They are stronger than anything that anyone else can do to them. It's as if they've all been acting in different plays and have suddenly all found the same script. For the first time everything is making sense. Now that they all have their parts, know their lines, their exits and entrances, playing in the same scene, working together, they are synchronised. Their hearts beat as one. They inhale and exhale in unison. This team of eight is indefatigable. They are infinite in their kindness, compassion, empathy and love. She takes a deep breath. ***They*** take a deep breath. Strength flows through them and from them.

"Oscar, I've shown you how I felt." She tells him. She's calm and her voice is rich with kindness. "I choose to let this go. I don't want to feel this way anymore. I don't want you to feel this way anymore. I want you to let go of your shame. I want you to forget what happened. I want you to learn to be kind to people and to yourself. I forgive you. Now, you have to forgive yourself. Will you do that for me? Will you do that with the help of Robert? Will you do this kindness for yourself?"

He's staring at her in disbelief. She supposes that it must be rather hard on him when she's just been yelling at him. She gives him time. She takes deep breaths. **They** take deep breaths. **They** send out compassion, empathy, unconditional positive regard and, of course, love. Oscar breaks his gaze with her to glance at Robert, who gives him an encouraging nod. He turns back to her and nods. He looks so very young in that moment. She sees that he's ready to find a way to move forward.

They sit a little longer. They look at one another and test what it feels like to be here in this room together. Time passes, but it doesn't drag.

"May I hug you?" She asks. "I understand if you'd rather not." She glances at Robert, but he's expressionless. Oscar stands and takes one step towards her. She can see that he can't speak. She approaches him and opens her arms. He steps forward and scoops her into him. She clasps his back. She feels him heave a sigh. They stand there for a moment and then another moment. She feels their heart beats synchronise. She releases him, he releases her and takes a step back. They're smiling but also crying a little. Their relief is like another person standing beside them.

"Thank you, Oscar."

"Gracias, Estella. De verdad. Gracias."

They hold each other's gaze, and she smiles at him. He looks washed out.

"Tomorrow night, Oscar; shall we make a grand entrance? Shall we give them something to remember?" They look into each other's eyes. She sees his smile in his eyes before it reaches his mouth.

"Sí, Estella. ¡Por supuesto! Let's give them something spectacular."

"Perfect!"

Red Carpet Take Two

Oscar and Estrella arrive at the premiere of season three of *Los Amores de Oscar* in a horse-drawn carriage. The crowd goes wild. All that's visible to them from the carriage is a sea of mobile phones capturing this unexpected moment. Oscar takes the collective breath away in Tom Ford, a white dinner suit with a white shirt and tan lace-up Oxfords. He leaves the top couple of buttons of his shirt undone in a highly uncharacteristic leaning towards informality. He's let his hair do its own magnificent, wild thing. He looks more relaxed than she's ever seen him. Estrella is in an Ozai N Ku long white linen gown with a black trim and black rectangles across the breast. As it's late November she has a luxurious black velvet wrap that she has draped over one shoulder. As they pull up to the red carpet, Oscar leaps down to a shimmy of gasps and screams and turns back to assist Estrella. He takes one hand, and she places the other on his shoulder as she descends. He crooks his arm, and she places her hand on the inside of his elbow. They smile excitedly at one another. They pose for photographs. She lets go of him to let him take selfies and sign autographs. She fixes a smile on her face as she prepares to wait. The crowd seems very excitable.

"Well, hello, Miss Estella! I have to say, that haircut is sensational." She turns to smile at him. Black suede suit with a biker jacket, see-through black gauze shirt, hair flattened with product into a shiny skull cap. Bloody hell, she thinks, what is it about this person that speaks to her with such passion? Why does he inspire so much love in her? Then there's Bram. A little further up the carpet they meet Arlo and Seamus. Estrella is not as surprised as she ought to be that some people want selfies with her and her autograph. There are interviews. Estrella sees handsome, unassuming Víctor also making his way up the carpet. He has a dedicated following of love-sick fans. She hooks her arm in his and pulls him into the sphere of the Boy Friends, the Love Struck and Oscar. Oscar looks pleased to see him. She's a bit bored with the circus, but one of the young people is always asking her something or making a joke. When they get to the official photographers and they're standing in front of the Netflix/*Los Amores de Oscar* hoardings, the photographers get Víctor and Oscar to stand on either side of her, Arlo and Bram next to Oscar, and Santi and Seamus next to Víctor. It's a breathtaking shot and the bevy of shutter clicks and flashes is almost overwhelming. That's one for my wall, she thinks. They shoot her with Oscar. They shoot her alone. They shoot Oscar and Víctor. Finally, they get inside.

The screening is met with applause and gasps of surprise, especially at the end, which is an arrested shot of Nito and Oscar kissing. The Q&A is rather tedious, but Oscar and Víctor do brilliantly. She receives questions about the scripts and what it was like to play Oscar's mother. She tells the journalist that it felt very natural and reaches out a hand to Oscar, who takes it and gives it a chaste kiss. Another explosion of flashes. Eventually, it comes to an end. Arlo gestures with his head for her to join him and Seamus and by the time she gets to him Santi and Bram are also there. Oscar's on his way over too, with Víctor.

"Where for dinner?" Asks Arlo as Oscar and Víctor arrive.

"I've booked a place," Oscar tells them. "Let's exit through the stage door."

They make their way backstage and through dressing rooms to what looks like a fire door that gives out onto an alley. The young people take care of Estrella in her long gown and heels. When they reach the pavement of the busy street, Oscar hails a couple of cabs. He puts Estrella, Santi and Bram in the first and gives the cab driver the destination. He and Víctor, Seamus and Arlo get into the second.

Bram sits in the front with the driver and scrolls through his phone, posting pictures from the launch. Santi sits in the back with her.

"I warned you!" He says crossly. She nods and mimics his explosion gesture with her hands. "Are you okay?"

"I am now, yeah." He shakes his head.

"He's different. Chilled. Are you okay being around him?" She looks at his lovely face, smiles and nods.

"It's all good now. Nobody can hurt me anymore." He looks her in the eye and slowly his mischievous grin takes hold of his mouth and he begins to nod his head.

"So I see!" He tips towards her and scrutinises her with a wondering smile. "Who are you now?"

"Yo soy Estrella. ¡Encantada conocerte! *I'm just divine, me!"*

He shakes her hand and they dissolve into hysterical giggles. Bram turns back from the front seat with a huge smile and rolls his eyes at them.

The restaurant is an Italian chain called Circolo Popolare with an entire wall comprised of floor-to-ceiling shelves filled with bottles of spirits; backlit and dazzling. After fifteen minutes of maddening selfies and autographs they finally get to their table. Oscar seats her between Víctor and Santi and places himself next to Víctor. Seamus sits next to Santi. Arlo sits by Oscar and Bram between Arlo and Seamus. Then they start drinking; telling stories; telling jokes; singing. It's magical. When Chico comes to the table, Oscar stands, looking confused, but Estrella gets up too and Oscar sits down again.

"¿Lista, Estrellita?" He asks her. The young people are a little stunned at first, but they soon start to exchange knowing looks. They smile at Estrella and size-up Chico.

"Sí, mi amor." She turns to the table of beautiful young people. "Thank you, my darlings. It's been another wonderful evening. Thank you for taking care of me." They're all a little sad to see her go, she can feel it, but her surprise is short-lived when she realises that she's sad to leave them too. They start to wish her a good night. She steps round the table to Oscar, who looks up at her from his seat. "Buenas noches, Oscar." She kisses him lightly on the forehead. He smiles at her.

"Buenas noches, Estella. Gracias por todo."

She walks over to Chico, takes his hand and leads him to the exit.

END OF PART THREE

EPILOGUE

Each of us carries around with us our personal, unique, intangible wounds. Sometimes they're lodged in our minds, others in our hearts and others still in joints and muscles. These wounds are the result of the things that happen to us and the things that don't happen to us. The things that are said to us and the things that aren't said to us. The things people do to us and the things that they fail to do *for* us. Often, they're the result of not being loved in the way that we need to be loved; perhaps we're not held, or the love given is conditional or inconsistent. Wounding can occur when people choose not to give us respect, refuse to hear what we're telling them, or they fail to be careful with us. We can be hurt in an infinite number of ways. We are hurt with alarming ease and like all wounds, if we don't take care of them, they become diseased and they never heal.

Many of us become attached to our wounds and we make them a part of our personality and let the disease that forms in them define and limit our lives. We don't allow the wounds to heal and sometimes, like Estella and her physical wound, we plunge a thumb into them to ensure that they continue to bleed. To make sure that they don't heal. The choice to do this is a decision not to move forward, a rejection of progress and the future. We sometimes make these decisions out of fear, overwhelm or a belief that it's impossible for the wound to heal.

For some of us, our wound is all consuming, all demanding and blinds us to any sense of perspective. It's so rare, after all, that one person gives another empathy, unconditional positive regard and compassion and rarer still that two people give the same to each other in the same conversation at the same time. This sort of reciprocity is almost a thing of legend. We're so tempted by the ease of becoming the victim. The momentary relief and satisfaction of showing our hurt and outrage. The temporary relief of sharing with and shocking another person with the awfulness of our experience and the depth of our wound. The relief that's only temporary, because we've shared our pain, but not released it. We are truly brave when we reject victimhood, release our pain, forgive the people who have hurt us and truly desire to move forward without our wounds. The courage to heal and forget leads us to freedom. The journey to that freedom may take us a lifetime; we may feel the desire to give up. We may make the journey in stages, taking rest between the different steps.

At fifty-eight, Estella, with the help of Vera and the practice of releasing blocked energy, allows her wounds to heal. It takes time. There are a good number of them, but once she makes the decision to heal, the process takes on a momentum of its own. The relief of forgiving her parents, her siblings, her lovers, her friends, her enemies, her teachers, random strangers and herself leaves her in a state of peaceful anticipation. She senses constant possibility. She knows that everything will come in its own time. There's nothing to force. There's no hurry. Her liberation from the predictability of working from nine to five gives her imagination and creativity full capacity and control. She writes every day with excitement to see what comes next in the stories and scripts that she conceives. She often receives offers of small parts in films and series, which she embraces with excitement, committing herself to bringing the parts to life and speaking their truth for them. She travels. Sometimes with Chico, or Igor; other times alone. When travelling alone she still plays her travel game: *who is that mysterious, stylish older woman, travelling solo, looking familiar and intriguing?* Her house in Hereford is now without jagged nails, is no longer unpainted and she has unpacked all the boxes. It's still full of colour, books, beautiful things and yet more beautiful things. When Chico sees it for the first time, he smiles and says that the house is a physical embodiment of her personality. The cats take to him.

Once or twice a year she finds herself at the same premiere or award ceremony as those young people she's so very fond of. Despite castmates or lovers, they always find her, and the press is always eager to photograph the seven of them. Víctor's one of them and indispensable at these gatherings for his wit, humour and kindness. There's almost always a meal, drinking, storytelling, laughter and singing. Sometimes they dance. There's now a tradition of getting their lovers/partners to come and break the party up in honour of Chico's arrival at the Madrid restaurant. There's often speculation about whose significant other will arrive first and who that significant other will be.

Igor is a good friend. He keeps returning to Herefordshire to work with Vera and stay with Estella and the cats. When he meets Chico, he declares him to be *good person,* and they get along brilliantly. Estella and Chico take him to Menorca and they see the dancing horses together. Anna also comes with them.

Oscar sees Adela almost every day when he's in Madrid. He takes her out for walks, to go shopping, on daytrips and she always brings a sketchbook. She has art classes twice a week with a young woman that Chico recommended. She's taken swimming twice a week by another young person that has been through Herminia's rigorous interview process. Oscar and his mother don't speak more than they have to, but she lets him pay for Adela's activities. Neither is interested in the other. The trust fund is set up and Herminia no longer need concern herself daily with worries about Adela's future. It hasn't made her any warmer, but she does leave the apartment now that Adela has other people looking after her. Oscar recently made contact with his father and is considering going to DF to meet him, but he's reluctant to leave Spain for more than a few days at a time; he has Adela to think of, and he sees Robert once a week, sometimes twice. At Robert's suggestion, he's started the process of getting a diagnosis for ADHD.

Víctor finds Oscar to be transformed; a kind, careful and thoughtful man who still struggles at times with anger, but has techniques that give him control. Their friendship is as solid as it once was before the fateful kiss. They have fun with a group of friends that they have made amongst other actors, artists and singers of their generation. Víctor is dating the lawyer of one of these friends. Oscar confessed to him a few months after the premiere of *Los Amores de Oscar* season three. He now knows the worst of him and the best of him and he's happy to be friends again. He thinks that Oscar's unlikely to look for love until his quest to understand himself has progressed further; perhaps not even then. Víctor loves him, but he's no longer ***in*** love with him.

Estella publishes a novel every year or so and is a firm favourite on chat shows where her cheerful frankness and sense of humour make for good conversation. She's a mine of ever so slightly shocking stories about her younger selves, which she tells with self-denigrating humour and excellent dramatic timing. It makes for dynamite television. There are still periods of darkness and loss of self-possession, but she recognises them now for the temporary states that they are and she finds the pain, releases it and moves on. The young people tell her that she looks younger every time they meet, which makes her smile, because every day and in every way, she has more energy, more love and more peace. They all do. They are so peaceful that they never let go of one another. There is always someone holding her, loving her, caring for her and putting her first. They can do all of that for themselves.

THE END

Stella
Miss estrella
Estella

Author's Note:

Estella is a work of fiction, but it is also an attempt to explain my experience of life. Like Estella, I experience the emotions, moods and feelings of people around me and sometimes become overwhelmed by them to the point of losing my sense of self.

It has been suggested to me that I might be an HSP, a highly sensitive person, but I am wary of labelling myself. Having worked in education on and off over my adult life I have met many people with labels like HSP, ADH and ASC and I have been distressed that their label sometimes blinds people to their individuality. Whilst there may be shared characteristics in a group of people diagnosed as having ASC, their individual personalities and preferences are utterly unique.

I am more concerned that as human beings we spend our time getting to know each other with love, compassion, unconditional positive regard and empathy. I would prefer that labels don't encourage us to prejudge people. If we are kind to one another, labels are irrelevant.

Another aspect of *Estella* that has a grounding in my experience of life is the transformative practice of Trinity

Coherence, a system of releasing trauma and unhelpful emotions in order to open yourself up to the infinite possibility of existence.

More information about this can be found at https://trinitycoherence.co.uk/ I have also described some of the tools that can be used alongside this technique, which I discovered only two years ago, and which have made a huge positive difference to my life. These are Trinfinity 8 and Ascension 11. https://www.nancygiuliani.com/trinfinity8

It has been through the practice of Trinity Coherence and the use of Trinfinity 8 and Ascension 11 that I have reached the self-knowledge and self-compassion to write this story. It has been a lifetime in the making and I am pleased that I am sharing it. I hope that it may be a comfort to others who have experiences similar to my own.

Gratitude

Unlike Estella, I am surrounded by people who love and care for me and support me patiently in every mad escapade that I conceive. They are also there to pick me up when things, not infrequently, go wrong.

My brother, sister-in-law and my nieces and nephews bring me huge joy and love.

I was fortunate to have two teachers who made all the difference to my self-esteem. The incomparable Colin Gray and the fearsome, brilliant Dr Elizabeth Brennan. I was also blessed at seven years of age to meet the most amazing librarian, for librarians are real superheroines and heroes, who later became a fantastic colleague and a dear friend. Thank-you Annie Jones.

JB, WGB and the Parentals keep me grounded, listen to me despite my banging on endlessly and we enjoy our food and wine together.

Lizzie, Nicolato and the girls provide infinite support, conversations, laughter and tasty treats. They were amongst the first readers of the first draft.

Newty read the first draft too. I can't live without her unconditional positive regard and indefatigable empathy.

N-Ro is always there and never fails to lift my spirits.

Without my fierce, personally selected daughter, her lovely husband and gorgeous child, my life would be much less rich. I never imagined that I would be a grandmother; thank-you.

My Menorcan family has been my refuge and my safe place since I was a teenager and has been there to help me recuperate and reinvent myself too many times to mention. My gratitude is fathomless.

Tracy made all the difference to the quality of my life by helping me to release the trauma that I had been nursing for a lifetime and gave me the chance to live again. I know she's there whenever the waves get too choppy.

I am also deeply and sincerely grateful to all the young people that I have had the privilege to get to know through my career in education and community development. I have learnt so much from them and continue to do so. How blessed am I?

Mummie and Daddy, I wish you were here for this. I miss you every day. Thank-you for making me think, read and ask questions.

I also thank the universe for my ***interesting*** life. **It is quite the rollercoaster being me.**

Questions for Book Clubs/Self Reflection:

1. At the start of the book, Estella is unhappy and feels bored; why does she feel this way? Have you ever experienced feelings like this? Did you find a way to get over them? What would you do if you became aware that a friend felt this way?

2. Estella has seven versions of herself. Do you ever use an alternative personality or version of yourself to deal with difficult situations in your life?

3. If you could go back to a past version of yourself or a particular time in your life, what would it be and why? What was it about you at that time that you feel the loss of now?

4. Why do you feel Estella has to maintain a distance from her family and work colleagues?

5. How and why does Estella manage to maintain her relationships with Win and Anna? Is this the same as her relationships with Igor, Elvira and Santi?

6. If you were to meet Estella, would she find that you give or take energy? Are there people in your life that take energy from you and others that you feel energised by?

7. Are you or have you ever known a Highly Sensitive Person (HSP)? What do you imagine the drawbacks and super-powers of being an HSP to be?

8. Estella chooses to forgive Oscar; why does she do this? How does she do this?

9. Do you think that Estrella and Chico will stay together?

10. Will Oscar be happy?

About the Publisher

DBI specialises in publishing impactful literature on the human condition, social justice, exposés, anthropology, and cultural cohesion. Our books aim to create positive, lasting change and provoke thought and powerful discourse, inspiring readers to see the world through a more conscious and empowered lens.

While we often publish non-fiction, we also publish fiction. Our non-fiction includes memoirs, autobiographies, and anthologies with up to ten contributors. We also welcome ethnographies, creative non-fiction, and selected works that amplify marginalised voices. Our fiction range is one which challenges beliefs and ideas, whilst celebrating relationships with self and others, and amplifying political or cultural narratives.

Our authors are dedicated individuals committed to creating high-quality, influential works, ready to invest the time, effort, and resources necessary to make a significant impact. We support our authors in navigating the publishing process authentically and confidently.

DBI works closely with an international team of experts to help our writers share their stories genuinely.

Founded by Dawn Bates, an award-winning, international bestselling author with a global reach spanning five continents, DBI is grounded in experience, expertise, and a fierce commitment to social change. Dawn's background as a leader, entrepreneur, activist, and world traveller enables her to coach writers with insight, guiding them to embrace their unique voice and navigate the journey to becoming a published author.

In addition to publishing, Dawn serves as a biographical writer, researcher and developmental editor, as well as an exceptional author coach, supporting writers who work with agents and other publishers.

DBI also offers thorough manuscript assessments, which include basic copy editing, marketing strategies, and suggestions for brand expansion and creating additional revenue streams. These assessments are designed to equip authors for the realities of publishing and build a successful career beyond the initial release.

To learn more about DBI visit https://dawnbates.com

Printed in Dunstable, United Kingdom

70595278R00170